Kia Lui Media, LLC

LOVE'S AWAKENING

A BILLIONAIRES OF MISSOURI ROMANCE

Evolving

KIA LUI

This is a work of fiction. Names, characters, places and incidents are the product of the author's imagination or are used fictitiously. Any resemblance to actual persons, living or dead, events, or locales is entirely coincidental.

Love's Awakening - Evolving
Copyright © 2022, Kia Lui
Self-published by Kia Lui Media, LLC
(cskialuimedia@outlook.com)

ISBN: 978-1-7333198-1-2

Cover design by: Kia Lui

Cover images by Kia Lui and C. Gerard Studios

www.kialuimedia.com

Printed in the United States of America

-Evolving-

If relationships are to survive, they must evolve. This can only happen with parties who are willing, who can communicate, and who can listen.

Previously, in "Love's Awakening – The Beginning", a serious problem Zion felt needed resolving led him to stop communicating with Lea. As is his usual practice, when he encounters a problem, he works it out and fixes it. He's never had to include anyone in his decision making. People follow his lead and do what he tells them.

But being in a relationship you can't do that. It's not only about him.

Lea opened up and gave herself to Zion in a way she had never to any other man. She told him exactly what she wanted, needed and desired. And he was all for it.

Their days together were glorious. Their nights were even better. Then it stopped. She didn't hear from him. She felt relegated to booty call status.

Fuck him I don't have to chase after a dick.

BUT OMG, THAT DICK WAS SOME GOOD DICK.

Lea picks up her broken heart.

Zion makes plans to get his Lea back.

The story of Zion and Lea, Love's Awakening is Evolving.

-1-

It's my wedding day. The decorations have turned out perfect. The lights sparkle. The flowers, some of them are withering. I pluck them and put them in the trash before anyone can see them. I'm ready to walk down the aisle. My dress is sexy. Oh, a thread. I pull the thread and a small seam opens. That's okay I can make it through the ceremony before anything happens. The closer I get to the alter, the more the seam opens. I look around and the flowers in the chairs are turning brown and falling apart. The lights are burning out. Where is he? He was there a minute ago. Waiting for me. Smiling. My Adonis. My Bear. "I said I didn't want you Lea. Now die. Die alone. You could never be my wife."

Lea awakens from the nightmare. She lays in the bed, adjusting to her surroundings. Reaching for her phone, she checks the notifications and as usual there are no messages from Zion. But why would there be? They broke up. Right? She sits up in the bed, reaches for a pillow and screams into it.

These fucking dreams have got to stop. The man is gone. I can't keep doing this. I'll drive myself nuts.

When Lea stopped hearing from Zion, the opportunity to get out of town was a godsend. She's been traveling on business the last few days. Being alone in her hotel, she cried out her heartbreak. Fighting the need to call and text him wanting answers, expecting him to tell her what was going on, drove her to suffering migraines and having reoccurring dreams of not being wanted, dying alone. After her second one, she decided it was time to accept what she had with Zion was over, and it was time to move the fuck on.

It was nice, but there will be someone after him. It may not be as good, but hell, it'll be close to happiness as I can get.

YOU NEED TO CALL ZION AND GET BACK WITH HIM.

You need to shut the fuck up. Never again will I chase after a man who doesn't want me.

The Sex Diva decides to take a mental break.

Lea's first step in moving on from Zion is getting back into socializing starting off with being a bridesmaid in her friend Bobbies' wedding. After all, they are known for quick hookups. Due to some issues with her vehicle at the airport parking lot, Lea is being picked up from the airport by one of Bobbies' relatives. This chatty woman keeps up a fast-paced conversation during the drive to the Cheshire Inn, and that takes Lea's mind off Zion.

Arriving at the hotel, they go straight to the bride's suite to get dressed. With so much going on, no one notices Lea quietly getting ready. When dragged into the conversation and pictures, she puts on her happy face hiding her misery. The ladies are taking shots and Lea takes two for courage. She can tell; it's going to be a long partying night before she can get home and rest. Bobbie is gonna turn up until the wee hours.

I'm just gonna sit in the corner and rest my feet after my bridesmaid duties are over.

Looking around at the available men, their scrutinizing looks, the way they act and how they approach her, she decides this is not the place she'll be finding her replacement for Zion. Even a temporary one.

An hour into the reception after all the wedding duties are completed, everyone is having a ball. Bobbie has dragged Lea to the dance floor numerous times, and she dances each and every one, working to tire herself out so she hopefully has no dreams of the 'breakup'.

Or is it a breakup? Lea muses. *At some point I'm going to have to clarify that with him. And get his account switched.*

Lea finally gets a break, hiding behind a tree on the edge of the reception room. She keeps thinking about him wondering if he would have attended a wedding with her.

Hell no. Can't see that happening.

She puts her head down wishing he were here or that she'd heard from him.

DAMMIT, HOW CAN WE GET THAT CLOSE AND STILL LOSE OUT.

It's my dream in living color.

Bobbie's five-year-old daughter Ashley finds Lea in her hiding spot. She's adorable. They're in matching color teal green dresses. Ashley's, of course, is Cinderella poof and she's wearing ballerina flats. Lea's is strapless, form fitting with a small train on the bottom and she's wearing peep-toe gold sandals, toenails painted iridescent, but this time with a hint of green. Ashley is carrying a slice of cake and is about ready to drop it.

"Ashley, what are you doing?"

"Bringing you a slice of cake."

"But I don't want any more cake."

"Well, may I have it?" Ashley asks knowing what she's up to.

Five-year-old can't fool me.

"Yes, you may have it. How about you sit down and eat it here at the table."

Instead of sitting at the table, Ashley moves to sit on Lea's lap to eat.

They sit there talking about her ballet shoes as she eats her cake in bliss. Finally, Ashley gets up and goes away dancing toward her mom and dad. A happy loving family. Something Lea feels she'll never have. She turns away from that view, looking out the window.

Zion stares at the information Crystal gave him regarding Lea's upcoming schedule for the next couple of weeks. Mom's doctor appointments, a wedding, and a four-state business trip. He makes the decision to go looking for Lea at the wedding reception to apologize and do whatever it takes to get back into her good graces. He has Sam drive around the parking lot looking for her car and doesn't see it.

He exits the SUV in front of an entrance hoping to blend in with a group of wedding guests. A few women speak and attempt to get his attention, but he's focused on finding Lea. He figures he'll go to the bar and hang around. After about fifteen minutes of waiting, he spots her hiding behind a tree sitting at a small table. A little girl approaches her.

He sits outside the room watching Lea with the girl sitting on her lap eating cake.

I would love to hear their conversation.

The little girl is animated, almost dropping pieces of cake numerous times, but Lea catches it, licking icing off her fingers.

Damn, my dick went hard thinking about her licking icing off me. She's so patient with the little girl. I wish I could give her a child.

Zion's mesmerized watching them. They laugh at something and the little girl hops down and dances off. Lea puts her head down rubbing her temples as if she's in pain and wipes a bit of moisture from her eye.

Oh, baby, I'm so sorry.

He notices she has a clutch with her. He texts her phone, not even thinking she may not have it with her. Four times, he texts her, and she never even reacts.

Maybe she doesn't have her phone. Naw man, she has it. He tells himself.

Instead of approaching her, he has the waitress deliver a card on a silver tray.

Man, I hope this works.

The waitress bends down presenting the card to Lea. Lea asks her whom it's from, but the waitress smiles, shrugs her shoulders, and walks toward the dining room of the hotel, being sure not to walk pass the bar and Zion, in case she's being watched.

Lea picks up the card to read it. She's not familiar with the looping handwriting.

"Please check your phone."

She takes out her phone seeing three, no four text messages from Zion. She figured she wasn't going to be hearing from him anytime soon so she set his text and ring tone on silent. The elation coursing through Lea seeing the notifications from Zion makes her want to stand up and scream "yes, finally, oh hell yes". Her hand shaking she unlocks her phone to read the messages.

Zion: *Lea, you look beautiful.*
Zion: *Kitten, answer me. May I come say hello?*
Zion: *Lea, I know you're angry with me.*
Zion: *Lea. Babe.*

Lea smiles at the texts. Then she gets pissed and tosses the phone back in her clutch.

Fuck him. What the hell is he doing here of all places?

FUCK HIM? ISN'T THIS WHAT WE BEEN WANTING FOR WEEKS NOW?

Yes. No. Hell, I don't know.

WELL DAMMIT FIGURE IT THE FUCK OUT CAUSE—.

Lea feels a presence behind her. Looking up, she catches her breath. Zion is standing there, looking magnificent in a black tux.

HE'S FUCKING HOT. EXTREMELY FUCKING HOT. NOW THIS THE WEDDING HOOKUP WE NEED. BETCHA YOU FIGURING SHIT OUT NOW AREN'T YOU?

Lea lets out the breath she had been holding.

Working on it Sex Diva. I'm working on it.

-2-

Mentally, Lea agrees with the Sex Diva. She wants to hop up into his arms and beg him for a forgiveness she has no clue what of. But she remains sitting. Staring. Forcing herself not to move even a pinky finger. Her mother would be proud. That constantly being told to sit and not move as a child has worked in adulthood for a change.

Where she's hiding, Zion can't sit down, so he pulls her up and into his arms.

"Zion, what are you doing here? How did you know I would be here?" she asks, stunned to see him.

He puts his hand on the side of her face. Lea pulls away from him.

"Lea, don't ever pull away from me like that. Ever," he growls.

Her pulling away angered him more than it hurt. He won't allow her to reject him.

"Why didn't you respond to my texts? I almost left thinking you didn't want to see me. Although, I don't blame you considering how I've treated you. Lea, I'm sorry. Please, don't send me away." He continues to stare at her, softening at the uncertain look in her eyes.

"You'll do whatever you want anyway." She stares at his lips wanting to kiss him. He smiles and lays one on her that makes her nipples harden and her groin ache. Her hand presses against his chest then clutches his bicep. He places his hand over hers.

Zion relishes the feel of her lips on his. He pulls her against him forgetting where they are.

"Lea and a sexy man kissing behind a tree. K-I-S-S-I-N-G."

Lea pulls away and looks into Bobbie's dark brown eyes. Her husband Ferguson is standing behind Bobbie smirking at them. Zion turns with a smile ready, not letting Lea move from his embrace.

Wiping his lips slowly, unaware Lea has on a lip stain that doesn't come off, he addresses them with a devilish smile on his face. "I'm sorry for crashing your reception. I wanted to surprise Lea. I'm Zion, her boyfriend."

The move of him wiping his lips causes the Sex Diva to awaken every sexual nerve in Lea's body. She jumps at the word 'boyfriend'. "Ha. That's funny."

Okay that flew out of my mouth before I could stop it. Zion looks at me as if he could strangle me.

Lea cracks a small smile then turns serious. "Boyfriend, my ass," she says staring at him, "You mean client, or how about business associate?"

"Boyfriend, significant other, your man, your boo. Whatever label you desire to use, 'cause you're mine." Zion says with a look daring her to defy him, staking his claim.

Lea says nothing. Stunned silent. No man has ever claimed her so publicly before.

Bobbie and Ferguson are staring at them watching the silent sparks fly between Lea and this man, a man Bobbie is so wanting to know more about. In all the years she's known Lea, she has never seen her interact with a man outside of business like this. She's heard about them, but has never seen it in action.

Lea accepts the shocked looks from Bobbie and Ferguson at the surprise of her having a man. They 'ooo' and 'aah'.

"I didn't even know you were dating," Ferguson said while looking at Zion.

Zion shakes hands with them and thanks them for the warm welcomes, continuing to keep his hand on Lea's waist possessively, caressing her.

Lea exasperatedly says, "I'm not dead. Just unattractive." She moves to step out of Zion's embrace but he grips her, forcing her to stay or create a scene.

Bobbie drags us out of the corner for pictures and to show off my 'boyfriend'. I could scream.

"Why didn't you respond to my texts?" Zion asks her after the attention refocuses on the bride and groom.

"What's with the boyfriend crap? I silenced my ringtone for you because obviously we're back to a business relationship. Nothing is going on with the Landon Enterprises project that I need to be on call for. You wanna explain to me what's going on?"

"Yes, after I get you home." Zion can't stop smiling at Lea's exasperation. To know that he affects her this way strokes his ego. And the fact he's so excited to just be around her blows his mind. He's never been this stimulated around a woman. Not even his temporary fucks.

We need to get the hell outta here before I make a fool of myself doing something an out of controlled teenage boy would do.

"How much longer do you have to stay? May I have your phone please?"

Zion looks at her like he wants to ravish her, and she can't tell if that's in a good or bad way.

Lea clutches her hand over her purse. "Why would I give you my phone?"

"Lea, give me your phone. Now!"

She stares at him.

He takes her clutch out of her hand and pulls out her phone noticing the card from the tray. He smiles and gives her a side look. Looking back down at her phone, he asks her to unlock it.

"Bite me."

"I will later. Unlock your phone. Please."

"Nope. Not till you tell me why."

"So, I can change my ring tone," he says. "Unlock your phone, Lea." He whispers seductively.

LORD ALMIGHTY THAT VOICE. OPEN YOUR LEGS WHY DON'T YOU, the Sex Diva annoyingly pops up.

They are locked in a staring contest. Lea loses and unlocks her phone.

Zion goes into the contacts searching for his phone number. "Really, you referring to me as Landon Enterprises Project?" he changes his contact name to "Bear, Lea's man". This makes her giggle.

He slides through her personal list of tones, selecting 'Summer Madness' by Kool and the Gang for his ringtone and 'Sure Thing' by Miguel for his text tone.

She tries to snatch the phone back before he can see the picture she uses as a wallpaper. Too late; he scrolls through her apps to get to the last screen to get a full view of the image. It's one of him standing on the other side of the water fountain. She has him in focus and the water in front of him out of focus. The image is haunting, as if he's untouchable.

Looking at her he whispers, "You're a fantastic photographer. When will you let me see more of them?"

Lea looks away from his questioning gaze. "I'll send them all to you."

Bobbie sneaks up behind them. "You guys can go ahead and leave if you like," she says. "People are taking off earlier than I thought. Zion, can I depend on you to get my girl home safe and sound? You look kinda safe and all, even though I just met you. If you can't take her home, my cousin will be more than happy to do so; that was the original arrangement." They look at the guy standing, talking with her husband.

He's rather cute, Lea thinks. She looks back at Zion.

An emotion of jealousy grips him seeing the look Lea gave another man. He's fixing their relationship status and making sure no man gets what's his. "Oh, hell no. Not another man," Zion softly murmurs.

Lea looks at him, questioning his last comment. "Huh?"

"Bobbie, the services of your cousin are not needed this evening. I promise to get Lea home safe and sound. I'll even tuck her into bed and read her a bedtime story if she asks," Zion says pulling her into his arms and nibbling her on the side of her neck.

Lea pulls away. The look Zion gives her pins her in place like a two-year-old caught snatching a cookie.

"A bedtime story huh? Good night, Lea. Good night, Zion, it was nice meeting you." Bobbie leaves gliding toward her husband and cousin breaking the bad news.

Lea turns back to Zion. "I'm hungry. For food. Can we get something to eat? Please?"

I don't forget my manners; I'm electing to be a smart-ass using them. Boyfriend, ha, that's still funny.

He kisses her, pressing her body into his. "I've missed you, and yes, we can get something to eat. Whatever you like. And I'll be biting you and fucking you hard, later." He glides his finger over the curve of the top of her dress. Lea grabs his hand and moves it to his side while staring at him.

"Stop it Zion. What is with you? We're in public. You know what I said to Crystal?"

"Lea, I don't give a shit. I want you, you're mine, and I'm staking my claim. Now, shall we leave?" he says leaning in for another kiss. "Kitten, I heard the entire conversation."

She steps away, and he pulls her back into his chest lifting her chin to look at him.

"Defiant today, aren't we? Keep it up. I'm enjoying this. It arouses me. As well as you," he says staring into her eyes.

Lea sucks in a deep breath not denying what he said. "Zion—."

He quickly kisses her. "Lea, go gather your things so we can go home."

She walks with him following closely behind her, grinning like a Cheshire cat.

Fitting grin for the place we're in. Lea muses to herself.

-3-

Lea has stored her suitcase and computer bag behind the front desk instead of up in the room for a quick exit. As she walks toward the desk, Zion is stopped by numerous women complimenting him, offering to buy him drinks or exchange phone numbers. Lea turns, talking to the front desk clerk. She hears Zion reject the women.

GEEZ THAT VOICE, THAT VOICE. CAN PICK HIM OUT OF A CROWD BY THE WAY IT SLIDES UP AND DOWN OUR SPINE.

Lea moves her neck from side to side reacting to Zion's voice with goosebumps popping up on her arms. *Yes, my body reacts to that man's voice leaving it inflamed.*

"Ladies, ladies, you're all beautiful and I'm sure other men want you, but I must send you off to hunt elsewhere. You see, I'm here to pick up my girlfriend. I'm taken, ladies. Good night and enjoy the rest of your evening." Zion turns away from them and walks toward Lea.

She watches the women behind him, watching him. They look her up and down and shake their heads. Lea's insecurities take over and she starts comparing herself to them. She feels like a frump.

BUT HE'S COMING TO US.

Yes, to frumpy, dumpy Lea whom he ignored for weeks.

YOU GETTING ON MY NERVES. I'LL BE BACK WHEN THE SEX KICKS OFF.

"My, my, my. All that attention and you're rejecting it. They're all beautiful."

"Lea Adams, if you keep this up, I'll toss you over my shoulder and carry you out of here. And they don't come close to your beauty. Let's go." He reaches for her things, and they walk to the SUV.

Damn fucking SUV.

Sam is standing by the rear hatch ready to open it. She says hello, not making eye contact.

I'm just the piece of ass his boss was fucking. No loyalties to me.

Lea walks to the back door opening it. She stands staring, wondering how to climb in with her dignity intact and her head held high while they are storing her things. Stepping up into the truck in her dress will be difficult. She'll have to lift it up to the knee, put one foot on the truck's foot rest, and lift herself in. She looks down at her dress considering widening the split.

Zion watches her. Right as she is about to rip the dress, he walks up behind her. "As much as I would love to see more of your beautiful thigh, there is no need to destroy such a sexy dress."

Lea turns around facing him ready to say something. He grips her by the waist, lifts her up and places her on the seat. She lets out a small peep as she lands on the seat and moves as far away from him as she can, assuming he's going to get in next to her.

He gets in on the other side instead. "What would you like to eat?" he turns his body toward her, gazing at her pointedly.

I wish he would stop fucking staring at me like that.

"Silent Grill. Thai Chili Wings and Parmesan Frites. To go please."

"We can sit and dine in if you like."

"Dressed like this? Are you nuts? I wanna go home. To my home. I wanna change."

His ass is not taking me to his apartment to fuck me into agreeing to forget how I've been ignored. Fuck that.

BUT EARLIER YOU WERE WANTING TO JUMP INTO HIS ARMS AND BEG FOR FORGIVENESS.

I was confused.

DAMMIT YOU GOT US BOTH CONFUSED. MAKE UP YOUR MIND. I WANT ME SOME ZION.

"I never imagined you having such a smart-ass mouth, Lea. I'm not sure how to respond. Spank you like the spoiled brat you're acting like or kiss you. Chill out with the attitude." Zion takes out his phone and looks up Silent Grill and calls in an order.

Sam drives to the restaurant and Lea sits with her hands in her lap staring out the window. All prim and proper. She turns away from him, hiding that he's right and what he said hurt.

Lousy jerk. Who the hell he thinks he is rolling up like this? He can't tell me how to feel and act.

"Kitten, I know you're angry with me. You have every reason to be. Lea, please look at me," he cajoles, caressing her shoulder.

She jerks away. "Stop talking to me like that. You ignore me then show up here. I'm going to kill Crystal. Did you tell her about us? She's the only one who could have told you about this wedding. Damn meddling-ass woman. Why are you in a tux to show up for something like this?" she asks, firing off irrational and illogical questions and statements as quickly as she can.

Zion unbuckles his seat belt and reaches for her face kissing her. She breaks the kiss.

"Stop kissing me, dammit. I can't think." Lea tries pushing away from him by turning her head, but he pins her in place holding on.

"I don't want you to think, I want you to feel. Just feel. This between us. How do you feel, how does this make you feel?" Zion keeps kissing her, holding her, refusing to let her overthink.

Lea hears Sam get back into the SUV, carrying bags of food.

When did we arrive at the restaurant?

"Zion, stop it. You have me confused enough. You ignore me then come back like nothing has happened. Stop with the attempts in seducing away how you've treated me. Tell me the truth. Are you with another woman and making me a side piece? Cause that can go both ways."

"I don't have another woman. I'm all yours. I had to handle something, and I'll tell you all about it. I promise. Anything you want to know. Everything. Come on, let's go in. By the way, there is no way in hell on this earth I'm letting another dick get to your pussy. You can forget that shit right now. I be damned if another man will ever take you away from me," he says in a biting angry tone. "And there is no way you will ever be a side piece to me. You the one and only in my life Kitten. Give me your house key."

We've arrived at my house? Lea distractedly hands Zion her keys and he gives them to Sam. She's stunned again at the way he has staked his claim.

AND WE FUCKING LIKE IT, RIGHT?

Sex Diva, yes, I kinda do like it. It doesn't scare me or make me cringe. What the fuck is wrong with me?

MAYBE WE LOVE THIS GUY.

Oh, see now you going way to far with that word. No ma'am. Shut the hell up.

Sex Diva giggles walking off into the corner of Lea's mind.

Handing Lea's key to Sam was Zion's sneaky way of having her house checked without her knowing it's being checked. He wants to explain it all first. They get out with Sam carrying in the food and her bags from the back.

"Lea, where's your car?" Zion asks her.

"In the shop getting tires replaced. They got slashed at the parking garage. That's why I had to get picked up from the airport. Why? What's it to you?" Lea snaps at him again.

Zion stands, staring at her. His mind is reeling from the news of slashed tires on her car and the tone of her voice. He remembers Crystal said she had car trouble, but tires slashed? This bothers him.

"What, Zion?"

"Check the tone of your voice, Lea. I get I'm in the dog-house right now but seriously? Is this attitude really called for?"

Lea hates being chastised. Especially when she knows she's in the wrong. And he's done it for the second time.

Lea, get a grip. Even your mother would put you in check for the way you're acting right now.

"You're right. You are in the dog-house. And no, my tone and attitude aren't called for. I'm hurt and not dealing with it well," she takes a deep breath and continues, removing the temperament from her response, "I get my car Monday. Shit happens when leaving your car parked at the airport. It's no big deal. The manager at the parking garage say they got slashed on the same day I dropped it off. It took me three days to find a place that was willing to pick it up, keep it safe and replace the tires. Not to mention a huge fortune. Satisfied?"

"I'm sorry you're hurting. I'll make it all go away." He walks over to her, standing close. "I'm bothered about the tires on your car being slashed. Where there any other cars damaged?" he softens his tone, speaking to her.

"Not that I'm aware of."

"Did you make a police report?"

"Yes, it was the only way my insurance would tow, cover, and get me a rental car if I needed one. Not to be snapping, but what is the big deal? It's just car damage. Next week, I'll take a taxi to the airport and leave my car at home. I'm going in."

Lea turns and looks at Sam being sure not to direct her sour mood at him. "Good night, Sam. Thank you for carrying in my luggage." She takes her keys back from him.

The interaction at the Moonrise Hotel still rankles me but there is no need to take it out on him. He was simply doing his job.

"Good night, Miss Adams. And, your welcome." He says, intently making eye contact with her. He gets back into the SUV and drives off being sure not to look at Zion. He can be fired for wanting to convey a comforting message to Miss Adams.

What the hell? Secret looks between my security and my girlfriend. This some bullshit, Zion thinks.

He texts Sam regarding Lea's car, not mentioning the look he just gave her.

> Zion: *See if you can find out anything about her car. Try to get the police report. You know whom to call if needed.*
>
> Sam: *Yes sir. I will send you the information as soon as I get it.*

-4-

When they go into the house, Lea walks straight to her bedroom to change clothes.

Manners, Lea. Where are your manners? He's already chastised you twice.

She returns to the living room. He's standing, waiting, looking fuckable with his hands in his pockets. She turns on the TV and hands him the remote. He doesn't take it, shaking his head no; instead, he leans against the door staring at her.

She drops the remote on the couch.

"Would you like anything to drink? May I prepare a plate of food for you? Did you rent that tux to show up tonight? Why are you standing there, staring at me? It's unnerving."

He walks toward her speaking, "A glass of wine would be great. I'll wait for you to eat. No, I didn't rent this tux. I own this tux, and if I had needed to rent one or buy one, I would have. I'm standing here staring at you because you are the most beautiful sight to me, and I want to hold you and make love to you all night long. Sorry to unnerve you but you unnerve me. Nothing to say about me not ever letting another man near you."

Lea stands with her hands clutched and fingernails digging into her flesh. She wants to accept what Zion is saying at face value, but being ignored brings out the smart-ass brat in her. Again.

"Nope, they're just words. Red or white?" she asks.

"Red" he responds, "and they're not just words. No man is getting you away from me. I'm it, baby. Accept it. I know when I've found a good woman."

"I wouldn't know that based on the last few weeks," she says, walking into the dining room, grabbing a bottle of his favorite red wine and two wine glasses.

That stings, but Zion takes it. For now. He follows her and she hands him the bottle and cork screw. He opens the wine, noticing the label. Looking at her with delight, he pours them each a glass. She stares at hers.

What he said sounds good, but they are just words.

She glides her fingers up and down the stem of the glass. How many times has she told herself she's wanted to hear the things this man is saying? And now that she's heard them, she doesn't believe them. She gulps down the wine, returning to the table to refill the glass.

Zion can't decide if he's offended, angry, or amused by Lea's sass tonight. He gets it. She has a right to be angry with him. But no woman would ever talk to him this way if she wanted to keep seeing him. Then it strikes him. Lea doesn't care. She'll walk away instead of staying and accepting the way he treated other women. He's not having that. He strokes her arm, needing to touch her. "Lea, you were going to change. Don't let me stop you. Do you need help unzipping your dress? And where would you like me to bite you? Nipples, clit, or ass?" He watches her, settling on amusement.

"It's a side zipper, thanks for offering." She storms off to the bedroom.

"Anytime." Her sass awakens him. He follows her, leaning against the door waiting.

Fuck it. He wanna watch? That's on him.

She kicks her shoes off toward a corner in the bedroom. Unzipping the dress, she shimmies it over her ass and lets it drop to the floor. Lea is left standing in a flesh tone bustier, flesh tone lace boy shorts, a flesh tone garter belt with black bow ties on them and glittery flesh tone thigh high stockings. She unsnaps the garters from the thigh highs and leans on the bed to take them off bending over showing her ass.

Yep, I'm profiling.

She undoes the bustier by untying the bow in the back and lets it fall to the floor. She slides the garter over her ass and down her legs, letting it drop to the floor with the bustier.

Zion is breathing heavily. He has his arms crossed over his chest with one hand covering his mouth, hiding his grin.

My very own striptease show. If I throw out hundred-dollar bills, she'll ring my neck.

Lea grabs a tank top from her dresser drawer and puts it on. She picks up the dress and bustier hanging them on the bedroom door.

"Ready to eat?" she asks him.

"Yeah, in a second," he says hoarsely.

Zion stands in the doorway blocking her escape and takes off his tux jacket, tie and shirt and hangs them on the bedroom door next to her dress. He takes off his shoes and socks along with his belt and unbuttons the top button of this pants. He takes her into his arms.

"What are you doing? We're not having sex."

His skin is soft and hot.

"You're right. We're not having sex. I'm going to make sweet, passionate love to you. We need to talk first." He kisses her neck.

"Are you staying?"

"I'm staying as long as I need to stay to convince you I want you, and I'm sorry for ignoring you. However long that takes, we'll be locked away in this house until its done."

"That won't happen. Let's eat." She attempts to move out of his embrace and slide past him, but he tightens his grip forcing her to look at him.

"What won't happen?"

"Staying in this house, locked away."

Zion releases her, allowing her to walk past, smacking her on the behind. "After you, Kitten."

She turns and gives him an attempt at an evil look after the smack, but can't.

"Excellent. That means I can convince you how sorry I am, and then we'll be making love."

"I didn't say that."

"You haven't denied it either."

They go into the dining room and Lea serves up wings and fries. Zion sits down at the table watching her every move. Each time she gets close to him, he touches her. She pushes his hand away attempting to stay mad at him, but his touch is softening her mood. She puts the place settings far away from each other, he moves them closer. She sits down refilling their glasses.

Zion explains what's been happening during his absence from her, "The Sunday I left you so abruptly was because I got a call from Saul. Something about emails. A shitload of emails, popping up in my email account. He thought they were a virus or phishing scam, but it turns out they were from an ex of mine. Addison Raymond. The 'she' I mentioned earlier." Zion looks away from Lea when saying 'Addison Raymond'. He tenses up and chomps down hard on the wing he had in his hand, biting into the bone. He picks up a napkin, wiping his mouth and spitting the bone into it, laying the napkin to the side, staring at it. Lea brings him back to the conversation.

"Go on," she prompts him, wanting to hear more about what could be making him so angry.

"Addison introduced me to BDSM. Or, in her mind, what she thought was BDSM. She got off on being beaten and treated like shit. It aroused her. Every fight, argument, disagreement would become physical, brutal sometimes, and she loved it. It was good at first. Then I hated it and myself. During therapy, I realized it was sadomasochism, the worst part of BDSM. But she took it to the extreme."

"You were in therapy?"

"Yep. Addison couldn't be happy if things were going well. Drama and misery excited her. Kept her aroused. When she broke it off to be with someone who was truly willing to beat her, I had to get some mental help. I had a choice: become mean and brutal or not. It was a long, celibate three years, but Crystal, Tom, my sister and the therapist helped me through that time. Crystal and Tom, as much as they could, helped me get through the roughest time in my life along with my parents, considering the little I told them about the situation."

He breathes in and out.

"It took a while, but I had to learn the difference among good sex, bad sex, and demeaning sex. I'm learning the relationship part, now, with you. You're my first relationship in twenty-five years."

Lea stares at him with a 'yea right' expression on her face.

"Don't give me that look. Women wanted me but wanted kids more. I couldn't give them that, so it was easy to stay away from relationships.

"Anyway, back to the last few weeks. I had to increase my security for my family and the office. I had a background check run on Addison. The difficult task was finding out all I could about her and keeping everyone close to me safe. I could've put a security detail on you, but that wouldn't have worked without a lot of explanations that I couldn't give as we were not talking.

"I had no idea what Addison wanted until I talked to her. The night you saw Sam, and yes, Sam told me he saw you, I felt like shit that I couldn't come and find you. But I couldn't. Addison and I were in the restaurant at the bar talking. She wanted to rekindle the sex. I told her no, that wasn't going to happen. Not ever. She started getting angry and aroused. I wanted to get away from her. She's married, and her husband allows her to fuck on the side when she's off her meds to work out her sexual aggression."

Zion links his fingers with Lea's on the table. She squeezes them, hopefully encouraging him to continue. He gives her a look of tenderness and keeps talking.

"When I got the emails, she was off her meds and claimed she was back on the drugs when we met to talk. I didn't believe her because she was too eager to get a room and fuck. I sent her away in a taxi and told her to stay away from me, my family, and friends."

"How did she find you?" Lea asks, "And were you even tempted?"

"A picture of you and me at Tom's wine tasting." He shows her the picture of the clipping he has on his phone. "Why would you even ask if I was tempted or even think that? No, I wasn't tempted."

"I ask because people like going back to past relationships. They're safe, familiar. It happens all the time. So, what now, Zion? Where do you stand with her, or where do you think you stand with her?" Lea asks.

"I would like to say it's done and over with, she's gone back to her husband or whoever and is leaving me alone. I don't want any of my past relationships, fucks, temps, or whatever I called them, Lea."

I can't believe she asked if I was tempted to go back. I have to get her to understand that no other woman has tempted me away from her since I first kissed her.

"But you don't believe that do you? That she's going to leave you alone?" she asks ignoring his last sentence, staring at him, wanting to catch a lie.

"I'm thinking and planning ten steps ahead right now. Only a handful of people know about us, and I would like to stick to the plan of, if not asked don't offer, but if asked, don't lie. I'm never going to deny you and I are together, but I'm not going to invite strangers into our relationship either. I have never invited people into my personal life, and I don't see any point in changing that now. My private life is just that, my private life."

"Are we together? You told my friend you're my boyfriend, but is that what you really want?"

I ask him giving him the chance to walk way.

"Lea, this is what I want, without a doubt. I came looking for you because I want you. I hated being away from you." He leans in close to her, caressing her thigh.

She looks down at his hand not saying anything. Then she looks up at him, her expression unreadable.

"What Lea?" he asks her, "Talk to me."

"Your first relationship in twenty-five years. Am I your test relationship? Maybe to see if you can make one work and find someone more to your rich lifestyle. Better looking eye candy maybe?"

I ask him, my insecurities showing in the questions.

"Lea, I don't want a relationship with anyone else, and I'll do whatever it takes to reassure you of that. You're my future. You're the sweetest eye candy I've ever had."

"For now. People change, Zion. Things change. Circumstances change. I guess we won't be having the kind of sex I was talking about us having, will we? I mean if it will take you back to a time that could rehash old memories, then we shouldn't do it," Lea suggests.

"Let's take it a step at a time. I want to try things with you. Things I want to do to you. Things I want you to do to me. I'm not going to let anything in my past dictate my future with you," he says leaning into her, wanting to be close.

"I guess." She stands up and walks away from him going to the couch.

Zion panics, "What're you doing?" he asks, thinking she's going to make him leave, but she goes to get her phone from her clutch.

"Texting Bobbie. Letting her know not to post any pics of you and me online and to send them to me instead."

Might as well protect his privacy as much as I can if I'm going to stay in this. Which I would like to do.

YAY HE STAYING, YAY YAY YAY. SEX NOW.

"You don't need to do that. If she posts them, I don't care. I'm okay with it."

The relief in my gut is palpable. I can't believe the stomach churning feeling I felt thinking she was about to ask me to leave. I still have to regain her trust, but at least, she isn't kicking me out.

"I would prefer not to invite crazy into my life if you don't mind. Besides my life isn't online; it's offline. Now what Zion? I didn't like that you felt you had to shut me out. It hurt. But I can't say I won't do the same thing in keeping you safe someday. I guess I need to work on my trusting skills," she admits.

"And I need to work on giving you a reason to trust me by talking to you and letting you know what's going on. I'm not perfect, remember? I thought I was doing the best for you by keeping you out of this. When issues arise, I go into automatic mode. I've never really had to include anyone in my decision making. I'm more of a 'see a problem, solve the problem' person. This relationship inclusion is new to me." He caresses her leg wanting his soft Lea back. "I've missed you."

This Lea is cold, stand-offish.

"I've missed you, too," Lea says. She clears the table wanting to get away from his intense gaze. "Why are you staring at me now? I'm just cleaning up."

"I'm staring at you because I can't believe how stupid I was to stay away from you. To exclude you. I'm sorry about that. Say you forgive me, Lea."

She returns to the table looking at him. "I forgive you Zion."

"Kitten, why are you not angrier with me? Is this it? Aren't we going to fight more or yell?"

Lea moves to the doorway of the dining room. "Zion, I've had time to think. I'm determined to do things differently from my past. Yelling and screaming is the old me. People can't hear through the yelling and screaming. I needed to listen. Because I'm calm doesn't mean I'm not hurt. You told me what happened. If you were secretive or shutting me out, I'd be gone. This would be over with. I'm glad you confided in me. It makes me feel like I mean something to you."

"You do," Zion says remembering what Crystal said.

Man don't say those words. Now is not the time.

"Look, why don't you go watch TV while I finish cleaning up?" Lea says, going back to the sink and washing dishes. She needs a few minutes to think about the last hour and all the information Zion has given her.

As is her norm, when washing dishes, Lea finds herself standing at the sink with her hands in dishwater, her mind a million miles away thinking. She hates the thought of having to give up her ideas about their sex life, denying herself of what she wants again.

LOOK, WE DON'T GOTTA GO DEEP INTO BDSM. SOME BONDAGE. SOME DOMINANCE. ROUGH SEX MAYBE? THAT ADONIS AIN'T NO GENTLE LOVER.

Lea flexes her neck and shoulders, loosening the tension she's feeling.

You right Sex Diva, he's not afraid to man handle me. We simply take it slow. No S&M but lots of B&D.

YEP, NOW HURRY UP. I'M HORNY.

Lea has been quiet and in her own world too long because when Zion kisses her shoulder, she jumps, splashing water over the front of her tank top. Looking down she sees the outline of her nipples peeking through the thin fabric of the shirt. She pulls it away quickly but not fast enough because Zion says, "Nice and perky. Me likes."

-5-

Zion sits at the table watching Lea wash dishes. He's amused at her rolling her shoulders and moving her neck back and forth. He snaps a few pictures of her with his phone without her noticing. After a few minutes, she stilled. He approaches from behind, wanting to hold her, to ease the tension.

She's so beautiful. Crystal's right. I'm in love with her. But I ain't saying it yet.

"Lea, what are you thinking about?" he asks, massaging her shoulders.

"Nothing," she lies.

No point in showing my uncertainties.

Zion kisses her shoulders, moving to her neck, lightly biting her. He moves his hands placing them under her breasts enjoying the weight of them.

Lea pulls away right as he is about to kiss and caress her at the base of her neck and spine. If he kisses there, she'll want to let go, feel, and react. But she's unsure of herself now. That's the weakest spot on her body. She moves out of his embrace, pressing her back up against the wall staring at him.

Shit, he can't hit that spot. We ain't ready for that.

I'M BACCCKKK. AND YES, WE READY.

"What's wrong, why did you pull away? I don't like it when you pull away from me."

He's staring at her with a hunger she can surpass right now. She wants to suck his dick so badly. Her mouth is watering at the idea of it. She could pounce on him and scare the hell out of him with her desire for it. She bites the inner portion of her cheek making her lips purse together. She quickly glances down to his crotch then looks up at the ceiling taking in a deep breath.

The words rush out of her mouth in almost a hiss, "No reason. Let's go to bed. I'm done here," she says hoping to distract him.

I can't pounce and devour the dick. I mean I can. No, I can't. That would be wrong. It's not like he would reject it. But he could reject and embarrass you. But he said he was yours. And being yours, you should be able to suck him off to the point he's crying for mercy.

MERCY MERCY MERCY BABY. STOP BEING SO WISHY-WASHY AND DO IT.

Zion watches her and stands up straight, squaring his shoulders.

"Lea, the back of your neck is a no-go zone? You keep moving away from me every time I go near it. I don't like you pulling away from me. When I find the spot, what will you do? Will you whimper for me? Will you beg for me? Will you be wet for me?" The seductive tone of his voice is making her nipples harden. Again, she pulls the tank top away from her breasts.

Zion stares at Lea's chest, her harden nipples and swollen mounds.

Mounds I want to open my mouth and swallow whole.

He wants to see what Lea will do if he kisses the back of her neck. This is the second time she has pulled away from him touching her. The night of the ball he just figured it was because so many people were around them. Now, he's thinking otherwise.

"Zion, I don't want you to confuse my reaction with what you have told me about your past experiences with Addison."

"Sweetheart, you're nothing like her. You're passionate, caring, and in your lovemaking, you're giving. When you let go, you make my blood boil, and I'm on fire for you. Don't hold back on me. Don't ever be afraid to fully let go with me."

"I'm not afraid. Everyone has their limits. And a man with your history should be careful what he asks for. We should go to bed." She makes a move to walk past him but he blocks her.

He grabs her by the waist and turns her around with her back facing him and places her hands on the sink. He places his hands on top of hers pinning her in place. "No. Show me, Lea. Baby, I wanna see. I trust you."

He kisses her shoulder, moving to her neck. She leans her head to one side giving him access. His kisses move closer and closer to 'the spot'.

Shit. Kiss it. Don't kiss it. Damn!

HE BETTER KISS IT, AND THE SECOND HE DOES, I'M TAKIN' OVER.

Oh, no, the hell you not.

Lea feels she's about to hyperventilate. Finally, he kisses and nibbles the top of her collar bone and her right leg buckles, pushing back toward him, moving between his legs. Her right butt cheek brushes against his penis. He presses into her, ensuring she feels how aroused he is. Lea grabs his head in one hand holding him in place rubbing her ass into his dick, maneuvering it between her ass cheeks. She places his other hand down her underwear, forcing his fingers to rub her clit.

Damn.

OH, FUCK YES.

"Zion, squeeze me."

He moves his hands upward, grabbing her breasts, squeezing and kneading them. Lea presses her body into his. He pulls away, leaving her frustrated.

Oh, hell to the fucking no! There is no pulling away from me now.

Lea turns around, looking at him. She grabs him behind the neck, pulling his head down and kissing him. She breaks the kiss and kisses his neck rubbing her pelvis against his, grabbing his dick through his pants. She licks, sucks and teases his nipples, causing him to jerk in response.

"Oh yes. Squeeze me," he begs Lea, putting his hand over hers. "Do it."

Before either one of them can react fast enough, before Lea overthinks the moment, and before Zion says stop, she has pulled down his pants and underwear and her face is looking at his dick, the tip, with pre-cum waiting to be licked off. He's about to say something, but she guides him to her mouth latching onto the tip, rolling her tongue around it.

Finally, I get to taste him. To feel his cock throbbing in my mouth. Feeling him jerk with pleasure. Caused by me.

SUCK THAT POPSICLE. WONDER WHAT COLOR CAN WE REACH.

"Oh. Fucking shit. Lea. Damn. Your mouth. Fuck."

Lea places Zion's hands on the sink.

"Zion, don't move your hands or I'll stop."

"Okay. Don't. Move. Hands."

Instead, he attempts to pull back out of her mouth, but she won't let him. She presses her face into the soft hairs of his crotch, breathing him in.

He actually trims his hair; he isn't overly bushy. I don't have to go digging for the stick in the bush. He smells so good. A combination of sex, sweat, cologne, and sex. Shit, I said that.

She licks around the tip of his dick, sucking in pre-cum. She uses her tongue to roll around the under skin of the tip. He jerks, and she feels more pre-cum hit her tongue. She uses it to lube up and down the sides of his dick, licking it like a lollipop.

Shit, this man's dick taste so good. Skin so soft.

She uses her other hand to lightly caress his balls. He throws his head back and growls. His moans are making her drip in her underwear. She adjusts them, so they aren't clinging to her clit.

"Oh, Lea. Stop. Please. Shit. Damn. That feels so good. Shit. Suck my balls. Please. Just a little."

She sucks in one of his balls gently rolling it in her mouth. He doesn't attempt to pull away, so she sucks in the other one. While sucking his balls, she uses her hands to stroke his dick up and down. He grinds his hips against her face. Letting go of his balls, she re-sucks on his dick. Up and down, using a combination of her tongue and the insides of her jaws to stimulate him.

I can't get enough of him.

She relaxes her throat and swallows him in as much as she can, moving back and forth. He grips her head, trying to push her off him.

Letting him slip out she reminds him, "Zion. Hands."

"Oh. Shit. Hands."

He places his hands back on the counter. She grips his ass, digging her nails into his butt cheeks and holds on. She can feel the sides of his dick throbbing on her tongue. He's so close to cumming.

I wanna taste more of him, but I can't swallow any more.

She keeps sucking, moving him in and out of her mouth, using her hands to grip his ass, leaving crescent moon shapes, so he doesn't plop out.

"Oh yes. Dammit. That's it. Suck it. Suck my dick. Yes. Suck me off. Shit. Your mouth feels so damn good. Oh. Lea I'm about to cum. Pull back now if you don't want me to shoot in your mouth," he groans.

Lea continues holding on as Zion is gripping her head, fucking her in her mouth. She doesn't admonish him about his hands this time, she focuses on getting that nutt. She moans and hums on his dick and he shoots. He unloads in her mouth and she catches all that she can. He jerks with each squirt of jism.

Zion moans some unintelligible words that even he doesn't understand what he's saying. The sensations Lea is causing him to experience hasn't happened in fucking ages. A combination of a shudder, heat flowing through his arms and legs. He has broken out in a cold sweat.

Oh, fuck shit. He mentally keeps repeating, but the words come out garbled. As Lea eases up, he doesn't want to let go of her head, he wants to keep fucking her mouth. He places his hands back on the counter, leaning against it, flexing his fingers, and of all things, his toes.

Why the fuck can't I stop flexing my fucking toes?

Feeling him getting semi-soft, she eases up, but continues licking the tip of his penis watching him. He grips the counter, his knuckles turning white, so she lightly licks him a few more times before completely releasing him.

She stands and turns on the faucet, splashing cold water on her face, rinsing out her mouth. He leans against the counter and holds on, catching his breath. Lea steps back, looking at him. She thinks about getting him hard and bringing him off a second time, staring down at his semi-soft dick.

I LIKEY THAT POPSICLE.

So do I, Sex Diva. I likey the man it's attached to even more.

Lea walks over to the table, pouring a glass of wine, drinking it, watching him. Bending down, she grabs his clothes from the floor, twirling the underwear around her middle finger. "You sleeping in these tonight or do I need to hang them on the bedroom door with your other clothes?"

"Burn the damn things for all I care," he says standing there with his eyes closed.

She walks off, twirling them in the air like a flag, leaving him in the kitchen to get his senses back.

WONDER WHAT'S ON TV, the Sex Diva says, smiling confidently.

Yes, let's find something to watch on TV.

Lea grins twirling his underwear on her bed like a spinning toy.

36

-6-

Zion finally takes a few steps away from the counter. He can't believe it. His legs are shaking. Again. He's never had shaking legs after sex, and she's brought him to this point twice.

What a fucking blow job that was. Let's not get it fucking twisted. I've had my dick sucked on. Plenty of times. But not from a woman who does it because SHE ENJOYS IT. Wholly fucking shit. And she walked her sexy ass away, leaving me here. I completely lost control and submitted to her. She had all the power and control, and I fucking loved it. I need to learn another word besides fuck. BUT WHOLLY FUCKING SHIT.

He wipes his hands across his face and head and grins. It's taking every ounce of his will power not to yell 'yes, yes, yes'. He stands up straight, attempts to adjust the silly grin on his face he knows is there and calmly walks into the bedroom and see's Lea sitting on the bed flicking through channels on the TV. He climbs in, crawling up her body, taking the remote from her hands and pressing the off button. The room goes silent.

Lea could never be Addison. She's so much more than that woman is in so many ways. I'm making love to this woman over and over and over as much as I can. Nope, you can't base a relationship solely on sex, but I be damned if we not gonna be gettin' it in every chance we get. Starting right now.

He lays on top of her, looking down into her eyes.

She's so damn cute.

"Hi." She says to him.

He grins back devilishly, "Hi."

He kisses her, putting as much of his feelings into that kiss as he can. He'd like to tell her he loves her, but he's never used those words with any of his temporaries. But he can show Lea. He kisses her lips, her eyes, her cheeks, her neck, and her shoulders.

Oh god, she's so sweet and precious.

He takes her hand and kisses her palm, flicking his tongue in the middle of it. She jumps, causing him to smile.

Yes, that's it, Kitten, enjoy this.

He nips at her wrist and trails kisses up her arm to the bend and kisses there. She giggles.

"Lea, you ticklish?" he asks. She moans in agreement. "Good, 'cause I like to hear you laugh."

He moves over to her other arm and repeats everything there. She puts her hand on his face and he leans into her, kissing it.

I'm home. I've never been this relaxed having sex. That feeling of get in, get off, and get out, is gone.

He slides down, admiring her breasts.

So, so, so damn perky in her tank top.

Her nipples are standing at attention. Usually, women won't have sex with the light turned on. Lea has left it on and is watching his every move. Probably looking for uncertainty.

Oh no, baby. You won't find any uncertainty from me.

"Hhhmmmm, Kitten. You're good at giving head. Where did you learn such skills?"

"Do you really want me to answer questions about my sex life? Especially, while we're having sex?" she asks, teasing him.

I really don't want to do that, but if he presses me I will.

"No. Never mind. Forget I asked," he smiles. "Lea, I need to take care of you, you should be ready to explode by now."

"Hhhmmmm, maybe."

Zion moves down gently removing her panties. He licks the opening above her delectable love button. Swirling his tongue around the juncture. He avoids touching her engorged member. As she gyrates her hips to get him to flick her clit, he pins her in place and continues to lick the area above it in a circular movement. When he thinks she can't stand the pleasure any longer he latches on and Lea jerks back.

That was totally unexpected. She hadn't braced herself for that immediate oh so delicious shot to her groin thinking he was going to stay above her clit. He latches on and sucks it in, rolling his tongue around it and pressing it between his lips.

"Oh, Lordy be. Hell yes." Lea moans.

Zion stops before she cums.

IS HE FUCKING KIDDING. I'M BOUT READY TO EXPLODE AND HE STOPS. WRAP YOUR LEGS AROUND HIS NECK AND PUSH HIM BACK DOWN THERE.

Before Lea can move her legs Zion lifts up looking at her.

"See? You need to be taken care of. And I'm the man to take care of you. Always," he nips the skin on her waist, on her thigh.

"Then why the heck you stop? Get back down there," she orders him.

"That's it, Baby. I like it when you order me to please you." He comes up and kisses her on the mouth, having her taste herself.

"Ride me Lea. I want to watch you. Ride your dick."

"Oh, so it's my dick now, is it?"

"Yes, it's your dick, my body is yours, just as you're mine. I claim it. I'll pleasure it; I'm not giving it up. Come on Kitten. Ride your dick."

Zion lifts up and lies down on his back scooting over to the middle of the bed.

Lea sits on top of his pelvis, positioning his penis between the folds of her pussy, gliding on it, making them slick. He stares down at the 'v' of her woman hood moving back and forth, watching the tip peak out.

So slick, so wet, he thinks. *Oh, she knows how to move.*

He bites his lip, watching her.

Oh yes.

"Lea, you're so good, when you gonna stick it in?" he asks, looking at her smiling.

"You want inside of me?"

"Yeah, you know it."

She slips Zion into her pussy, slowly opening herself to fully take him in. She glides down on him and he pushes up to feel the insides of her walls gripping him. Lea leans back and stretches to take him in, to feel him filling her up, expanding and throbbing inside of her.

She rides him slowly, moving up and down, grinding her pussy into his groin, into his soft hairs. They tickle her clit as she bends over to gain more traction to move better. Zion grips her breasts, rubbing and squeezing them, playing with her nipples. He rips the tank top into two pieces, wanting to put a breast in his mouth.

OH GOD, WE AIN'T GONNA HAVE NO CLOTHES LEFT WITH FUCKING THIS MAN. WE COME TO BED IN THE NUDE FROM NOW ON. YES, RIDE 'EM GIRL. RIDE. HIM.

"Zion you feel so good inside me. Oh, fucking yes. Damn your dick so fat and long."

"No, this your dick. Come on. Ride it. That's it, Kitten. Fuck your dick. Oh yes. Take it. Fuck it Lea. Cum on baby. Fuck."

Lea moves faster with every word he says, knowing that he likes what she's doing and he wants her to keep doing it, telling her his dick is hers. She feeds off his lust for her.

God, I hope this is always like this between us.

Zion grips her ass and Lea grinds as hard and as fast as she can wanting to, needing to cum. He pumps into her, pushing her into him, holding on. She leans over him, her breasts brushing up against his chest.

The hair on his chest. It's tickling my nipples.

"Oh, Zion, I'm getting ready to cum. Oh, shit yes."

She can't help herself, he can probably tell, but she needs for him to know. He pumps into her as fast as she is sliding up and down on him and she cums. Drenching them, having squirted for the second time from his love-making. He holds her face with one hand and her ass with the other hand, slapping her ass cheek hard.

Damn, she squirted all over me. He shoots and cums. "Oh. Fucking. Yes. Lea."

Zion is bucking inside her, draining himself with Lea squeezing his dick as hard as she can with her inner muscles, milking him dry.

They slowly come down off their sexual mountain peak. Lea tries to move. He holds her on top of him, not wanting to let go. After a few minutes, she moves a leg, stretching and flexing it.

"Where do you think you're going?" he asks.

"Warm towel. To get a warm towel," she laughs. "My house. I'll get the towel. Yes, we need warm towels to clean up." But she hasn't moved from his chest. Repeating herself.

"You keep saying that, but you haven't moved yet."

"I don't want to. I like it here."

"Beautiful, go get that towel," he says and kisses her, pushing her off him. It feels pretty darn cold right now.

Lea grabs two towels, one to clean herself and the other to clean him, soaking them in lukewarm water. Returning to the bedroom, she leans over him and wipes him down, gently. He's lying there, sprawled out, taking up her entire bed.

"Uhhhmmm, that feels good," he whispers.

She throws the towels into the hamper and climbs in bed, with him pulling her into his arms.

So very nice to have him here.

VERY NICE INDEED.

-7-

Zion and Lea are still lying across her bed after their last love making session. He's propped up on her pillows leaning against the headboard and she has her head on his lap with her feet propped up on the wall. The sounds of smooth jazz are playing in the background. They're 'discussing' the torn tank top that's now hanging half on and half off her nightstand.

"Look Lea, you make it a habit of walking around naked, and we won't have to have this talk about torn clothes," he tells her.

"Zion, I'm not that comfortable walking around nude as you are. It's just a tank top and boy shorts. Can't I get a pass on that? Please?"

"Okay. How about this? A tank top ONLY when walking around the house but in bed NUDE. That's all I can agree to at this point." He's loving this conversation. "If you come to bed with clothes on, I'm making no promises about what they will look like in the morning."

"But Zion, you were the one who said I should be in silks. Now I can't—?"

"Silks my ass. They cover too much. Tanks only while walking around and nude in bed. That's all I'm giving in to."

"Will you promise to at least put on gray sweatpants for me. Please?"

"Oh my God. Woman, seriously? Gray sweatpants?" He sighs. "You got it. And no underwear." He roars with laughter.

"And no underwear," she says, feeling she has won at least part of the discussion.

"Zion", Lea says becoming serious. "Will you tell me more about Addison?" She's feeling curious and wants to know what she could be dealing with and whose memory she needs to erase.

"Baby, she's nothing you need to worry about. I won't let her hurt you."

"If she's determined to be with you, she'll keep coming after you. Besides, it's not that I'm only worried about her getting to me. I want to know about her. And your relationship with her. Think of it this way, knowledge is power. In more ways than one," Lea says.

Zion looks at her, wondering how much he should tell her, really tell her.

I told myself I gotta give her a reason to trust me and me trusting her with my past is a start.

"I do have some say so as to whom I will and will not be with. As I said, we met in college. Things were good the first year. Typical relationship stuff. Dating, partying, and studying. We had plans of being together forever. We were getting business degrees, so of course, we had a lot of the same classes, talking of opening our own business, but we had no clue what the business would be. We had the typical disagreements. I was into passing all my classes, making my parents proud by doing better than average. She was cool with being below average, barely passing, getting in her homework late or not going to class. She made sure she went to the classes we had together, but if we didn't, she wouldn't go to hers or would go half the time. We argued about that."

Zion plays with one of the curls in Lea's hair while speaking.

"After freshman year for the summer, she went home to New Mexico, and I returned to St. Louis. We kept the relationship going. When we got back to school for our sophomore year, something was different about her. We would argue more about stupid stuff, and after the argument, she would want to fuck, and I mean that in the negative way. The bigger the argument, the more she wanted to have sex. The sex wasn't off the chain, but it was good sex. Oral, doggy style, missionary, nothing to brag about, but in my late teens, early twenties, that's what I knew about, what we knew about. It got to the point that she couldn't get aroused unless she was angry or had been angry. At first, it was nice because the arguments were in private, between us. Angry sex was some exciting sex. But she would make them public, she would physically fight, hitting me, and she wanted me to hit her back."

Lea caresses Zion's legs hoping, to comfort him. She doesn't know what to say, but she wants him to continue. This has to be details about his past no other woman has ever come close to knowing and he's opening up to her. Something she can't remember a man ever doing in her past relationships.

Zion continues. "Hell, I was young; I was thinking, okay, this is 'our sex life'. Then I started listening to people talk about their relationships and sex lives, and theirs was nothing like what I was having with Addison. I started getting sick of her and everything about her. I had friends talking about how happy, how loving, and how intensely erotic their love lives were. Mine was hateful, tiring, and evil. I made sure we no longer had classes together. I started going home more often, really distancing myself from her. Finally, I had a talk with my dad about it. He noticed how stressed I was, and he made me tell him what was going on. He told me I was never to hit a woman, always walk away, and I was never to be the type to hit a woman unless it was in self-defense, fearing for my life.

"He said 'Son, I have heard about BDSM, but what you have is sick'. I didn't even know what BDSM was when he was talking about it. I was not feeling that conversation. I knew hitting and fighting and arguing with Addison had to stop, or she had to go. But I didn't do it quickly enough. Turns out, when Addison went home that first summer, she fooled around with some guy who introduced her to BDSM, or what she thought was BDSM. And she loved it. When she came back to college for sophomore year and me, she assumed she would introduce me to it, but she wanted the demeaning, degrading, beating, and hateful part of it. The S&M of BDSM.

"I was an 'A' student my freshman year, but ending my sophomore year, I was barely pulling in a 'B' average because of all the shit with her. I had to let that go. Over that summer, she would call me, arguing, cussing me out for no reason. Hours later, I would get a call and she would be apologizing. Turns out, she would start an argument with me, go fuck and get beaten by ole boy, and then come apologize to me after. I didn't find this out until after we broke up though."

Zion hesitates remembering back to Addison and those calls. The sound of her grating voice, calling him names, begging him to love her. Not to leave her, then she telling him to get the fuck out of her life because he was a weak son-of-a-bitch. The feel of Lea's caress brings him back to the present.

"Prior to my junior year starting, I made a detour before going back to college to see her. She was hateful to me. She would start an argument, hitting me, throwing things at me, and this was in her parents' house in front of everyone. She didn't care. Then she would get all soft and say how sorry she was. Her parents informed me she was not going back to school. They were not going to be supporting her failing all her classes. They were forcing her to get a job. I left thinking we were still going to be together doing the long-distance relationship thing.

"We did for about three months, but I got tired of it. My stomach was in knots when she would call, and when she would manage to come see me. We would have sex after an argument she started, then she would be nice, apologize, go home, and it would start again. After my junior year, she ended our relationship because she was marrying someone who could give her the sex life she needed, and, of course, the babies I couldn't give her. Her parents told me to walk away. Their exact words were, 'Run, disappear off the face of the earth from her, and don't have anything to do with her ever again'. With this coming from her parents, I listened and walked away.

"I managed to make it through the summer with my broken heart. That summer is when I became distant in my relationships with women. When I went back to school, I perfected my playa status. I dated all the women I rejected for Addison. By the time graduation came around, I could compartmentalize everything in my life. School, family, friendships, and fuck buddies. I finished in the top five percent of my class, and started my path to billionaire status. By the time I had made my first million, the partying and working started wearing on me. Those around me noticed and suggested therapy. I was in therapy for three years to understand what happened and figure out who I was. I became the respectful 'playa' you met three months ago. I wasn't about to stop enjoying life. I managed to do it respectfully. Wow, has it been three months already? Wow Lea, three months," he laughs.

"Yes wow. It's been a kinda nice three months except for these last few weeks."

"I didn't know what else to do at the time. I had to find out what was in that woman's head. I followed her parents' advice. I made sure to keep my circle of friends tight. No one gets close to me unless I allow it."

"Do you miss any part of the life you had with Addison?" Lea asks, wanting to talk more about BDSM to see if he is open to discussing it and having some aspect of it in their relationship.

"No, none. It was nice in the first year of the relationship, but all relationships are like that. I don't miss her idea of sex. I enjoy our sex life, as you can tell by looking at the sheet. You playing with my hairs like that so close to my dick is keeping me semi-hard. Stop it 'cause we're supposed to be talking." He places his hand over hers, halting the caress.

"Sorry, they're so soft." She pulls her hand away and looks at him.

"What are you thinking about? Have I scared you away with what I told you?" he asks as he caresses her cheek.

"No, you haven't scared me away. That first year getting to know someone is always nice, you say. It's been a while since I've made it to a year of getting to know someone. It rarely has gotten past four months."

"Asking what kind of men you've been meeting and dating is a waste of a question for me. I was like one of those men. I'm looking forward to getting to know you. This 'with you', I like it a lot."

"Zion, I want to share something with you, but I don't want to take you back to a time where you're uncomfortable or re-hash old memories."

"If I can't handle it, I'll let you know. I promise," he says.
THE BOX! YOU GETTING OUT THE BOX!

-8-

Yes, I'm actually getting it out and sharing it. I've never shared this part of my life. I have explicit instructions for it to be given to Gordon and the contents burned without opening should I die before he does. Now I'm about to open this Pandora's box and let Zion into my utmost secret desires.

HE BETTER NOT EMBARRASS US.

Lea gets up, walks over to her closet and pulls out the 'box'. Her 'toy' box. Zion sits up in the bed. She sits down, pulling the sheet up to her breasts. She starts removing items and laying them between the two of them: a feather, a Miniature Whip/Tickler, Ben-Wa balls, dice, different gels and creams, blindfolds, books on oral sex, sexual positions, black erotica stories and poetry, vibrators – most for clitoral stimulation and a couple for G-spot stimulation.

He picks up each item and holds it. He flips through the books and notices she's read each one. They have dog-eared pages, highlighted passages, and marginalia. He moves onto the vibrators.

Lea grabs some batteries putting them in the toys that need them and plugging in the other ones that need to charge. Zion watches her every move. She turns on a vibrator and hands it to him. He tests out the speeds of each one and hands it back to her. She removes the batteries, placing the toys back in their storage bag.

"Why don't you keep the batteries in them?" he asks.

"I rotate them out. Batteries explode when they get old. I don't want to ruin my toys."

"And the one you plugged in. It needs to be fucking charged?" he asks incredulously.

Lea grows unsure of herself at his tone and starts putting things away.

Okay maybe this was not a good idea after all.

"Lea, no. Don't stop. I'm sorry. Don't take it that way. I've never seen anything like this before, that's all. Keep going. Please, keep going." He sits up and kisses her. "The women I've been with before you would never have brought out sex toys. Continue."

She pulls back from the kiss, feeling less confident than before. Wrapping the bed sheet around herself tighter, she proceeds.

He doesn't mention the move. Instead, he opens the case with the Ben-Wa balls in them and feels their heaviness in the palm of his hands.

"Remember our discussion at the restaurant?"

He nods his head.

"Well, these are them. Strengthen inner walls to—."

"Help you grip my dick tighter," he finishes for her.

"Yes."

He picks up the dice and looks at the words on a couple of them. Lips, shower, suck, lick. He smiles putting them back in the bag.

Next, he picks up the miniature whip. On one end is a feather, on the other end are leather strands. He slaps it against his thigh trying out the leather strands end. He hits himself four times, each time hitting harder.

Lea's nipples say 'hey'. She glances at his hardening dick.

He likes the whip.

HELL YEAH, WE MAY HAVE TO INVEST IN A LARGER ONE.

He next looks at the different gels and creams. They're pretty much self-explanatory: Deep Throat, to make a throat numb to last longer giving oral, warming massage gels, and clitoral stimulation gels.

Zion is thinking, *I'm a fucking virgin when it comes to this type of sex play.*

He picks up a catalog and flips through it. Vibrators, gels, clothing, books, bondage items. They have handcuffs, but you can use one contraption to strap one's wrists and ankles to a bed, no headboard or footboard needed.

Hell, I figured you would use ties or scarves or something like that. Shit, Addison had no fucking clue about BDSM. Lea, can teach me a lot about this. And I want to learn. With Lea as my teacher.

"Do you only purchase this stuff via a catalog or do you go into stores?" he asks her.

"I've been to stores numerous times."

Lea puts things away, feeling unsure now, but she opened this subject so she might as well answer his questions. As she unplugs the other vibrator, he grabs it from her hand, turning it on, testing out the eight different speeds. She reaches for it to put it away, but he tightens her hand over it with his.

"When was the last time you used this?" he asks.

"The day of our meeting, I was going to use it that night. But I used my fingers instead." She looks at him warily.

Shit, what is he getting at? I'm not throwing this away.

THAT IS OUR MOST EXPENSIVE ONE. WHAT HE THINKIN' CAUSE IT AIN'T GOIN IN THE TRASH.

"Show me." he demands.

"Pardon?"

OKAY, WE CAN DO THAT.

Say huh?

HE WANTS A SHOW. WE GONNA GIVE HIM A SHOW.

"Lea, you know what I'm asking you to do. Show me how you use this on yourself," he says as she looks him in the eye. He doesn't smile, not wanting her to think he's mocking her. He wants her to feel encouraged by his words, to do as he says. To be vulnerable for him. He pulls the sheet away from her body, wanting to see her nakedness. He knows he made her feel unsure. He gotta watch his mouth. Can't take two steps forward and one step back.

"You don't feel threatened by me having a box of sex toys?" Lea asks remembering having conversations with other men and how they would get highly offended at the thought of it.

"Lea, this is going to sound extremely conceited, but I know my skills. I may not know sex toys, but I sure as hell know how to please a woman. I want to learn this with you. Proceed."

She grabs the vibrator from him and places it next to a tube of lube on the bed.

"Why do you need lube? You have no problems with getting slick for me."

"I've never done this in front of a man. Call it performance anxiety. I may not get as wet or take to long to get to the mountain top." Lea giggles, "A little help with warming gel won't hurt."

"Baby, I can lube you up," Zion says licking his lips and fingers.

"You are supposed to be watching, not participating."

"Right. Do you beautiful. Do you." Zion strokes himself under the sheet, increasing the hardness of his penis.

DAMN HE GOT A PRETTY SIZE DICK.

Sex Diva, pretty. Really?

Lea takes her eyes off Zion and his stroking hand, looking him directly in the eye, "All right. Scoot over so I can get comfortable. My queen bed is perfect for me but you devour it."

He obliges. "It's perfectly cozy for the two of us. You can't get far." He props himself against the headboard turning toward her, slightly leaning on two of her pillows.

Lea climbs into bed with her head at the foot and her feet facing him so he can see what she's about to do. He doesn't touch her, propping himself up farther. She closes her eyes attempting to clear her mind of him next to her and that he's watching.

I don't know if I can do this, but I'm going to give it my best shot.

"Come on baby." he whispers above the music.

"Hush," she whispers back, smiling at him.

He grins.

Lea tunes him out, visually and vocally getting into her groove. She starts with caressing her lips, thinking about Zion kissing her. Wanting his lips on hers. Even though she can feel his body next to her and feel his heat every time her leg brushes up against his, he doesn't touch her. She pretends he's a pillow. She turns on the vibrator, gliding it over her nipples, changing the speed of the vibration as she does so, squeezing her tits.

Oh, Zion squeeze them hard, lick my nipples, suck them, oh please.

She pinches her nipples hard, visualizing Zion biting them. She moves the vibrator down her stomach, letting it sit on her belly button, feeling it vibrate. She slowly glides her hands down to her pussy gripping the vibrator.

Shit, this feels so good.

She pretends Zion's hands, his mouth, his lips, his tongue are on her.

Oh God I wanna feel his tongue on my clit. Lick my clit, suck it.

She presses the vibrator against her clit, squeezing the folds of her pussy around it. She slowly lifts her bottom up and down moving to get that orgasm.

Oh fuck, yes, shit, make me cum Zion, fuck me. Shit yes, baby yes.

She moans, still rubbing the vibrator against her clit. She can feel the orgasm building for release, about to explode. She feels the bed dip. Opening her eyes, she watches Zion move and place himself between her legs, watching her masturbate. He's holding his dick, moving his hand up and down the shaft.

"Lea, let me put it inside of you? I wanted to watch, but I can't. I want to feel you when you cum. Shit, you look so good."

"Do it."

Zion pulls Lea up to his waist and slides into her. She keeps the vibrator pressed against her clit. He moves in and out holding her legs apart, watching her. She closes her eyes, enjoying the action from him and the vibrator.

Oh yes, this feels so titillating.

"Oh, shit baby. Don't stop. That's it. Keep playing with your clit. Shit, let me see you get yourself off. Get us both off. Yes. Baby, fuck your dick. Shit yes."

Lea moves her body up and down, closer to cumming.

Zion tried to sit there and watch her, but she looked so damned sexy. Playing with her tits, and moving down to pressing that vibrator against her clit. He's watched women caress themselves prior to him fucking them, but this with Lea is different.

Fuck, I was so jealous of the damned B.o.B. I needed my dick inside of her. I needed some of that action. She's feverishly fucking my dick and stroking her clit. Oh, fucking yes.

"Come on baby. Cum for me. Oh yes. Baby. Yes."

Zion keeps pumping into her. She's moaning and breathing hard and then she cums. She drops the vibrator and grips his ass, pulling him into her deeper, stroking him. She has him pinned to her, pumping his dick feverishly up and down, in and out of her tight pussy.

Oh, fuck yes, this feels so damn hot.

"Oh yes. That's it. Fuck. Me. Damn. Lea. Oh. God. Lea. Baby. Ooooooooooooooooooooooo. Shit. Yes." Zion cums, pumping into her pussy.

"Oh, Zion yes." She cries from the force of the orgasm she's having. *Oh god this feels so damn heavenly. I don't want it to stop.*

Zion jerks inside of her, draining himself, plopping down onto her chest, slowly gyrating inside of her until he becomes soft and slips out. He slightly lifts his pelvis and lays his softened penis on top of her pussy.

Yes, this woman has me as her prisoner, locked up tight.

He raises, propping himself on his elbows looking at her. He kisses her tears away, smiling at this wonderful, sexual human being he has under him.

"Hi my sexy Adonis."

"Hello my beautiful, sexy, Nubian queen." They lay there hugging each other kissing.

Ima need to do some research to keep up with her.

Zion and Lea sleep late into the afternoon. They finally get up and have French toast, bacon, and eggs for lunch. He texts Sam and tells him to pick him up around four, wanting to spend as much time with Lea as he can. He may be doing a lot of traveling in the next couple of months and he doesn't plan on passing up any moment of being with her. Another first for him. Arranging his schedule to ensure he's spending more time with a woman. No more thinking a woman will make herself available for him.

"We have yet to discuss our limits and our safe words. Tell me, what are your limits?" Zion asks.

"No threesomes, I'm not sharing you. Only you can watch me. No video. No anal play. Nothing gets stuck up my ass. But you're more than welcome to lay your dick between my ass cheeks and rub yourself off," Lea says trying to look innocent.

Zion almost chokes on his drink and shakes his head grinning, "Geezus, woman you keep blowing my mind. Okay, I agree, we're not sharing each other. I don't even want you sending me sexy pictures, and even sexting makes me a little nervous. We'll have to talk in code. I don't do anal play either, but that rubbing off using your ass cheeks sounds wonderful. I look forward to phone sex with you, we must have plenty of verbal phone sex."

I dry dishes while she washes. Zion Landon is doing domestic duties. Ha, that's funny, but I'm loving every bit of it.

Continuing with their conversation he says, "Safe word. We saying no or stop, won't work for us. We need a word between us that will cause us to instantly halt and put a break on what we're doing when it's too much for either of us."

"How about Ocean? When I have my dreams of being left alone, I feel like I'm in the middle of the ocean and everyone is sailing away from me. I'm drifting in the middle of the ocean. Ocean can mean to stop, to halt."

"Okay, Ocean is our safe word to halt. What about to ease up? How about Halo? When we don't need a halt on things but want to ease up for a moment, we can use halo," he suggests.

"Ocean to stop and Halo to ease up. I like those," she says.

"So, do I," he smiles. "How about we test them out. To make sure they work."

"Good idea." Lea pulls him by the front of his shirt toward the couch.

Kia Lui

-9-

Sam arrives on time to pick up Zion. He's doing the walk of shame, leaving Lea's house in his tux. Closing the door behind him after watching the car drive off, Lea walks around talking to herself and rehashing him being there.

Maybe I need to clear out a couple of drawers and some closet space. In such a short time, this man has come to mean a lot to me and I don't think that's all good. He can still walk away. He has more options than I do. I can take the attitude to enjoy the moment and not worry so much about the future. Sometimes you do nothing about the past, then it decides to almost kill any future you could have. His Addison could kill our future.

Lea goes online and checks her social media accounts. On her own pages, she doesn't post much about her personal life. She's more active in groups. She keeps her friends-and-followers list low. Looking through the lists, she doesn't notice anyone out of the ordinary and hasn't received any new requests in over six months. She closes and cancels three accounts she forgot she even had. The settings of current accounts are changed to make sure any pictures posted or tags from friends have to be approved and set to private.

Zion doesn't even have any personal social media accounts. All of his are related to business, run by his marketing department. Little to no information is posted online about his social life outside of the typical gossip items found. Lea runs across his sister's page and hers is private.

I'll continue to keep my life off-line and enjoy the moment.

Lea calls Zion before going to sleep. He answers on the first ring.

"Hey you."

"Hi Bear. I have something of yours."

"Oh, is that right? Now what did I manage to leave behind?" he asks smiling. Talking to a woman on the phone like this has not been a part of his life. He can talk to Lea all day about nothing and everything.

"Your handkerchief was on my dresser. Monogramed with ZL. Smelling so much like you. Oh, and your scent is all over my bed. I don't think I'll be washing my sheets and comforters for a while," she says while lightly brushing his handkerchief against her cheek.

"Ah, so I did leave it at your house? Good. Can't have strangers getting ahold of that. They may perform some voodoo to try and woo me."

"Maybe I'll perform some to keep you."

"You don't need to, you have me, no worry. I miss you, babe. Already I miss you in my arms."

"I miss you, too," she tells him. "I'm not going to ask when I'll be seeing you. Don't want a repeat of before. I'm traveling for business this week."

"Actually, you'll be seeing a lot of me this week." Zion is staring at Lea's travel schedule. He's made arrangements for her to fly in and out on his plane, and he'll be right by her side. He doesn't have any scheduled meetings with clients, which is perfect. He can work from anywhere. Wednesday through Friday he and Lea will be traveling together and going out on dates. He'll be showing her a little of his world.

"What's that supposed to mean? I'll be out of town on business this week. I'll be in and out of airports."

"Well, we'll be in and out of airport hangars, but your flights are chartered. You'll be flying Landon Enterprise Airlines to and from all your destinations. I'll be by your side. You'll be handling your business during the day, and at night, we'll be enjoying ourselves seeing the sights of Atlanta, Miami, and Chicago."

"Zion what are you talking about?" she says sitting up, excitement flowing through her veins.

"Crystal gave me a copy of your schedule. I've cancelled all your flights. I've changed all your hotel reservations. We fly out Wednesday on my company plane and return Friday evening. I want to take you all over the world, but for now this will do."

"Zion, you're wonderful. And a bit heavy handed. What if I wanted to say 'no' to all of this?"

"I would kidnap you and surprise you. Are you saying no?"

"Hell no! Pass up the chance of traveling with you. I'm not crazy. Do I need to pack anything extra for going out?"

"Nope, only your business attire. I'll take care of the rest." Zion smiles into the phone. "Get some sleep, Kitten. I'll see you Wednesday at my office."

It never even crossed my mind Lea would say no to me about changing her travel plans. I need to be careful of that. Lea isn't like the other flashy women I used to date. She has a strong mind and opinions of her own.

"Goodnight, Zion."

"Goodnight, Lea."

Lea ends the call and squeals. Her bag for the week is packed and ready to go. He cancelled all her flights, so her itinerary is worthless. She tosses it into the shredder. She'll be traveling in a private plane with a sexy Adonis. Her sexy Adonis.

PACK THE DEEP THROAT. YOU MAY NEED IT. YOU'RE GETTING YOUR PERIOD THIS WEEK. WE'RE NOT LEAVING HIM HANGIN'.

Lea stays with her mom Tuesday night to ensure she has everything she needs for the week and reminds her to call Gordon for anything. Lea hasn't informed her mom much about Zion.

After Lea's last heartbreak her mom felt there was no need to meet any man her daughter wasn't seriously dating. Ms. Adams considers them temporary flings.

Ms. Adams once had a 'discussion' about Lea's dating style. She was frustrated seeing her daughter hurt every time she gave her heart to a man too soon. They had a come to Jesus meeting one day with Ms. Adams telling her daughter to have some fun and stop trying to turn every walking penis into a husband. "Lea, I want you to date, have fun, relax getting to know men. Don't mean you gotta sleep with them and you definitely don't have to marry. Especially if you thinking I'm looking for you to do so. Are we clear on that?" Her mother asked.

"Ma, what happened to you having a good girl?"

"You will always be the good girl I raised you. Stop being a carpet for idiotic pencil dicks. Enjoy life."

"Yes ma'am."

Lea smiles, remembering the conversation. Her mother tells her to have fun, call every night, check in and be careful.

On Wednesday, she goes in to the office early to clear up anything waiting for her. Instead of going to Lambert International Airport, Sam will be picking her up at ten and taking her to Zion's office. They will drive to the Chesterfield Airport to board his plane. It's been fewer than forty-eight hours since she has seen him, but it seems longer.

Crystal asks her, "How are things with the two of you?" She's closed the door, plopped herself in Lea's office chair, and is waiting for details. "Zion is saving us eight-grand this week I see."

"It's strange as hell. Crystal, I'm dating a client, a billionaire, and he's fucking hot. He may be saving us eight-grand but I think about what this is costing him."

"Lea, stop worrying and enjoy it. I'm so thrilled you two are together. When you were out of town, he was pissed."

"I guess he's told you about this Addison Raymond?"

"Yes, he informed me she resurfaced. Trust him. He can handle it. If you notice anything strange, report it. It may be nothing, but let's not be naïve. The woman could be really nuts. Tom has upgraded the office security system by the way. We have video surveillance now. You can connect to it on your phone twenty-four/seven. I downloaded the application to your phone this morning and added all the passcodes. All the staff has been made aware of the changes."

"Thanks, Crystal. Is this a Zion suggestion?" Lea displays mild anxiety in her question.

"Nope. Tom had been in the process of upgrading the system anyway. He got the idea from what is going on with the Landon Enterprises project and contacted the same company they are using, Essensecurity. The man is a bigger techno geek than you are. We remember what Zion went through with Addison. Nothing can be out of the ordinary when it comes to being cautious. Have fun on your 'business' trip. Try to get some work done while having sooooo much sex. Everything okay with your mom? You need us to look in on her?"

"Gordon said he will, but if you could give her a call, that would be great?" Lea asks.

"Will do," Crystal says, leaving her office.

At ten o'clock, Lea meets Sam in the lobby of G-TEE. He grabs her bag out of the front closet along with her backpack. She holds onto her purse, needing something to do with her hands. She says goodbye to Crystal and Tom and gets on the elevator with Sam.

"Sam, I'm not good at chit chat, but how have you been?" She tries to make them feel comfortable with each other.

"I'm good Miss Adams. It's okay, you don't have to make chit-chat. I understand how you may feel about me after you saw me that night."

"I know you were doing your job. He's the boss and that's where your loyalties lie. I'm just—. Well, we're good. I don't want it to be awkward between us. I want you to know I understand you were doing your job."

"Yes ma'am, we're good." They look at each other in the mirror of the elevator and smile.

Sam senses Lea has stopped at saying she's just a piece of ass. This would have been the first time in his employment he would have had to correct a woman about her status in his boss's life. He was ready, consequences be dammed.

Lady, a piece of ass you're not to Zion Landon.

They arrive at Landon Enterprises at ten-forty-five. Sam escorts her to Zion's personal office. She's been here a handful of times, but was always escorted to a conference room, the IT department, or the server room. Today, it's straight to the executive wing. She walks into the waiting area outside of Zion's office where Morgan greets her.

"Hello, Miss Adams, Mr. Landon is expecting you. You may go on in." Morgan walks her over to the door and opens it.

Zion is on the phone and Lea feels uncomfortable, as if she shouldn't be here. She hesitates, then attempts to back out, but he freezes her in place with a look and mouthing, 'Don't you dare leave'.

Lea walks in. He has a view of interstate two-seventy. The furniture in his office is minimal. Desk, chair, meeting area to the right of his office doors, and a small kitchen area to the left. He keeps talking to the individual on the phone not taking his eyes off Lea, grinning.

"Look, Mrs. Casey, your son is of age. He has every legal right to fire my company as his financial consultants. There is nothing I can do to stop him. No, ma'am, your financial portfolio is completely separate from his. He only knows what you tell him. As your financial advisor, I'm not allowed to discuss your business with him unless you designate him as a beneficiary or point of contact. Yes, ma'am, I'll continue to be your advisor as long as you would like. I'll be out of town for the next few days but my assistant, Morgan, can reach me should you need anything. Thank you ma'am. You take care, too."

Zion ends the call, takes out the ear piece and walks over to Lea for a kiss. "Hi beautiful. Welcome to my office."

"Good afternoon Mr. Landon." Lea kisses him.

"Hhhmmmm, you haven't called me Mr. Landon since the day we met. I'm still not sure if I like it. Is it a sign of respect this time or something else? Miss Adams." Zion caresses her ass while kissing her neck.

Lea presses her pelvis into his. "Something else," she says leaning into him, loving the feel of being in his embrace.

"Lea Adams, ocean," he says testing out their safe word.

Lea pulls away and walks over to the conference table, taking a seat. Smiling, he adjusts his dick in his pants and walks back over to his desk. While keeping an eye on her, he responds to a few more emails then packs up his computer, putting it in its case.

"Let's get going."

As they leave Zion's office, he hands his computer case off to Sam, stopping to have a conversation with Morgan.

Lea steps to the side to give them privacy. Zion looks over at her, his face showing displeasure.

Well, it's a habit. If I'm not a part of the conversation, I back off a little. Give people privacy.

They walk to the elevators and he pushes the button. "Why did you step away from me back there?" he asks.

"To give you privacy. That's the respectful thing to do, right?"

"I guess. I didn't like it. It felt like you were excluding yourself. Don't step back like that."

"Okay." She plasters a silly grin on her face.

They get on the elevator with other people, so there is no making out. He grabs her hand and links their fingers, tightly. They smile at each other, thinking the same thing.

No kissy, kissy face this time.

Usually, Lea dresses in leggings, an oversized shirt and khaki shoes when traveling, but today it's nine-to-five from head to toe. Coral button-down silk blouse, black vest, black slacks, and coral heels. When they land, she has a meeting with a client at an elite furniture store, Modern Memories Furnishings. Zion will go to the hotel, and Lea will go meet with her client. They get into the car and Zion pulls her as close as the seat belts will allow.

Neither of them notice the individual standing across the street staring.

Addison.

She has managed to locate Zion's offices. She was about to go up to see him when she saw him coming out of the building. As she was about to rush to him and announce her presence, she halted at the way he put his hand on the back of a woman that came out the door before him. At first, Addison assumed he opened the door for her to step out, as the gentlemen he is. But seeing him place his hand on her back, she hesitated watching. This looks like they have some kind of familiarity with each other.

Who the fuck is that? Oh, hell no, she's not getting my man. This bitch better be someone he fucking works with and even then ima need to set her ass straight. Stay the fuck away from my man

Kia Lui

-10-

In the car, Zion and Lea are turned facing each other, not paying attention to what's going on outside.

"You look sexy in silk after all. Any chance we can make out on the plane? It has a bedroom; we can join the mile-high club."

"We can make out only if you promise not to rip my clothes off me so I'm not meeting my client in the nude."

"I'm not making such a ridiculous promise." Zion lustily stares at her.

"You want to rip my clothes off me, still?"

"Yep, every time I see you, I keep thinking you have on way too many clothes," he states. "We'll be landing at two forty-five. You meet your client. What time do you think you'll be finished?"

"Don't know, I'm pushing for no later than six."

"May I see your phone please?" He asks stretching out his hand.

"Why?" She reaches for her purse to get her phone. "Why do you want my phone this time?"

Lea holds it out of his reach. He puts his on the seat between them. His screen saver is a picture of her standing at her kitchen sink, looking down into the water, a million miles away. He's cropped it and put a filter on it so you can't tell she's in a tank top and boy shorts. She looks at him, then down at his phone. She reaches for it and stares. He gives her the code to unlock it, 091672. Her birthday. She doesn't remember ever telling him that.

"Yes, Kitten. My unlock code is your birthday. You mean that much to me," he whispers.

"I didn't know you were taking pictures of me. It's beautiful."

"Lea, you're beautiful. Turn on your Find My Friends and add me, I'll add you to mine."

I give him my phone and the code: 202122. He sets up our phones to be able to find each other.

"Our first date, our second date, and our third date," he says. "Why are you so quiet Lea? What are you thinking?"

"Your code is my birthday. Is that a coincidence or on purpose? You allowed me to unlock your phone. Why? You noticed my code is of our dates. A man has never given me his code to his phone, handed me his phone, has ever had me saved as his screen saver that I'm aware of. I'm stunned, happy and ecstatic. You really want me, don't you?" She asks not looking at him.

"Lea, look at me. Yes, I really do want you. I'm not going anywhere. Tell me, what are you thinking?"

"Zion, I've never been with a man that knew exactly what he wanted, didn't hesitate about going after it, and it was me. You're sexy, and you can have any woman you want. Plain Jane, actress, model, or the girl-next-door. I don't know where I fall into those categories, sure as hell not model or actress. Maybe the Plain Jane. But you want me. Me, Lea Adams. I'm accustomed to being with men who have one toe in a relationship and the rest of their body out looking for something else. This is so new and different to me. I still don't know how to act at times," she admits to him. "There goes my flow of the mouth disease again. Sorry if I went too far."

"Lea, you haven't gone too far. This is all new to me, too. I haven't been in a long-term relationship since college. I don't know at times if what I'm doing is right or wrong with us, ima just do it. I shut you out so I could deal with Addison. That was wrong. Now I'm doing things that hopefully are right. My entire body, mind, and soul is in this relationship. I say, do what feels right. As for me dating models and actresses, it's not what it's cracked up to be. It was something to do. I like this relationship, let's enjoy it,"

Zion says, hoping he's reassuring her, but he's actually reassuring himself.

"Plain Jane? Lea, there is nothing plain about you. I can remember the girls next door from my past. I will say you're the most unique woman I've ever met. You have a career you love; you aren't into the social scene. Woman, all this is so out of the norm for me. I'm accustomed to superficial and materialistic women where status and money is priority one. This with you, I'm assuming is how dating should be. This is how our dating is going to be."

I pull him toward me, kissing him, putting all my feelings into that kiss. I don't say the words 'I Love You', but hope the kiss I give him shows that love and more.

Zion pulls away, breathing hard. They've arrived at the airport. Stepping out of the SUV, he walks her to the plane. Lea's eyes bulge with wonder.

I'm going on a private plane. I need a fan to cool myself and calm me from the excitement I'm experiencing right now.

His pilot, co-pilot and two stewardesses greet them by name. Sam and another security guy are traveling with them.

Well, no making out and joining the mile-high club on this trip for sure.

The second guy is Zach Ryan. He will be Lea's driver to and from her appointments.

I don't know this man. I'm not feeling this.

Ryan, as he has requested to be addressed by his last name, seems to recognize her hesitation. He explains he has been working for Mr. Landon for over a decade and she is safe with him.

Yeah, right, okay. Not. But I say nothing of my fear. Only thank you.

They walk onto the plane and Lea stops dead in her tracks with Zion bumping into the back of her.

"Lea, what's wrong?" he questions, catching her by the waist before they could fall.

I whisper to him, trying not to let Sam and Ryan hear me.

"I keep forgetting how fucking rich you are. Shit. Zion, I'm on a fricking private plane." She turns around looking at him, "Sorry about the language, but fuck, you're shit loads rich."

He grins and kisses her. "Baby, you keep making me the happiest man on earth. I so love that you can forget about the money and see me, Zion, the man. Now let's take our seats so we can get going."

Lea sits down and Zion buckles her into a seating area across from him. Ryan and Sam are sitting around a table, buckled in. The plane has separate seating areas for conference meetings and traveling. Lea looks around in awe.

Zion watches Lea looking around the plane. Other women would be primping, placing themselves in sexy positions, adjusting clothes, hair, checking makeup. Lea is looking around like a kid in a candy store for the first time. He takes his seat staring at her smiling.

This woman keeps a smile on my face like no other woman has.

Bending over the armrest, Lea is looking toward the back of the plane and sees a door slightly ajar. She assumes that's the sleeping area. She wants a tour, but the flight is too short and the men start talking business. She takes out her tablet, busying herself with her own work.

During the flight, Zion, Sam, and Ryan discuss security issues with the new building. Zion keeps glancing at Lea, wanting to go sit next to her.

Ryan and Sam take notice, saying nothing but giving each other knowing looks. Zion has never traveled with a woman and discussed business. He looks relaxed as if everything happening is second nature to him, like Lea has been on numerous trips with him and he can discuss his private matters. This is not the Zion Landon the men are accustomed to being around.

Lea listens and takes notes in case any of what they are discussing may be good to know for the Landon Enterprises project. "Mind if I ask a few questions?"

All three turn to her expecting to hear a question about dinner or shopping. "Go ahead," Zion says, wondering what she could possibly want to know about his office security.

"Your security cameras. Will these be viewable on your smartphones and tablets?"

"Yes," Sam responds.

"Who all within your company will be able to view these cameras and their footage?"

"All my security detail, head of my IT department, and myself," Zion responds, intrigued with her questions. He turns his body facing her, leaning back in his chair with his hand playing with a pen. "What are you getting at Lea?"

"Will you be viewing them from your home office?"

"Yes, whenever and wherever we need to. What's up?"

"You will need more powerful computers for whomever will be viewing these cameras and footage. Your phones will need to have as much memory and speed as you can get. For your home networks, you will need to purchase a separate router and have the camera feeds on that router alone. Otherwise, your network connections will keep dropping. If you keep them on separate routers they won't interfere with other devices on your network. Your cameras can be on a faster gigahertz speed than, say, your home printers or smartphones. Keeping your laptop and cameras on a different one makes more sense."

All three men sit looking at her, stunned. "What?" Them looking at her like she's grown two heads aggravates her.

Yes, gentlemen this lil lady can talk business just as well as you three. Jerks.

"This is what I do. I've run into this issue before. And this is why you hired me, but please go ahead. Continue on with your discussion. I'll address your issue later. When your video feed stops working and y'all can't figure it out. See how much extra that will cost you."

She takes out her phone to find a game to play until they land. Zion gets out of his seat, goes over to her and lifts her head up kissing her.

"Damn woman, you're a total package. Smart, sexy, knowledgeable, and mine. All mine. Gentlemen, make sure to implement all her suggestions." He kisses her again.

I almost tell this man I love him; his kisses are so satisfying.

"I may need to steal you away from G-TEE and have you come work with me."

"Uh, no. Not gonna happen. I love my job. Carry on."

They arrive in Chicago thirty minutes earlier than what she would have if she had taken a commercial flight. As they deplane, Lea notices two cars. A red Porsche Panamera Turbo S and a black Lexus LS 600h L. Ryan walks to the Lexus and Sam walks toward the Porsche with their luggage. Zion walks up behind her, putting his hands around her waist.

"Boys and their toys. I get to test it out to see if I want to purchase one."

"Have fun and be careful." Lea smiles at him.

"Oh, baby, always. Call me when you're done. We'll meet in the hotel lobby for drinks, then go to dinner."

Before he can move, Lea grabs him and steals one last kiss, then walks away.

I've always been hesitant in showing affection in my relationships for fear of being rejected. With Zion, I'm going to give in to what I'm feeling, like the man said. See where it takes me.

Zion watches Lea walking to the Lexus. He beams.

She's mine, all mine.

Sam watches Zion watching Lea. *That boy is finally in a relationship and enjoying the love of a special woman. Not that fake shit he been fucking for years. Thank the heavens. Finally.*

Kia Lui

-11-

Ryan pulls up to Modern Memories Furnishings for Lea's meeting with her client, Parnell Carr. Why Mr. Carr is paying G-TEE to fly her to Chicago to do a furniture consultation for his new office is beyond her comprehension. He's paid for this, so here she is.

Ryan parks in front of the store and opens the door for Lea and she steps out. They observe the empty parking lot. "Ma'am, are you sure they're open?"

"It does look closed, doesn't it? Ryan, will you care to join me? If I go in there alone, Zion may ring my neck. Better safe than stupid, don't you think?" Lea uses Zion as an excuse instead of admitting to herself that she really doesn't want to do this. If she were alone, she would've turned around and left.

"Of course, Miss Adams." Ryan wasn't going to allow her to walk in there alone and her suggesting it takes away an argument he felt may have taken place.

They enter the store noticing it's deserted, except for what looks like a salesman and he's backing off into an office and closing the door.

What the fuck? Lea and Ryan are thinking. Ryan slips his hand toward his gun, unsnapping the leather holder, ready to extract if necessary.

A noise attracts their attention from somewhere, and they see Mr. Carr descending some steps.

"Hello, Lea," Mr. Carr greets her.

Parnell is fifteen years younger than Lea. He attempts to live large, putting on a front. During their first conversation, Parnell turned Lea off by calling her 'Dear', 'Ma', or 'Ole Gal'. She hated those eighties pet names. She cussed him out after the 'Ma' reference, and he has been a semi-gentleman since, other than trying to bed her in subtle ways. She'll get this visit over with and ensure he never asks for her assistance again. The check cleared so she goes into business mode.

"Hello Parnell," she responds dryly, "shall we get started?"

"Who is this?" Parnell looks at Ryan.

"He stays." Lea looks at Parnell daring him to say something. Ryan is here for a reason. It may be Zion's reason but there is nothing wrong with taking advantage of the security he represents.

Lil boy is pissed. Yeah buddy. I got your number. This cougar is not interested in your young ass.

"Okay." Parnell dismisses Ryan with a smug look and focuses on Lea, turning on the charm. "I'm furnishing my new office, and I wanted your opinion and suggestions on the best furniture that would look well. You know my tastes of old furniture, but I don't want it to look ancient old. And, of course, some of it may need to be altered to accommodate my business needs and equipment."

"Bull. You know what furniture you like," she says, staring at him.

"Please, Lea."

His 'please' sounds like fingernails on a chalkboard.

Lea rotates her neck and squints her right eye, fully displaying the discomfort she's feeling at his words. "Fine, let's shop. Shall we?"

They walk around and he points out couches, tables, chairs, and desks. Lea likes some of his choices. Everything selected would fit into an office or a home. One selection he made was a media piece that a previous owner changed the walls and doors to iron mesh. This piece would eliminate his electronic equipment, such as printers, and wireless boxes overheating. She points out things he could hide his equipment in and how it can be altered to fit wiring. He tries to get close to her, attempting to touch her, but Ryan keeps making his presence known. After touring the store for two hours, her patience is gone, and Parnell can tell.

"I'm boring you?" he asks.

"You're wasting my time, and we know it. It's your money and our scheduled appointment is over." Lea makes a move to leave.

"Wait. May I take you to dinner while you're in town?"

I laugh to myself. No way in hell.

"Thanks Parnell, but I have plans already."

"Lea, you don't have to lie. I know you're single. I'm sure an older woman as yourself can utilize a young man like me. We could be good together. I could tame you. If you get past this age issue, I could be the man of your dreams." Parnell reaches to touch Lea but she steps back.

"You funny. No. You hilarious."

Ryan moves to protect Lea, but she halts him before he can check Parnell. She has been wanting to do this for some time and she's not letting this opportunity pass. Turning to Parnell she squares her shoulders, straightens her spine and lets loose all the words she has wanted to say to him from the first 'Ma' reference he laid on her.

"Tame me? Man of my dreams? Utilize you? Where in the hell do you get these ideas from? You would be more like the man of my nightmares. Lil boy, mentally, you are young enough to be my child. Even in my heaux phase, you wouldn't get a play. Tame me, that's funny." Lea walks toward Parnell and gets within six feet of him to make her next point.

"This cougar would have your ass in a corner in the fetal position sucking your thumb, begging me not to leave. Pleading with me. Telling me you MY bitch. Your inexperience is shouting you have no clue how to treat a woman, let alone an older woman." Lea looks him up and down in disgust. "Your attempt at being an alpha male is disgusting to Alpha Males. As I said the check has cleared. This meeting is over. Good day, Mr. Carr. Tame me my ass. Boy, you just sad." She turns and walks away.

Parnell stares at Lea, wanting to prove her wrong and snatch her back, making her kneel before him, ramming his dick down her throat. He had plans for the salesman and him to fuck her. Hell, why else would he spend all this money to get her here? Naw, she was gonna be his bitch. He looks over at Ryan thinking maybe he can take him. Ryan opens his jacket, putting his hand in his pocket; displaying his Glock G19 pistol. Parnell looks Ryan in the eye, calculating what to do next. He backs off, watching Lea leave the store.

"Don't make me dog walk your ass, lil bitch," Ryan says chuckling. He follows Lea, keeping an eye on Parnell and the door where the other person he knows is watching and listening.

They exit the building, striding to the car. Ryan doesn't say a word but opens the car door for her, then turns toward the building and checking their surroundings to be sure nothing will happen before he can get them out safely.

During the ride, Lea texts Zion informing him her meeting is over and she's on her way to the hotel.

I would say I can't believe what just happened, but this isn't the first-time men have looked at me as being needy and treating me as if I was desperate for the small 'consideration' they were giving me. Oh no baby, not this cougar. I don't have time to train little boys.

Zion calls. "Hi Kitten, all go well."

"Sure," she says, dead panned, making eye contact with Ryan in the rear-view mirror, "I'll explain later."

"Is everything okay?" Zion has gone into savior mode.

"A lil boy trying to play grown-up games. I'll tell you about it when I see you."

"Okay. When you get to the hotel, go to the front desk. Give them your name. There's an envelope for you. Follow the instructions. See you in about an hour."

"An hour! Zion?"

"An hour." Not only has Zion been test driving the Porsche, but he's been shopping for Lea. He's set out the attire he would like to see her in tonight and has packed the remainder.

Damn, it was nice shopping for her, imagining what she would look like. In and out of everything.

Ryan pulls up to the Peninsula Chicago. When Lea gets out of the car, she looks at him. "Go ahead and laugh. You gonna bust a gut holding it in so long."

He grins. "I'm sorry ma'am. I can't get the image out of my head. Fetal position and all."

She smiles. "Good night, Ryan. And stop calling me ma'am. I'm not that old."

"Good night, Miss Adams. I'll try."

Lea goes straight to the front desk giving them her name. She is handed an envelope containing a card key to the Executive Suite and a note from Zion:

> *"Baby, go up to our suite. Your clothes are laid out*
> *for you. Take a nice hot shower, smell good for me.*
> *Come up to the Z-Bar at seven-thirty." Bear*

Grinning broadly, she looks at the time on her phone. Six-twenty. Walking toward the elevator, she taps the card to her nose smelling the scent of him. Lea slips the note into her purse, keeping the card to the suite out.

Okay, I'm not going to over think this nor will I be nervous. I will, but I'm not going to give into it.

-12-

Zion watches Lea enter the lobby, pick up the envelope, and step to the side to read it. Men are watching her. She has no clue. Even a couple get up and walk past her, speaking. She speaks back but gives them no play. She has no idea how attractive men find her.

That's my girl.

A corresponding smile breaks out on his face, knowing the note she slipped in her bag will end up with the one he wrote her from the Cheshire Inn. He watches her move to the elevators going upstairs. Ryan comes over and tells Zion about the meeting with Lea's client. He boils with anger, this boy coming on to her. Ryan tells him what she said. Zion shakes his head and roars with laughter, attracting admiring looks from women mingling in the lobby of the hotel.

"She really called him all that?"

"Yes sir."

"Thanks Ryan. I'm glad you were with her. Be ready to leave tomorrow after breakfast around ten-thirty. We fly to Atlanta."

"Yes sir. See you tomorrow," Ryan gets up to leave, handing the keys to the Lexus to Sam then walks off to enjoy his night.

Zion looks over at Sam. "Feisty, isn't she?"

"Yes, she is and you seem to be handling her well," Sam comments.

"I'm not handling her, I'm in love with her. Can you believe it? Me in love. She's handling me."

"It's about time. So, are you getting the Porsche?"

"Yes. They will deliver mine to St. Louis in a few weeks."

"Nice birthday present to yourself?"

"Yep, turning fifty," Zion shakes his head. Forty-nine and first time he has ever fallen in love.

"Let's get going. Lea and I should be outside by seven forty-five."

"Yes sir."

It's seven twenty-five. Zion goes up to the hotel bar to wait on Lea. He texts her to come into the lounge and walk toward the bar where he's waiting.

When Lea gets to the room, a dress is laid out on the living room couch. It's black down the sides and brown in the middle, with crisscrossing threads of gold, down the bodice. The dress is form fitting, curve hugging, baring minimal cleavage.

If I had boobs big enough, my cleavage would be popping out all over the place. This will push my boobs up with a small amount of cleavage and lots of jiggle. Sexy but understated. Nice Zion. Really nice.

There are black stilettos, a black clutch and chocolate diamond studded gold earrings. He even purchased underwear, a lace bra and lace boy shorts.

Lea, is astonished, staring in awe.

He bought clothes for me. And jewelry.

The Sex Diva is prodding her to hurry up and get dressed. She showers, shaves, puts on the dress, and stands to survey herself.

Damn, I look good. This man has great taste.

She's done a smoky brown eye with red lipstick. She breaks out her Pure Instinct scent, rubbing it on all her pulse points. She feels a little bit, no, a lot, nervous, but takes a deep breath, grabs her clutch and heads for the elevators.

The elevator opens with five women already on. Lea steps on saying excuse me and moves to one of the corners. She glances at them and glimpses herself in the reflection of the elevator walls. They are chatting and talking about all the men staying in the hotel this week and how they'll be either catching a husband or some dick. One turns to Lea and asks if she had come from getting lucky.

She says, "No, I'm in town for business and don't know anything about the number of men staying here."

The woman informs her the black Greek fraternities are having their convention here this week. "Every woman is bound to catch a man. Even you. There has to be a few men that want your type."

Lea stares at her blankly, "Pardon? My type? What exactly is my type?"

"Well, if you gotta ask, obviously you lacking what we got. Good luck." The catty woman exits the elevator before Lea can cuss her out.

Oh, how sweet. Even I can catch me a man tonight.

Lea lets the other women exit then she steps out. Her heart races at the sight of all the black men.

Shit, I haven't been in a room this full of men outnumbering the women in like forever. If I wasn't going to meet Zion, I could definitely find something here tonight.

Groups of them are everywhere. She hesitates for an instant because she has to walk through all them to get to Bear.

Really? Seriously? Wholly Fuck! Now I see what ole girl meant about type. So much silicone and horse hair in this bar, it is utterly ridiculous.

Zion watches Lea standing at the entrance, hesitating.

Come on babe, come to me. You can do this.

She walks as if she heard him.

That's my Lea.

She walks through the throng of men and thirsty women. She speaks to the men who speak to her, but keeps moving. Five women have attempted to grab Zion's attention in the time he has been in here, but all he wants is Lea.

In she walks, scanning the bar looking for him. He winks at her when she spots him. She smiles and walks toward him, wanting to run. As she gets closer, a woman steps in her path to cut her off.

Man, not another one.

"Hey handsome. Wanna buy me a drink?" she asks.

"No. I much rather buy one for the beautiful lady you stepped in front of."

The thirsty one steps aside and looks at Lea. She steps past the woman into Zion's waiting embrace.

"Hi, Bear."

"Hello, gorgeous." He puts his arm around her waist and lays his hand on her ass possessively. "You want anything to drink?"

"I'll have a sip of yours."

Lea takes his drink, turns it around so her lips touch where his were and sips staring at Ms. Thirsty the entire time. Lea then hands the drink back to Zion, brushing her finger tips against his. Straight vodka with lime. She keeps her face expressionless, knowing Zion is inwardly laughing at her. Lea dislikes the taste of straight liquor.

"I guess I got extremely lucky," Lea says to the woman she recognizes from the elevator. "Uhm sweetheart, would you say I was your type?" Lea asks Zion smirking at him, hoping he plays along. She leans on him pressing her chest against him, forcing the mounds of her breasts together.

GOT DAMN THEM GIRLS LOOKING GOOD IN THIS DRESS.

He catches on quickly, "Not only are you my type, but you blow away all the caterpillar eyes, silicon ass, tits, and horse hair in the room."

The thirsty woman looks Lea up and down. "Seriously, her over me?" She flips her hair over her shoulder and walks off.

"Why that phony witch."

"Don't waste a second thought on her, Kitten. She's so not worth it. What was that type stuff about anyway?"

Lea turns toward the bar leaning against it and Zion bends down to hear her explanation above the noise. "I rode the elevator with her and some other women. She said some men might be here who would like my type. When I asked her what she meant, she made sure to insult me on the sly. Can we get out of here?"

He turns looking at the woman giving them a death stare. She would have been his type. In the past. Now it makes his skin crawl. "Sure, dinner and dancing are much better than being in this hookup factory."

Zion pays for his drink and they walk out with him behind Lea, his hands on her waist pulling her close to him whenever someone walks in front of them. While walking toward the elevator, Lea and Zion catch a few people saying his name. Aware he has been recognized, Zion secures Lea in his embrace. As he reaches the elevator and presses the button, a gentleman approaches.

"Zion?" The guy asks.

Zion turns toward him. Looking the guy up and down with a hard stare, the guy takes a step back and introduces himself. "I'm sorry. We went to college together. I'm Daniel Carter. Our girlfriends were roommates in college. She's my wife now. I simply wanted to say hi." Daniel stretches out his hand for a gentleman's shake.

Zion obliges. But he hasn't spoken a word. Lea watches the interactions. Daniel turns toward her to introduce himself. "It's Addison, right?" he asks of Lea.

"Why would you think her name was Addison?" Zion asks. Lea senses this is a moment where she needs to let the men handle this and she watch.

"You guys were so in love in college, I assumed you married her. And it looks like I have made a horrible mistake in my assumption. I apologize."

The elevator dings and the doors open. As people exit, Zion maneuvers Lea on. "Daniel, you have a good evening. We have to go." The doors close on Daniel before he can speak.

"Zion what was—? Why did you act like that? Not even introducing me. Are you embarrassed by me?"

"Lea, hell no I'm not embarrassed by you. Baby don't ever think that. I run into people from my past a lot. The ones from college set me on edge. With Addison reaching out to me and him bringing her up, didn't sit right. I have friendships with few of my college friends. Anyone that was close to me and Addison, I stay away from. This run in, I don't know if it was by chance or not, considering. No way am I going to let people I haven't seen in two decades meet someone I'm dating without running a background check on them first."

The elevator reaches the lobby. As the doors open Lea says, "Wow."

They step off and to the side, out of the way of others getting on.

"Lea, don't take what happened too seriously and please don't let this ruin our night or our trip."

"It's all good. I mean it was weird not getting an introduction but with my introvert ways, I probably would have said something stupid wanting to be funny or intelligent. Woulda came off embarrassing the both of us."

"Embarrassing, I doubt that."

"Zion, one time, I was introduced to a big important executive and got the hiccups. At first, I belched and then started hiccuping."

He laughs out loud again attracting attention. "My Kitten belching. Come on. Let's go enjoy our night."

They walk out the hotel to see Sam standing next to the Lexus.

"What happened to the Porsche?" she asks, filling relieved he is back to smiling and not frowning.

"Returned it."

"You aren't buying it?"

"Of course I'm buying it. Mine will be delivered for my birthday." They get in and are on their way to dinner at the Jazz Stranger Dinner and Dancing venue.

"Zion, when is your birthday?"

"July sixteenth. By the way, my sister is throwing a combined birthday party for her and me, and you are my date. All I want for my birthday is you."

"I'll add it to my calendar. But I'd like to get you something."

"Kitten, I already did. Nope. No getting me anything. You're all I want."

"I guess. Heck, I wouldn't know what to get the man who can afford everything anyway."

She checks her phone. His birthday party on July sixteenth is booked in her calendar as an all-day event.

That's what I get for giving him my code.

"Kitten," he says in that low seductive voice of his, "let's talk about your forty-fifth birthday. What would you like to do? Or do you have plans?"

"Nothing. I haven't celebrated my birthday since I turned forty. I claim the same rule. I want you and nothing else."

"Nope. We're doing something. Plan on it. Maybe Europe."

"What? Europe? That's—. Thank you for the clothes. You have great taste."

"Don't change the subject. We'll plan something for your birthday. It was my pleasure shopping for you. I can't wait to see you out of them."

Lea grins, slipping her hand into his. "Oh really?"

"Yes really." He brings her hand up to his lips kissing it. "How's your mom?"

"She's doing well. Told me to have fun and not to worry about her. She'll be good and not overdo it."

"Good. So, can I convince you to focus on us tonight?"

"Absolutely, Bear," she says as she slides her hand up his lap to his penis. Semi-hard. He puts his hand on hers.

"MMMhhhmmmm, I've missed that. But dinner first, play later."

"Party pooper," she gives his dick a squeeze and then pulls her hand away.

They arrive at their destination. It's a dinner lounge overlooking Lake Michigan. A club is upstairs for dancing and drinks. They're escorted to a secluded table, allowing them privacy.

The Sex Diva snickers, PLAY TIME.

Lea notices the dinnerware is placed close together as on their first date. She and Zion grin at one another and sit down. After reviewing the menu with Lea, he places their order. Wine, a stir fry with veggies, seafood, and pasta and sliced strawberries with cream for dessert.

She crosses her legs sliding her foot up Zion's leg every now and then. He looks at her and smiles. "My little sex vixen, behave," he orders.

"Yes sir." She moves her foot, putting her hands in her lap.

"So, Ryan told me about what happened with your client today. Fetal position sucking his thumb. Cougar. Is there something you want to tell me about?"

"Nope, not really, but since you asked. Parnell Carr does have a business; graphic design. He doesn't need the office setup he thinks he does. It's a status symbol with him. How he found G-TEE, I don't know. He's been wanting a consultation with me, for months. I was always on other projects and I made Crystal price the consultation out of his range, even telling him he would have to pay for traveling expenses. It didn't dissuade him. I knew he wanted to sex me. During our time apart, I agreed to do the meeting to get out of town and away from you, figuring I would be returning your account to the original project lead. I didn't wanna be running into you so soon in the office, so I accepted the job with Parnell. Well, I did the consultation and it's over."

"Our time apart from each other. A nice way of saying it. What about this cougar stuff?" he asks.

"I'm forty-four and look thirty-four. I can pass for thirty, depending on the hair style. I've always dated, no let me change that. In my past, I messed around with younger men, never my age. I figured young ones had stamina, old ones were slowing down. Stamina they had; everything else they didn't. Gordon used to tell me I had the mentality of a dude: fuck 'em and leave 'em. It was self-preservation. Trying not to get hurt. Do not ask me a number. If you do, I'll deck you."

He puts his hands up. "I'm not that stupid. You aren't a virgin. No matter the number, I'm focused on the knowledge. I'm not going to sit here and judge you, that would be hypocritical and really, stupid of me."

"Anyway, I shredded my cougar card at forty and decided to go for a higher quality man than what I was getting. Turns out quality is harder to find than quantity. Was harder to find." She puts her hand on his thigh. He covers it with his and squeezes it.

"I recognized the game Parnell was playing from day one. I figured he would realize I wasn't interested and move on. He didn't, so I introduced him to the Lea of my cougar days. Client lost."

"I think cougar Lea and Zion the playa could have given one another major headaches and grief. When will I get to save you? Martin, and now this Parnell guy. I'm beginning to think you have me around for my looks and body," he says.

"Zion, these were two business situations. Even if we had never met, I would still have to handle them some way. That doesn't take away from you and what you are to me. I know I have a strong personality. When you aren't around, I want you to have peace of mind knowing I can handle myself. Don't knock them looks and body. I'm enjoying every bit of it. As I hope you are with me."

"Most definitely. It's strange being with a woman who can get things done. It's an adjustment. I keep thinking I need to save you to prove to you I'm the one," Zion says.

"Well, you have shown me you're the one by opening up and sharing your past. You coulda kept it a secret and given me minimal information. I value that."

He lightly caresses her cheek smiling. "Hhhhmmmm. I'll keep that in mind."

Lea and Zion have enjoyed their dinner and conversation discussing more details of their past and sharing more secrets. The waiter comes to clear the table and informs them their reservation upstairs is ready. As they exit the restaurant, Lea excuses herself to go to the bathroom to freshen up. As she is re-applying lipstick, three women come in.

"Good lord, did you guys see that chocolate hunk standing in the lobby?" Girl One asks.

"Damn, girl. Yes, I so hope he's going upstairs. I wanna grind against that muscle-bound giant," Girl Two chirps in.

"Hold up, I spotted him and pointed him out. He's mine," Girl Three informs them.

OMG, three women arguing over Zion. Wholly cow.

"Look, maybe he can handle all of us tonight. Shit, he looks like he can."

Lea turns around, looks at all the ladies, and says, "Sorry, ladies. That chocolate hunk is mine. He belongs to me, and we don't share. Y'all have a wonderful evening. Love your shoes," she says to them, complimenting Girl Two.

Lea walks out and into Zion's arm's, knowing she has an audience watching him kiss her on her temple and caressing her ass. He smiles at her, questioning her look, and glances behind her. When they get upstairs, she explains to him what happened in the bathroom.

"Yes, baby I'm all yours and no one else's," he says.

Lea and Zion dance and people watch for the next couple of hours. When the ladies in the bathroom arrived upstairs and spotted them, they gave Lea head nods, fake swoons and thumbs up signs. Zion plays along by shrugging his shoulders and picking up Lea's hand to kiss it.

This man is perceptive to what is going on around him. He's not detached or distracted like other men I've been out on dates with. I like this a lot.

Around midnight, they leave, taking a late-night drive around Chicago enjoying the sights on the Magnificent Mile and the Chicago Pier. Lea is tempted to take out her phone to get pictures. Instead, she focuses on her cuddle time with Zion. As they pull up to the hotel, Lea's phone vibrates. She checks to be sure it isn't her mom. It's her client she's supposed to be meeting tomorrow, Carol Jackson. It's almost two-thirty in the morning in Atlanta.

"Zion, I need to answer this."

He motions to Sam to wait before opening the door and says, "Go ahead."

"Hi, Carol. How are you? Is everything okay?"

She's crying. "No, my husband's mother has passed away. I need to cancel our appointment tomorrow. We have to fly to Salt Lake City, and I don't know what we will be doing after the funeral."

"Oh, I'm so sorry. I understand. Don't worry. If you need me, call, okay?"

"Thanks, Lea. I'm so sorry for the late call, but I wanted to catch you before you flew out."

"Don't give it a second thought. Take care of yourselves."

"What happened?" Zion asks Lea after she ended the call.

"My appointment for tomorrow cancelled. Her mother-in-law passed away. I need to email Crystal and Tom."

Lea sends an email explaining what happened and asking if G-TEE could refund her deposit and send flowers. Zion stares at her taking care of business.

He enjoys watching Lea work, responding to a client's crisis how he would. He's impressed and proud of her. He's been wanting to kiss her all night, but she's wearing that red lipstick she put on the night he saw her at Jazz at the Bistro. It has the same affect now as it did then. Woke him up.

Lea smiles at him mischievously. "Zion, why haven't you kissed me?"

"I want your red lips on my cock."

She licks her lips. The lipstick stays in place. "Well, let's go."

96

-13-

Getting out of the car at the hotel, Zion tells Sam the change in plans. They won't be flying out until three, leaving the hotel at one, and for him to inform everyone.

Lea squeaks, "Good night, Sam," as Zion pulls her behind him.

He stops at the desk and informs them he will be checking out late. He moves toward the elevators so quickly that Lea has to skip to keep up with him.

"Zion, slow down. What's the hurry?"

"I'm trying to get us on an elevator alone."

"Oh. All righty then. Move it. Faster."

They get to the elevators, and he makes her stand in front of him, pressed up against his dick. She feels him hardening. She moves her hand back to touch him but has to drop it. Five other people are coming to get on the elevator with them.

"Shit." Zion says under his breath.

Zion and Lea are the first to get on and move to the back in a corner after he presses the button for their floor. He stands against the back railing with his hands on it giving Lea a challenging look. She walks up to him, turning around, pressing her body to his, making sure his cock is positioned between her ass cheeks. He slides down a little. Other than her ass enveloping his dick, they aren't touching each other.

The other people on the elevator speak and ignore them. Lea keeps clenching and unclenching her butt cheeks around his dick and he keeps flexing it.

DAMMIT, HE HAS SOME KINDA DICK CONTROL!

As everyone gets off, Lea and Zion are left alone to ride the remaining floors to their suite.

She relaxes back into his body. He places his hands on her hips keeping her in place.

"Shit, baby, your ass feels so good."

Lea moves up and down on his dick.

"Ooooooooo," he moans.

The elevator stops, and the doors open. They exit with Zion smacking Lea on her ass in the process. As they walk to the suite, she inches her dress up, showing more leg and thigh. Right as she is about to show underwear, he says, "Ocean."

She lowers her dress and halts at the door. He stands behind her, using his key card to let them into the suite.

Lea walks in and drops her clutch, pulling the dress off her shoulders and sliding it down. Zion closes and lock the door behind him leaning against it.

Wiggling out of the dress, she turns around, standing in her bra, lace boy-short panties, and heels.

Zion unzips his pants and pulls his cock out, above his underwear. No, Lea's cock. She walks to him, licking her lips, wanting to taste his pre-cum. Kneeling before him, she opens her mouth, taking him in, making sure he can see her red lipstick each time she slides his dick in and out, licking up and down. She helps him out of his pants and underwear, and he takes off his suit jacket and shirt.

"Oh, Lea. Suck me." he growls.

Lea hums and moans on his dick, pulling him out and looking up at him whispering, "Zion, you taste and feel so good. You like this, Bear?"

"Shit yes. Fuck yes."

She sucks on his dick, forming an 'o' so he can see the red lipstick. He hasn't taken his eyes off her the entire time.

Zion is enjoying watching Lea's red mouth on his cock, but he doesn't want to cum in her mouth. He's been thinking about rubbing his dick between her ass cheeks since the ride in the elevator with his penis squeezed in between them. He wants to shoot his jiz on her ass.

Damn, Baby, yes! That nice, firm ass.

"Halo," he breathes. Lea slows down and gently releases his dick. This gives him the opportunity to completely pull out and away from her mouth. He backs up against the door looking down at her. She's pouting.

How cute.

Zion helps her stand and takes her over to the couch. He bends her over the edge and rips off the underwear. Walking up behind her, he presses his dick between her ass cheeks. Zion alternates spreading her cheeks, sliding his penis between them, and squeezing them tight, enveloping his dick. Lea rubs back, grinding into him.

"Oh. Lea, your ass. Damn, Baby, ima shoot all over it."

He presses in between her butt cheeks, forcing her to press her pussy into the couch.

Shit, she's moving faster. She's about to cum.

He keeps rubbing his dick between her cheeks, squeezing them together with his penis poking out with each thrust. It is such a fucking turn on. He leaves trails of pre-cum in the crack of her ass each time he pulls back.

Zion has Lea pressed against the couch in a way that the edge of it causes her pussy lips to press and rub against her clit. Each time Zion grinds into her ass, it causes her pussy to grind into the edge of the couch. She's fucking loving it.

He can't take it any longer. His hands splayed out on her ass cheeks, pressing them closed around his dick, her grinding into him, he explodes, leaving trails of cum on her ass.

Lea cums, pressing her pussy into the couch, leaving her thighs slick with her cum.

"Oh, yes! Zion yes," Lea moans. She trembles through her orgasm, holding onto the couch.

They stand in this position for what feels like an eternity, him leaning over her with his dick pressed in between her butt cheeks.

"Zion," she whispers his name.

"Yes, Kitten."

"You have to stop ripping my underwear off."

He lifts his head. "It's okay, I bought you fifty pair. Let's go shower," he says and walks her to the bathroom, hugging her from behind.

In the bathroom, she slips off her shoes and takes off her bra while Zion turns on the water.

"Fifty pair? You bought me fifty pair of underwear? In addition to the dress, shoes and clutch, you bought me fifty pair of underwear?" she asks incredulous.

"Yes, and the earrings, two more dresses, another pair of heels, plus jeans, tops, and flats that are being delivered to my apartment. You won't be doing the walk of shame leaving my place ever again."

"I wasn't ashamed. Thank you for everything. The earrings—."

"They go with your necklace and ring. I know. At first, I wanted to put you in diamonds. Especially that night I saw you at the charity ball, but diamonds don't seem to suit you," he says.

"Nope, I like the colored stones. Do I need to clear out closet space and drawers in my place for you?"

"Well duh, yeah."

Or you can move in with me.

The thought pops into his head. He gives himself a mental kick in the ass.

Hold up man, hold up.

They step into the shower, lathering each other up. He gets hard and she gets moist.

"Tomorrow, because your client has cancelled, what are your plans? I received a call earlier to have drinks with one of my clients in Atlanta." While he's saying this, he's lathering her breasts, supposedly cleaning them, but only pinching her nipples.

"Enjoying yourself?" she playfully asks him.

"Yep. What about Atlanta?"

"I do have to make some calls on this project called Landon Enterprises and get status updates on how things are going at the building site. I need to type a report for the CEO. He's an important client of my boss."

While responding, Lea lathers his chest, running her fingers through his chest hairs, watching his nipples harden.

He groans from the touch of her caress, flexing his pectoral muscles. "Are you enjoying yourself Lea?"

"Tremendously." She moves down to clean his manhood.

STROKE HIM.

To stroke him.

BOUT TIME. GEEZ.

To stroke him. And where you been?

WATCHING THE SHOW. GOOD JOB.

I know right?

"You know you have too many male clients you deal with. I believe it's time I made you forget about all of them." He places his hands on her face and lifts it up for a kiss.

"Well, I can't forget about this one. I'm having a mind-blowing, tantalizing pussy-meets-dick affair with Mr. Landon. I must do a good job in pleasing him, in and out of the boardroom." She keeps stroking his dick.

"Not affair, Kitten. Relationship. Our relationship. I'm sure Mr. Landon appreciates the extraordinary effort you're making. Just remember, he's more into you outside the boardroom than inside. Unless he has you bent over and fucking you from behind on his boardroom table."

"He really likes to watch me play with my clit while he jacks off. I think I'll give him a show tonight."

Zion looks into her eyes with so much passion, heat and lust, she no longer feels embarrassment or shyness in front of him and wants to do this.

"Let's get this show started," he says, reaching to turn off the water.

Going into the bedroom, he plops her down on top of the desk. He puts a towel in the rolling desk chair then sits stroking himself.

"Baby, open them legs and play for me." Zion relaxes into position readying himself to enjoy what's about to happen. Releasing all tension from his mind and body, he gradually slips back into a moment years ago. With Addison.

Lea opens her legs. As she does, her pussy lips spread. Zion licks his lips at the sight of her glistening juices. He grabs his dick and squeezes it. Hard.

Damn. Looks like he's squeezing it too hard.

Zion steps back into another time. Back in his past. A night when Addison kept edging him on to jack off. To squeeze harder and harder. In order to get through the pain and please her, he closed his eyes. He could hear her whispering 'harder dammit you fuck, squeeze harder' and he would do it. To please her. To make her happy. And after cumming he would hate the sight of her. Needing to punish her with pain. He is so far into the past, Lea doesn't exist. He doesn't hear her.

"Zion. Ease up."

WHAT THE HELL LEA. GET HIM TO BE GENTLE.

Zion doesn't take his eyes off Lea's fingers playing with her clit. He's off in his own world, masturbating. Up and down the shaft of his penis, he strokes and keeps squeezing harder and harder. He reaches for his nut sack and even squeezes them hard. The skin around them stretching.

Shit that looks painful. Lea thinks absentmindedly stroking herself.

DAMMIT. WILL YOU DO SOMETHING TO MAKE HIM STOP. SAFE WORD.

Lea watches the ecstasy on his face, unable to look away or speak. Realizing seeing her masturbate takes him closer and closer to finishing, she opens her pussy lips more, sticking her fingers inside of her, hoping the visual will help to get him there quicker. She takes her fingers out and licks them. He explodes all over his stomach, jerking in the chair. He keeps squeezing and tugging. The veins on the back of his hand contracting.

Lea has never experienced a man doing this and it has left her frightened. She sternly says "Ocean", hoping he hears her through his fog of whatever he is reliving.

FINALLY. WHAT THE HELL TOOK YOU SO LONG?

I didn't... I was scared... I've never seen... experienced... Shit now what?

He doesn't stop.

He didn't hear me. Fuck.

Lea closes her legs and hops down off the desk. "Dammit Zion! Stop it! Now!" she yells nudging his shoulder.

He stops. Lea reaches for the towel that was left on the floor and holds it in front of her, like a shield of some kind. But she has no idea what she's shielding herself from. Surely not her Bear. But this man, she not liking at all right now.

He stands up, and stalks toward her. Pulling her to him, he kisses her hard, bruising her lips.

"Zion, OCEAN." Lea mumbles against his mouth.

He pulls back not understanding why she would be saying their safe word.

"Are you okay?" she whispers.

He focuses on what she's saying.

"You were squeezing and jerking yourself so hard."

Looking down at himself, he stares. His crouch is covered in sperm, and his penis is red with his hand print. As realization dawns on him, he feels the intense pain coursing through his body. He bends over grabbing the edge of the desk, knuckles white.

A low growl rumbles from his gut and he hisses lowly.

Lea catches him, laying his head on her shoulder, holding him. He's trembling. "Oh Zion. Baby." Lea says anguished.

Zion concentrates on riding the wave of pain. He wants to yell in agony. Not from what his penis is feeling but from the fact Addison and that part of his past has encroached on his and Lea's world.

Dammit, I went there. I fucking jacked off hard, punishing myself like I used to with Addison because she liked to see me in extreme pain. Shit, fuck. Breathe Zion. Fucking breathe through the pain. Deep breaths. Concentrate. Stop allowing Lea to see your physical pain reaction. Get a grip. Hold Lea. She's not Addison.

"Lea, Kitten?" he hisses lowly. Zion brings Lea into his shaky embrace, attempting to calm himself down. She doesn't allow her pelvis to touch him.

"Don't reject me. I'm sorry," he pleads, "I—." A shiver racks his entire body, from the pain in his groin, from what he thinks is Lea rejecting, and from the cold chill in the room.

"Zion, I'm not rejecting you, and you have nothing to apologize for."

She gently allows her body to relax into his. When he presses her against him, she can feel the muscles in his stomach and waist constrict as he holds her.

"Honey, you're in pain. I don't want to make it worse. Come on, let's go take a bath this time."

Zion gingerly walks behind Lea toward the bathroom. She runs them a bath. He's standing at the sink, gripping the edge of the counter. She turns off the water and walks up behind him, hugging him.

"Zion, it's okay. Bear. I'm worried about you. Promise me you won't hurt yourself like that again. Please? I don't ever want you hurting yourself like that, ever. We don't need that. Okay? Come on." Lea pulls him with her toward the tub.

She gets in first. He looks down, not looking at her, climbing in, resting his head against her, submerging his glorious, throbbing manhood in water to help ease the pain. Lea turns on the jets of the tub on low. The waves of the water slowly help to ease the pain Zion is feeling. He gingerly strokes around his penis and thighs sloshing the water to remove the remnants of sperm.

He grabs her other hand and links his fingers into them, leaning his head on her chest with his eyes closed. She caresses his brow and his cheek, soothing him. They sit in the water, relaxing and not saying a word. When a shiver runs through his body, Lea makes him get out. She dries him off, avoiding touching his penis. She's unsure if it's still hurting, but, in case, she makes sure not to brush up against it. She looks up at him and kisses him directly above his penis in his pubic hairs.

"I love you, Lea," Zion says, not taking his eyes off her.

"I love you, too, Zion," she whispers, standing up. "Let's get some rest." She caresses his cheek.

"Kitten, what about you? I don't want to leave you hanging like this," he whispers.

"I'm fine. I'm cramping, which means my period will be making an appearance any time. I can wait. Right now, it's about you."

They get into bed and Lea turns on the TV. Zion lays on his hip facing Lea, propping pillows under his head and between his legs. He's unable to stretch out on his stomach and pelvic area. He brings Lea close to him, holding her tight. "Zion, I don't want you hurting yourself like that again. For me or anyone else. That kinda pain for sexual gratification is not necessary. Promise me you won't do that whether we're together or not."

Zion shows a vulnerability with her in this one moment he never knew he could feel or express. "Lea, I promise. Never again." He grips her harder, drifting off to sleep.

Lea tries to get comfortable and sleep, but every time she moves, he reaches for her pulling her close into him. He grimaces when she comes into contact with his pelvis.

"Zion, wake up." She whispers. "Lay on your back."

He groggily turns over, and she lays her head on his chest, and places a leg over his, pulling the pillow from between them. She caresses his pubic hairs above his penis, knowing it will soothe him.

He smiles at her twirling the hairs around her fingers. "Lea, I'm not letting you get away."

"Bear, sleep. I'm here and not going anywhere."

She gives up any chance of getting any sleep and focuses on comforting him.

WHAT KINDA CRACKED-OUT WITCH WAS HE WITH?

-14-

Lea wakes up the next morning with pain in her gut and side. She's cramping from her awkward sleeping position and from menstrual cramps.

Shit, the birth control keeps me from bleeding as heavy, but it sure as hell doesn't take away the pain. Oh, joy, Mother Nature has made her grand appearance.

She sits on the side of the bed, looking at her hand, smiling. During the night, whenever she would move it from Zion's fuzz or try to switch positions to give him some sleeping room, he would move her back, placing her hand splayed over his stomach, and her head on his chest with his hand caressing her back and ass. She gets up and goes in search of pain pills, orange juice, and tampons, trying not to wake him.

Zion, missing the feel of Lea in his arms, reaches for her. Before he can touch her, she gets up and goes to her suitcase and he's left gripping air. He watches her, falling in love with her more and more.

Lea, unaware Zion is awake, takes out a pill box from her toiletries bag and grabs a juice out of the fridge, popping two pills. She moves quietly grabbing clothes to go to the bathroom to change.

Zion's emotions sink. He wanted to hold her, feel her. He needs Lea right now.

We have hours before we leave and she's getting dressed? Is she ashamed of me for what happened last night? Fuck!

She turns around and sees him staring at her. She hesitates for a second, unsure of what to do, then smiles at him.

"I thought you were asleep. Sorry, I didn't mean to wake you. I'm starting my period. Needed something for the cramps," she says as she is walking back over to the bed, climbing in next to him. "Good morning, Bear."

Zion opens his arms and she crawls into them. "I love you, Lea."

"I love you, too, Zion. Do you mind if I take a look?"

He shakes his head. She lifts up the sheet and sees that he's limp, but doesn't look as red as he did last night. Fingerprint impressions are fading.

Shit, last night. I mean this morning. I still can't believe I went that far. Lea is not Addison. Lea doesn't want me in that kinda pain for sexual pleasure. Lea only wants me aroused and enjoying myself. Enjoying her.

He buries his face in her hair, closing his eyes, breathing in her scent while she surveys his limp manhood, not touching, but staring intently.

I don't want to see her disgust or disappointment. I feel her caress my pubic hairs and kiss my chest. God that is so comforting and calming. She put me to sleep when she did that. Made the pain bearable. I'm loving this woman so much right now.

"Want some pain killers? I have Aleve and Tylenol. Sorry, I didn't think about them—. Well, earlier. I guess they would have been a tremendous help hours ago."

"Tylenol would be great, Lea. You were a tremendous help hours ago. I'm going to have to go commando today. Haven't had to do that in years. Not since college," he says, opening his eyes looking at her, hopefully explaining away what happened without having her pry and thanking her at the same time.

"Commando, huh? All the ideas coursing through my mind right now. Never thought about a man being commando in dress pants. You won't think badly of me for staring too hard at your lower region, will you?"

"Kitten, stare to your heart's content." He smiles, slightly turning his head.

"Oh my, you're blushing." She kisses his scratchy cheek, gets up and brings him a bottle of orange juice and two Tylenol from her pill case. He gingerly sits up to take them. Lea notices him gripping the sheets but says nothing.

"Yes, I'm a grown ass man and you're making me blush. Only you Lea. Only you. Remember that."

"Don't worry, I will. I'll order breakfast. What would you like?"

"You. But I'll settle for bacon, eggs, toast, and fruit."

He reaches for her hand and brings it to his lips, kissing it. He wants to pull her into his arms but fears she might land on him.

Lea looks down at his crotch, then up at him, shaking her head. "Your pain and my period are our saving grace."

She goes to the bathroom to get dressed, leaving him speechless and grinning.

Zion lays there wondering why Addison crept into his mind as it did last night. Then he sits up remembering the run in with Daniel Carter and him mentioning her, thinking Lea was her.

Am I so fucking mentally weak that a run in with an old classmate, mentioning the woman I hate would send me into hurting myself? Reliving hateful experiences? Oh fuck no. That ain't gonna happen.

After Lea goes into the living room, giving him some privacy, Zion gets up slowly, walking to the bathroom to survey the damage.

If I was with Addison, she would be laughing at the pain I'm experiencing right now. Then we would fight and fuck. I would be in pain for days. With Lea, she's letting me heal, giving me time.

Thinking about Lea, he gets slightly hard.

Well, it still works.

He laughs at himself while standing in the shower, letting the cold water hit his stomach, cascading down, attempting to temper his arousal. Right now, there's no way he can give into what he's feeling and make love to Lea. He will never make love to her with any kind of emotions he could be feeling regarding Addison and his past.

Zion stands in the shower practicing the breathing techniques he learned in therapy to rid himself of thoughts and feelings of Addison. As the water washes over him, he feels the peace and calm taking over.

Don't worry Kitten, I'll never do that again. I'll never scare either of us like that again.

After the shower, he sits on the side of the bed, checking his emails, legs spread wide, allowing the cool breeze from the air conditioning to comfort him, thinking about what clothes to put on.

Man, I could use some sweatpants right about now.

Laying on his back, he laughs softly. His phone vibrates with an incoming call. It's from Saul.

"Saul, good morning. What's going on?" Zion asks.

"Sir, I wanted to let you know that Addison Raymond showed up at the office yesterday. Well, not the office, but the building."

Her again. He takes a deep breathe before responding. "What the hell you mean, the building?" Zion sits up, covering himself. He instantly steps into business mode.

"I tapped into the building's security and played around with some face recognition software I obtained from Essensecurity. The software isn't in production. It's just something we've been designing and toying with. I decided to take the picture you gave me of Ms. Raymond and scan the building's security video. We came up with a match."

"No way!"

Saul continues, "Yes sir. Yesterday, outside of the building and at the building's security desk. They did their job of not allowing her up to the floor, but she hung around. She saw you leaving, sir. Security didn't even inform me of her arrival. They somehow convinced her to leave. They won't tell me what they said to her."

"Shit, man. I wasn't even paying attention to people around me outside the office. I was so focused on Lea. Dammit!" Zion says, frustration in the sound of his voice and word choice. Rarely does he cuss in business mode. "We need to get the fuck outta this building. I'm done trusting this place. Thanks for the call. Keep me aware of anything out of the ordinary."

"You're welcome. I will, sir."

While getting dressed, Zion thinks about what this could mean for his business, family, and especially Lea.

With my family, I can add more security. For my business, it's time to push the builders to get the new office space completed. Lea. I'm not going to stop seeing Lea. That ain't gonna happen. How can I keep our relationship going and her safe?

-15-

Unsure of how things will proceed after Zion's episode, Lea decides to get dressed and give him some privacy. Staring at her reflection in the mirror with her hand in mid-air holding her tube of lipstick, she remembers the look of ecstasy on his face. He seriously was aroused and enjoying himself.

HE WAS ZONED THE FUCK OUT. WE DIDN'T EVEN EXIST.

Sex Diva, I know. And I can't figure out if I'm jealous because of that look he had for someone else or scared shitless of it.

HERE'S THE DEAL. WE GOTTA PAY MORE ATTENTION. CLOSER ATTENTION. MAKE MORE EYE CONTACT. SAY HIS NAME DURING SEX. BE MORE VERBAL. SOMETHING. CAUSE THAT SHIT WASN'T COOL.

Yes, more verbal. Have him focus on me, Lea, and my voice and touch. We got this. Obviously, I won't be pushing any BDSM ideas. I'll settle for man-handling and intense sex. Do you think it would be wrong of me to desire some of what he displayed centered toward me.

LEA, GIRL, I DON'T KNOW. I MEAN WE CAN WANT IT BUT IT COULD BE HELLA DANGEROUS ATTEMPTING TO SAFELY GET IT. HOW HARD HE WAS SQUEEZING. IT'S KNOW TELLING WHAT ELSE KINDA PAIN THEY GOT INTO.

You right. Leave that shit alone. Intense sex. Focusing on what he can handle. We got this.

YEAH GIRL, WE GOT THIS.

She goes into the living room of the suite and calls room service to place their breakfast order. Sitting down she fires up her computer to get some work done. Thirty minutes later, breakfast arrives and Zion comes into the room as she's signing for it. The young lady rolling in the cart looks up at him and runs into the table. Zion has come into the room with his shirt open, dress pants on with some fuzz peaking from his pelvic region.

DAMN SEXY ASS MAN. GOT WOMEN LUSTING AFTER HIM. BACK OFF LIL GIRL, THAT'S MY MAN.

Sex Diva, calm down.

WHY?????

The server turns away from him, looks at Lea, mumbles thank you, and exits the room.

Lea closes the door leaning on it. "You don't mind if I busy myself with serving us instead of drooling, do you babe?" She smiles at him.

"I prefer the drooling, but I'm hungry for food, so serve away."

He buttons his shirt and sits down to eat. She watches him. When he walks over to the table, he wasn't walking as if he was in pain, but he could be hiding it from her.

After a few minutes, Zion speaks up. "We'll be flying out at three. We have time for some sight-seeing if you like."

"I can't." Lea considered doing some but decided against it. She doesn't want Zion having to walk too much. She wants him to sit in one spot, not move, and let himself heal.

YES, LET OUR DICK HEAL PLEASE. I'LL GO TAKE A REST.

Thank you!

GIRL, NO PROBLEM.

"I scheduled a conference call with Neil at your building site to get some construction updates. Tom and Crystal will be joining me. It starts in about fifteen minutes." Lea figured getting into business mode would distract them from the sex they wouldn't be having.

"Mind if I sit in on the call?" he asks. "There will be no need to repeat everything or re-read it."

"Sure." She walks over to the desk and places her phone next to her computer ready to dial into the call. When she turns around, she looks into Zion's eyes. He's staring at her intently. "What? What's wrong? Is my hair standing up? Why you staring at me like that?"

He smiles at Lea, gets up and walks over to her, lifting his hand to caress her cheek. "Nothing's wrong, beautiful. I can't get over how much I'm in love with you in such a short time. How good you make me feel by loving me. How can you love a broken man?"

"Zion, everyone is broken in some way. I'm far from perfect. Who am I to judge you? Someday, I may be asking for your understanding. I hope you give me that chance."

Lea hears the ping of her computer. Five minutes until the conference call. He steps back and they get into business mode. Lea sits down at the desk and Zion pulls a chair next to her. She places the phone between them, pulling her computer closer to her with his project files open for review. He can look on while she's typing in updates.

She dials into the call and Neil, Tom, and Crystal are ready. "Good morning, everyone. How's it going? Zion is also on the call." She avoids saying he's sitting next to her while halting his hand caressing her leg.

I would choose to wear the skirt I brought instead of the pants.

Everyone says good morning. Because this is her meeting, she starts. "Neil, how are things at the site?"

"We're eight weeks ahead of schedule. It has been the best weather and working crew I've had on any job. All the electrical has been run, plumbing is done, building inspectors have been out and signed off on approvals with minimal changes. Even the changes, including the additional security cameras, where approved by the inspectors. Because a lot of the materials are ordered and stored in warehouses, we can go in and lay flooring," Neil says.

"Great, how is the basement looking for the IT server rooms, video surveillance areas, and equipment? Has anyone been out to take a look around?"

"Yes, to the second question; two representatives from Landon Enterprises, Saul and Morgan. Saul was impressed with everything he saw and wants to bring out one of the new servers and racks to see how it would look in the space."

"Perfect. Tom, do you have anything you want to know more about?" Lea asks him.

"Yes. Neil, is there any way you can setup an area with a couple of cubes and furniture so we can see what things will look like?" Tom asks.

"Can do Tom. Mr. Landon, is there anything you would like to know about?" Neil asks him.

"Actually yes, and this will be a shock and surprise to Tom and Lea so, please, ignore the stunned silence and/or shouts of dismay you're about to hear. I would like to move in as soon as possible. Even if we have to do this floor by floor. I'm not feeling as secure as I want to in my current location. Whatever the cost, don't worry about it. I can discuss the logistics of this with G-TEE, but I would like to know if we can do this. There could be a bonus in this for everyone if we can make this happen, say within the next six to eight months."

Neil takes in a deep breath. "Let me take a walk around the site and check some things out before I respond yay or nay. I really don't want to make a fool of myself, say yes, and then have to back out. Give me about a week and I can let you know."

"Sure, Neil that would be great. You go ahead. Miss Adams is waiting to strangle me and I'm sure Tom and Crystal would like to reach through the phone and beat me. You should disconnect now," Zion orders him.

"Will do sir. Lea, I'll talk to you next week."

"'Bye, Neil."

They all wait for Neil to hang up and Tom lights into Zion.

"Man, what the hell is going on? You really want to move things up? I'm not for rushing this and doing a half-assed job here. I need an explanation. Lea, what you doing to this man?"

"What do you mean, doing to this man? Why it gotta be me doing something to him? He's a grown man, able to make his own decisions. This is news to me, too," Lea responds to Tom in the voice she had used with Martin. Zion recognizes it and attempts to calm everyone down.

"Look, guys, you all know about Addison. Well, this morning I was informed she may have seen Lea and me leaving my office Wednesday. I'll tell everyone more about that later. She hasn't contacted me directly, but I'm tired of not having any security control over my own office. I'm thinking ahead. If we can get into the new building any sooner than a year, I would love it. Any time before the end of the year, I would pay through my ass for it. Well, not through my ass but at least a fifteen percent bonus to all companies involved."

"Shit man. Lea, re-work the project schedule? We can send suggested deadline dates to our vendors and see which ones can meet the change and which ones can't. That will give us an idea if this is at all possible. Give me projections for end dates of October, November, and December." Tom tells her.

"Yes sir, will do. Is there anything else before we end the call?" Lea asks.

Crystal speaks up. "Yes, I have a question. Are the two of you having fun, sexing it up, and enjoying yourselves? Or is this just a business trip?"

"Crystal, shut up, go away, oh my god. What is with you!?" Lea screams and laughs.

Zion speaks up. "Goodbye, Crystal and Tom. We'll talk next week," Zion ends the call cutting Crystal off.

"I can't believe she asked that. What's happened, Zion?"

Zion harshly responds to Lea's question. In business mode he doesn't expect to be questioned by an employee. He expects action. "Like I said, Addison may have seen us leaving. Saul told me he was playing around with some face recognition software with the building's security and came up with a match for her. I want us safe. I want my business secure. Whatever it takes. Get the dates together, and we can take a look next week."

His tone makes Lea emotionally step back. *This is business Zion and not boyfriend Zion.* Before she responds, she takes a deep breath. She scoots her chair away from him a fraction of an inch, takes the pad and pen, placing it in front of her and steps in to professional business mode. "Will do. Are the suggested three dates Tom mentioned good or do you need more?"

"No, those dates are fine. Include bonus amounts of ten, fifteen, and twenty percent."

"I'll get on it right now." She almost said sir but managed to stop herself.

"Lea, I didn't mean to snap—."

She was about to address him as Mr. Landon to really distance herself from him but caught herself. Instead with a deadpan look and tone of her voice to convey she's the employee she says, "Zion, no worries. I'm your Project Lead. This is what I do. If there is anything else you would like to add or change, email me the details and I will get it included in the updates." Lea then turns to her computer, ending any more apologies he may offer her. She bites the inside of her lip in an attempt not to display the sting she's feeling.

It's not like I haven't been in a position of being ordered to do my job. Just never expected to get it from my boyfriend. Whom I'm working for and not with. He'll never be my boss again after this is done.

Zion moves over to the couch with his computer, emailing Saul and Sam about the possible changes in dates. He fires off emails to his department heads, letting them know move-in dates may change and to plan a meeting to discuss. Next, he emails Morgan to get a meeting scheduled with everyone. Knowing Addison was at his office has taken this to a new level. He watches Lea working with her back turn toward him. Her body is ram-rod straight. She's typing a mile a minute and writing notes on the pad even faster. He dislikes this work wall between them.

In addition to getting the information Zion, no Mr. Landon, requested, Lea makes a list of items to complete to return the Landon Enterprises project back to the original Project Lead.

Ain't no fucking way ima put up with this kinda attitude. Yes, he is the client, but he not about to treat me like shit. No ma'am. No sir. I can quit anytime I want.

Lea is writing and typing so frantically that her thoughts are intermingled with the requested updates. Re-reading it, she has numerous fucks, hell naws, bullshits, kma's, and bite me's.

Yep, this contract gonna have to be switched to someone else.
WHAT ABOUT THE RELATIONSHIP?
We'll see.

After the two-hour silence of working, Zion speaks up to break the tension in the room. "Sam will be up to get our luggage. Time to check out and get to Atlanta."

Lea relaxes her body and does a twist and turn movement. Sitting so straight has given her a cramp in her lower back. She wanted to move to the bedroom to work, but her conscience wouldn't allow her to sulk away from the 'boss'.

No sir, I was ordered to do my job and that's what the fuck I did.

"Okay."

As she stands and starts putting away stuff in her backpack, he moves to the end of the desk. "Lea. I'm sorry. Addison seeing us put me on edge and what happened this morning isn't helping. I don't want you thinking I'm taking this out on you."

"I don't Zion. This is business. It's what I do."

"It's not business. I've never fallen in love with a business colleague."

"Neither have I."

"I want to get back to before what happened after dinner."

"We both know that's not possible Zion."

Instead of using words, he brings her into his arms and kisses her passionately. Lea gives back just as much passion.

WELL I GUESS THE RELATIONSHIP IS STILL A GO.

Yeah Sex Diva, relationship is still a go.

Breaking the kiss, she lays her forehead on his chest and asks, "Would you like me to pack your things?"

His chest expands from the deep breath he takes smelling her scent, "No Babe. I'll join you."

HOW IN THE HELL HE GONNA LAY A KISS ON US LIKE THAT AND WE CAN'T FUCK?

They walk to the Suites bedroom. Zion brings out a garment bag and unzips it. It contains two dresses, shoes, and underwear.

"Uhhmmm, is there something you need to tell me?" She asks inching her way toward the bed.

"Maybe. Where are the dress and shoes you wore last night?"

Lea goes to the closet and pulls out a hanger holding the dress and purse and bends down to get the shoes. She takes everything over to Zion, hopping on the bed, attempting to be nosey.

"May I see?" she asks.

"Nope, you can't." He places the dress and shoes in the garment bag. "Wait 'til we get to Atlanta."

"Aawww, you no fun." She crawls across the bed to get a full peek into the bag. He thwarts her attempts by kissing her. "Not until we get to Atlanta. I like the switch in mood. We'll figure out this working and loving relationship. Eventually."

"I'm considering returning your account back over to—."

He shuts her up by kissing her again. "You do and I'll cancel it."

"You cancel it and G-TEE will sue you. With my help."

"Then things will stay as they are."

"Are you asking me or are you telling me? As much as I understand the dynamics of you being the boss and my man, don't think I will allow you to treat me any way you like."

"Lea, I don't want to work with anyone but you on my account. Will you stay?"

"Yes, Zion. Things will stay as they are. With us figuring out how to love and work together."

There's a knock at the door. "I'll get that." She goes to let Sam in.

Zion watches her leaving the room.

Reassigning my ass. And breaking up ain't gonna happen. Lea Adams, you mine.

"Good morning, Sam." Lea greets him.

"Good morning, Miss Adams." He goes and collects their suitcases and computer bags and they exit the suite.

During the ride to the airport, Zion, Ryan, and Sam talk about the call Zion received from Saul about Addison seeing them. He informs them about the chance of moving into the office early if everything can be worked out. Lea sits and listens, taking mental notes.

Zion wants additional security at his Clayton office. Sam reminds him of the security cameras he has requested for all access points in the new building. Ryan assures Zion that cars and drivers are in place should he decide to have his family be escorted at all times when leaving their homes.

Sam asks Zion a question he thinks Zion doesn't want to address. "Sir, what about security for Miss Adams?"

"What about security for Miss Adams?" Lea barks, "I'm not a factor in this equation. I'm just someone that works for him. There's no need for security for me."

"Lea—."

"You're not putting a security detail on me. Addison wants you. Handle it and leave me out of it. I'll be fine."

"I will not have a security detail put on you for now. But I'm reserving the right to change that should I see fit. Is that understood?" he says, daring her to argue.

"Understood," Lea whispers, turning away from all of them looking out the window. She tunes out their conversation for the remainder of the ride. She grabs onto one of the twists in her hair and starts twisting away in an attempt to calm the outburst she wants to lash onto Zion. Lea was never one of those people to have public confrontations. Recalling the outbursts and public displays Zion would have with Addison, Lea allows her silence and body language to convey her emotions.

Dude getting real close to me telling him to kiss my pretty brown ass, I know that much.

Zion leans back in the seat staring at her. Wanting to touch her. But the way she has turned away from him, tells him this is not the place or the time.

This dating a headstrong woman is annoying the fuck outta me. I'm used to women going along with whatever I say. Lea. Lea is gonna drive me nuts and keep me on my toes. The ride will be wonderful.

His airplane is sitting on the tarmac awaiting their arrival. Lea quickly gets out the car, sprinting to the plane not speaking to the others. Sam and Ryan take their time ensuring the luggage is loaded, purposely giving Zion time to board before they do. They understand without verbal communication, he and Lea need a few minutes alone.

On the plane, Lea takes a seat preparing to do some work on the Landon Enterprises project reviewing dates and numbers, using the pad and pencil she always keeps handy in case she has to store her laptop, which she forgot to grab out of the trunk of the car. Zion sits next to her not doing anything. He's always working, and for once, he's not doing anything. Not making calls, and not taking out his computer. But staring at Lea. She cocks her head to the side, looking at him.

"What now?"

"Nothing. Just waiting to get in the air so we can go to the sleeping quarters."

"Why? Don't you guys have more business to discuss?"

"I need to hold you, and I'm going to hold you all the way to Atlanta."

"What about work? You told me you wanted dates and cost."

"Work some other time. Business can wait."

"Huh?"

He grins at her. Zion got a quick glimpse of the page in the notebook Lea flipped opened. He saw the title of the page, "ToDo Returning Landon Enterprises Project", with a long list of items to be completed. He says nothing.

Sam and Ryan board the plane and take their seats, buckling up. Once the seat belt signs are turned off, Zion unbuckles his and pulls Lea up with him after unbuckling hers. She tosses the notebook aside but Zion grabs it.

They walk toward the sleeping quarters. He tells the others he doesn't want to be disturbed unless necessary. Lea didn't see the sleeping quarters on the flight to Chicago because it was such a short flight. He closes the door behind them, leaning against it, devouring Lea with a look of desire, standing in the middle of the small room.

There is a bed, a shower stall, a small sink, and even a TV on the wall. Enough comfort for a rest during a long flight.

She turns around, looking at him. Zion opens the notebook and shows her the page asking, "Are you staying on my account?"

Before responding, Lea bites the inside of her lip. He walks over to her, handing her the book. Lea takes it and tears out the page. She rips it into small pieces and tosses them above their heads. "Yes Zion. I'm staying on your account." She tosses the book onto the bed.

He puts his hands on her waist, lays butterfly kisses on her cheeks, forehead, neck, and her lips. Lea backs away from the embrace. She wants to press against him, to feel him, to get her a full body bear hug, but she's afraid of hurting him.

"It's okay baby. I'm fine. I know we can't do anything, but I want you up against me to feel that all is good with 'your' dick. Feel it." He places her hand on his semi-hard penis. "Still working properly. Still jumps to attention for you, no pain, no aches, no more hesitation, no more embarrassment, and no more hurting myself," he whispers into her neck.

He kisses her, keeping her pressed against him.

Damn me and my period.

They deepen the kiss and she presses harder into him wanting to be as close to him as she can get without having sex. She can feel an orgasm building. She tries to stop the kiss and pull back, attempting to tamper it down, but he won't release her. He keeps kissing, pressing her pelvis into him. He bends his knees slightly, opening his legs. The 'v' of Lea's pussy brushes against his semi-hard penis. Zion gently rubs against her until she cums. Lea whimpers into his mouth, her release of being close to him again, of having him make her cum for him.

"Oh, yes, baby, you know you needed that, and I needed to give it to you." Zion says, loving hearing her cum.

They lay on the bed cuddling and kissing during the remainder of the flight.

-16-

Landing in Atlanta hours later, Zion and Lea are in better spirits, checking into the Ritz-Carlton, Buckhead Luxury Suites. Zion has arranged an impromptu meeting with one of his clients in the lobby bar for drinks.

"I'll hang out here 'til you're done." Lea offers, not wanting to be in his client's private meeting.

"What the hell for? You're coming with me. So, get dressed," he says to Lea, ready for a protest. She gives him none.

He places the garment bag on the bed. Lea, finally getting her chance to see the contents, gets excited. The bag contains the gold and black dress, a second black dress, and a red wine dress. A second pair of shoes and clutches that match each dress. For tonight's activities Lea chooses the black dress, with gold sandal heels, with black rope details along the straps and the black clutch. The dress clings to her curves without restricting her movements. It has three-quarter-inch sleeves, exposing one shoulder, falling just above her knees. She removes all her jewelry except the earrings he purchased.

Zion is fully dressed, lounging on the bed and watching Lea get ready. She thinks she's putting on an understated outfit, but the minimal choices make her stand out even more. Her makeup, looks as if she doesn't have any on. If he hadn't been watching her, he would have never thought she was wearing it. This time, it's a lavender lip gloss on those kissable lips. She picks up a pink tube and glides it over her pulse points on her neck, exposed shoulder, and wrists. He gets up, walks to her, and grabs it before she puts it away, reading aloud; "Basic Instinct." He opens it and takes a whiff but can't figure out the scent. Then he places his nose to her neck smelling a floral scent.

"Is this what you've been wearing since we met?" he asks, "I have been trying to find this so I can buy you one for my apartment."

"Yes. It's a pheromone scent. The aroma can change each time I wear it. I'll order another one for your place."

"Please do. Soon. Do I even wanna know where you would order a pheromone scent from?"

"You saw the catalog when I showed you the items in my toy box."

"With all the vibrators and BDSM stuff? They sell perfumes? That's the second time I haven't paid close attention and missed out on something since meeting you. Lea Adams, you are truly a distraction."

"I'll stop distracting you if you like." Lea opens his shirt and kisses his chest, breathing in. "You smell good, too."

Zion is wearing a black suit, gray shirt, no tie, and black shoes, and he has a gray handkerchief peaking from the pocket of his suit jacket.

"Thank you, beautiful." For some reason a compliment from Lea seems different from the compliments he's received from other women. He blushes.

"Ready?" she asks him.

"No. I wanna cancel." He holds out his hand for hers, and they exit the suite.

Sam and Ryan are waiting for them. They take the elevators down; Sam having used a card to keep it from stopping at other floors.

They walk to the hotel bar. Upon entering Lea notes an additional two security guards outside the lounge and four more inside with the place closed to the public.

Wholly shit, who the hell are we meeting with?

Ryan and Sam follow them, taking seats closer to the door that allows access from the street.

My nerves are on overload; my palms are sweating. What's with all the henchmen?

Lea switches her clutch to her left hand, unclenching the right one, attempting to wipe it off on her dress on the sly and giving it some air so she isn't shaking hands with a sweaty palm.

Oh, the horror of that. But it's not as bad as the belching and hiccups. Remember not to swallow air and slow deep breaths.

They get to the middle of the lounge and a gentleman stands up. Zion's client is a well-known actor that lives here in Atlanta. He and his wife wanted to meet to have some drinks, to say hi, as they had not seen him for a while. Zion explains he's been busy with the construction of his headquarters and this trip was unexpected. He wanted to hang out with Lea during her business trips. Zion looks over at Lea, bringing her forward for introductions. She smiles.

God, that look! I'm in heaven.

The bartender and waitress bring drinks to the table. For the gentleman it's LOUIS XIII cognac with two long stemmed glasses monogrammed with the hotel's emblem. For the ladies a bottle of Quinta do Noval Nacional port with two glasses.

Lea is grateful they don't talk about the client's personal finances as she didn't want to have to leave. She doesn't think she would have allowed herself to sit in on that. She manages to hold her part of the conversation.

I'm proud of myself, I'm doing well.

After about an hour, they finish off their drinks and conversation, going their separate ways. Zion and Lea get into his rented limo with Sam and Ryan in the back with them. Dinner tonight is at The Whiskey Wok.

Instead of having Sam and Ryan sit at a separate table, they all sit together, enjoying dinner and light conversation. They especially enjoy the chef creating special entrees. Lea has tasted many different things tonight: lamb chops, sea cucumber, ahi tuna, wagyu beef, moose cheese, truffles, sea urchin, scallops, and foie gras. She refused to taste the fugu, squid, octopus, snails, eel and oysters. She took their ribbing good naturedly.

"Y'all strange. Just admit it. I'm the only one at this table that eats normal food. Eel. Naw, I'm good."

Zion laughs at her. He's enjoying dinner with his girlfriend and his security detail as if they're life-long old friends, and Lea has fit in perfectly tonight.

After dinner, they decide to take a walk through Buckhead with Ryan following behind them working off the fullness of their stomachs. Sam went to the limo waiting for Zion's call.

"Thank you for including me in your meeting with your client tonight. I'm glad I didn't embarrass you," Lea says to him, leaning her head on his arm.

"I never thought that. If I had any idea that would be the case, I never would have mentioned it. Besides, I want to show you off to everyone, and as soon as this Addison crap is over with, I plan on it. On my own terms of course. I do have some bad news though."

"What?"

"When we get back to St. Louis, I would like to tone it down with us. Only in public. I want Addison to believe you are a business colleague. I have someone following her, but until she does something, I can't take any kind of action. This is the only thing I can think of to keep you safe without putting a security detail on you. Please Lea, out in public only. In private, we're Zion and Lea, dating, in a relationship. Those who know will continue to know and those who don't, won't," he says.

Lea pauses slightly before answering. Her initial reaction would be to balk and run, believing she's being hidden away. But Zion is being open and honest about Addison. She feels she should trust him and she will.

He turns her face up to his, forcing her to look into his coal black eyes. He whispers her name, "Lea?"

Unable to look away, she unconsciously licks her lips and responds, "Sure, we can do that. Don't worry, I trust your judgment."

"Thank you, sweetheart. I appreciate that." He kisses her. "Let's get back to the hotel, we have an early checkout. I don't want this week to end, but tomorrow we're back to St. Louis." Zion looks back at Ryan and tells him to call Sam.

They stand off to the side, people watching while waiting.

Lea thinks about what Zion has asked of her. She agrees to deny herself what she wants in a relationship. Again. No BDSM. She has a man, but she can't be seen with him. She can't tell anyone outside of those currently knowledgeable.

He gets what he wants. What the hell do I get?

In the car, Lea's quiet, reflecting on what she's agreed to.

Same shit, different man. Yeah, I agreed to it. Don't mean I have to like it.

"Lea, what's wrong?" Zion asks her, uneasy with her silence.

"Nothing," she says, rubbing her thumb against his palm, staring at their clenched hands.

Lea wishes they could have stayed in Atlanta or stayed away from home a bit longer. There's no elevator play, nor is there any suite or bedroom play. The Sex Diva ain't happy and neither is Lea.

The Sex Diva is arguing with Mother Nature about her menstrual cycle starting this week. Lea is questioning her relationship with Zion.

What does 'not in public' mean? Will we ever go out? Movies, dinner? Will we be doing anything? Maybe he's ashamed of me or us, and this is an excuse to hide it.

Instead of approaching him about what she's overthinking, or that she's giving herself a headache, she works on packing and making sure everything is ready for tomorrow. Zion is on his computer answering e-mails. Lea is cramping again, so she runs a bath for a soak.

Zion looks up and notices she's nowhere in sight, but he does hear water splashing. He walks to the bathroom, stripping on the way. She's in the tub, eyes closed.

Poor baby.

"Hey there. Cramping?" He climbs in behind her, having her lay against him, this time soothing her.

"Yep, and waiting for the pain meds to kick in. Thanks for making this week enjoyable. I imagined myself in and out of airports stressed out about being alone. Sitting in hotel rooms, working the entire time, crying over missing you."

"You're welcome. I don't want you crying about us. You don't do anything else but business when traveling? No shopping or sight-seeing?"

"Depends. I would go find a museum to walk around. Food to go. Or if I was lucky enough to have friends or family in that town, I would visit with them. Honestly, this week, I thought I would be re-hashing memories of us. Making new memories has been much better."

"What's next week looking like for you? I didn't get your schedule from Crystal beyond this trip. I'm having dinner with my family Tuesday night but am pretty much open. I wanna be with you," he says.

"Whatever that means." Lea mumbles.

"Lea, it means, what we define it as meaning."

"I have my trainer two days this week after work. I'll go by and see how mom is doing. I'll be working and prepping for the Landon Enterprises move. And there's the schedule you want to see. As your project lead, I'll be putting that together."

"Meet me at my place Wednesday. No matter the time, be there after work. You have the key to get in," he informs her with an offhand remark while caressing the sides of her breasts. Perfect handfuls.

"Stop playing with the boobies. They're tender. What key? I don't have a key to your place," she corrects him.

"Yes, you do. The garage card key I gave you to get out of the garage unlocks the elevator and gives you access to my apartment. Only five in existence and you have the fifth one."

"Wait, you gave me the card quite some time ago. You were that sure of us getting this far?" She rubs her cheek against his arm. "Sorry I haven't returned it by the way. It's such a plain card. I believe its time I clean out my wallet.

Zion responds, with a slight grin, "That's ok. I had them designed to be plain. They don't tie back to my apartment unless told. Honestly, I forgot to get it back. I remembered tonight you had it. I was about to have it deactivated, thinking it was lost." Lea pinches him. "Ouch, that hurt. Ima tell my mama on you," he says playfully rubbing the area.

She laughs, caressing the spot, "Okay, I'll be there Wednesday. To hang out."

"Are you okay about how things are going to be when we get back home? You were quiet on the drive back to the hotel?" he asks her, wanting to know her true feelings.

How can two people date and not be seen?

"I'm not all that thrilled about it. It takes me back to times when I would date a guy but we didn't go anywhere. He would call after nine on a Friday, asking me what I'm doing. I would fall into his plan and he would say, 'I wanna see you'. Which meant sitting around my place. But he had plenty of time and energy to hang out with his family and friends."

"Lea, it's not like that. Believe me, please?"

"Zion, I get what's behind it, but it doesn't mean I have to like it. I'm being honest with you. There will be times I go out with friends. I'm not going to put your business out there, so I won't be discussing you. You don't have to worry about that."

"I'm not worried about you telling my business. I'm worried about you being out without me. I'm not liking that part of this. I'll figure something out. We'll figure something out."

"There may not be anything to figure out. Remember, I don't go out that much. I want you to know, it could happen. I will go out without you. I do have friends and family I like to spend time with. It's just that being asked to not be seen with you in public bugs me."

Zion caresses her arms, thinking about what she said.

Going out without him. We're a couple. We should be spending this time going out together. Not separately. And sure as hell not hiding.

"Are you angry with what I said?"

"No Lea, I'm not angry at all. Or at least I'm not angry with you. Just the situation. Anytime you wanna go out, we'll do so. I'll hire as much security as I need. And you'll get to introduce me to all your friends. Everyone will know you're taken. I'll make sure of that."

They get up early Friday morning, checking out and going to the airport, with breakfast on the plane. Today, Lea is traveling in jeans, flats, casual jacket and shirt. Zion surprises her dressed in a similar fashion. On their way to the airport, they go over schedules with each other. He'll be meeting with another of his clients, and she'll be going to hers to set up their home office and troubleshoot on their computers. There will be no hotel stay for this day of the trip. They'll meet back at the airport hangar at six, with Lea being finished with her client by five. The plan is to arrive back in St. Louis by eleven tonight.

On the flight back, Zion and Lea lay on the bed in the sleeping quarters of the plane, talking. She won't be seeing him this weekend as she'll be staying with her mom tonight through Sunday. They're having a girl's weekend, movie, dinner, and Lea running errands for her. Of course, she and Zion make out but no sex.

"I'm going to miss you this weekend after spending so many days together," Zion says.

"I'll miss you, too. I don't want you to get tired of having me around. Someday, when you come home and I'm in your bed asleep, I want to be sure you're happy I'm lying there naked and waiting instead of thinking, will she ever go home?"

"Go home? Never. Hell, if I could convince you to move in with me tonight I would. I'll let you go home and deal with missing you. I need to crunch some numbers to see how much this change in dates could cost me. I'll be working all weekend."

"Uhm, Zion, can we talk about this love, uhm, us saying 'I love you'?" Lea sits up crossing her legs looking at him.

"Why, are you saying you don't love me?" He looks crestfallen.

"No, I'm not saying that."

"Then what are you saying? Be warned I'm not liking the direction of this conversation."

"Oh well. Deal with it. You've only known me four months, and men don't fall in love as quickly as women. Especially a man with as many options as you have. I want you to be sure this isn't some fly-by-night emotion you're feeling. You said it while in pain."

"You said it while I was in pain, too. And let's talk about that why don't we? Are you sure you love me and your love for me is real?" Zion sits up ramrod straight, bracing himself. He's a little pissed at the direction of this conversation. He has not declared his love to every woman he's met.

"Yes, it's real. And you didn't answer me. Do you really love me? I'm giving my heart to you, no doubts, no turning back, you have it, it's all yours. You not sure of your feelings, I'll deck you for crushing my heart and leaving me alone to get over you. Leaving me to settle with a subpar human of a man. After you, no one will measure up or surpass you. Don't fuck with my emotions," she growls.

He relaxes his mind and body, "Oh, Kitten, that is the best declaration of love I've ever had in my life. Yes, I love you. Yes, I really love you. My heart is yours. No way in hell will I ever fuck with your emotions as I don't expect you to fuck with my mine. I'm sure of my feelings. Another woman not getting what you got babe. Are we clear on this?"

She smiles the smile of a two-year-old. "Okay."

"That's it? Just an, okay? After that speech all I get is just an 'Okay'?"

"Yep." And she lies back in his arms.

"Lea, you are going to drive me out of this world, and I'm going to love every minute of it."

"Good. At least now you understand what you're getting."

138

-17-

They arrive in St. Louis at ten forty-five. Lea calls her mom to let her know she's back and will be there in about thirty minutes. Her mom tells her to wait until tomorrow morning to come by, that it's too late for Lea to be driving to her house. It's not as if Lea hasn't driven to her mother's house this late before. With her hours, it happens often. But a chance to get one more night with Zion, she hops at it.

"Okay Mom, see you tomorrow."

"Cool, change in plans. Sam, drop Lea and me off at her house, you can take my luggage home. I'll be working this weekend. Go get some rest. I'll have Lea drop me off tomorrow and see you Monday morning at seven a.m."

"Of course sir," Sam and Ryan load up the SUV with their luggage. Ryan takes off in another vehicle and they get in the SUV to drive to Lea's house.

In the backseat, Lea caresses Zion's thigh gradually moving closer and closer to his crotch. "Kitten, don't do that. You're still on your cycle. I can wait."

"Zion, you need to hush and enjoy the moment. I would like to make sure you're thinking about me in a carnal way while you're working," Lea whispers to him, "Do you wanna safe word me?"

"Hell no. I want you. Always."

The privacy glass is up, so Sam can't see what they're doing. Lea caresses Zion's dick through his jeans, being as gentle as she can, but he increases the pressure by putting his hand on top of hers. She lifts her face up, looking for a sign of pain in his expression. He bends down to kiss her. She attempts to unbuckle his pants, but he unzips them, only allowing her partial access to him.

Lea moans in frustration.

"Baby, when we get home, you can do all you want, okay? Just caress and kiss me for now." He glides his hands under her shirt to caress her skin, making her hot all over.

They arrive at Lea's house about ten minutes later. Zion grabs her suitcase, laptop bag and the garment bag with the purchases he's made.

"I thought the garment bag was going to your house."

"There's a dress in there you will need for my birthday party. It's better off here with you."

"Wonderful. Gives me plenty of time to shop for accessories. Sam, thank you for everything this week."

Sam smiles at Lea. "My pleasure, Miss Adams. See you Monday morning, Mr. Landon. Call me if you need anything."

Zion watches the interchange between Sam and Lea.

What the hell was that fucking grin for? My girlfriend has tamed my head of security? This comfort is getting out of hand.

Inside Lea's house, Zion pulls her into his arms, wanting to be close to her instead of addressing the familiarity she has with Sam. He'll take that up with him later.

"Hi Kitten." He breathes into her neck.

"Hi Bear." She locks the door behind him.

Pulling back away from him, she unbuckles his jeans. "Zion are you up for this?"

His dick springs out of his underwear and practically stands at attention. "Lea, what do you think?"

She bends down with his penis at eye level. Instead of taking him in she helps him take off his shoes, jeans, and underwear. They walk over to the couch and he sits down. Lea grabs a pillow off the couch. Placing it on the floor, she kneels in front of him, taking off her top and putting her hair in a ponytail.

"Oh, shit, Lea, what are you about to do to me?"

"Nothing, I want us both to get very, very comfortable."

Lea spreads Zion's legs open, moving in between them, and pulling his head down for a kiss. He moans into her mouth. She pulls back, bending down over his dick, gently licking up one side and down the other. He slightly flinches.

"Zion, remember our safe words, okay. Say them for me."

"Ocean to stop and halo to ease up," he whispers looking into her eyes, not glancing away.

Lea watches him as she slowly lowers her head, opening her mouth and putting the tip of his dick in. They laugh at each other, both thinking the same thing.

Baby just let me put the tip in.

REMEMBER, WE GOTTA CONCENTRATE ON HIS REACTIONS. MAKE SURE HE'S THINKING ABOUT US. I MEAN YOU. WELL, YOU KNOW WHAT I MEAN. BUT DON'T—.

Sex Diva, will you shut the hell up. I got this.

Lea gingerly sucks and licks around the tip, making sure he's accustomed to it being Lea and her tongue and not associating it with any other memory. He eases back onto the couch, relaxing, allowing her to take control. She cups her hands around his shaft, gently working up and down, applying pressure. She gets into the groove of sucking him off while closely monitoring him.

Oh, God, he tastes so good. His pre-cum is slipping down my throat and I can't get enough of it.

She uses her right hand to gently play with his balls. He's loving that action. He lifts up so she can play with both of them at the same time. He scoots down farther on the couch and leans back to give her deeper access to his dick.

"Oh, Lea. Yes, baby, yes, suck me. Oh, fucking yes."

Oh, this woman knows how to suck my dick.

"Shit yes. Lick the tip for me."

Lea slides her tongue up the shaft, gliding over the veins pulsing on the sides of his penis. She returns to the tip, licking it all around, and flicking her tongue under the hood, making him jump and jerk with each flick.

"Baby, you ready to cum for me, to shoot down my throat?"

"God, yes, Lea, please yes."

She moves in closer to the couch, bracing her legs against it and placing her hands on either side of his thighs. He places one hand on the back of her neck and the other on the side of her face. Lea sucks on his dick, moving up and down. He pumps into her mouth, first slowly. His moves become feverish and erratic. She slows him down with the pressure of her hands on his thighs, forcing him to focus on the pleasure and to forget about past pains and movements. He gently moves faster, only this time as if she were riding his dick with her pussy instead of her mouth.

She looks up and sees him watching her. They don't break eye contact. He pumps harder, but nothing like when he was jacking off. The ecstasy in his eyes, the way his mouth is slightly open and then him licking his lips gives Lea confidence. With renewed, vigor she closes her eyes and attempts to deep throat him.

Oh, Bear yes, that's it, it's me Lea.

She moans, sucking his dick with increasing pressure. He reaches that point of no return, stills her head, shooting cum into her mouth, jerking with each squirt that hits the back of her throat.

"Oh fuck, yeeeessssss," he groans, holding Lea's head in place, not wanting her to move. "Oh, shit, this feels so good." His jerking movements cause him to scoot to the end of the couch, almost falling off. "Oooh yes." he growls. He releases his hand from her neck and leans back on the couch as Lea slips his dick out of her mouth, sliding her tongue along the sides and across the tip before breaking contact.

She gets up and goes to the bathroom to swish her mouth with mouthwash. Lea returns with a warm towel. When Zion stopped her, she didn't catch all his cum and some is in the hairs of his crotch. She returns, wiping him gently.

I'm amazed at her. Truly amazed.

Zion and Lea make it to bed. He falls asleep with her wrapped in his arms.

The next morning, they wake up late. "Where are we going shopping for accessories for your dress?" Zion asks her.

"What do you mean 'we'? You really wanna go traipsing with me in and out of stores trying to find the right jewelry and shoes? I can grab one of my girlfriends and go. Or go alone. No biggie."

"Oh, it's a biggie. We're going to do as many normal things as we possibly can within reason. Because we just got back to town, I doubt that I'm being watched or followed. Today we shop. Let's hit the stores."

Lea walks to the passenger side of her car, with Zion taking the driver's seat. Watching him adjust the seats and mirrors makes Lea think about getting another car. One where different driver's adjustments can be saved.

"What are you grinning at?" he asks her.

"All the adjusting I'm going to have to do when I get back in the driver's seat. Or get a new car. You know one that remembers different driver setups."

"Hhhmmmmm. New car. Shall we go car shopping too?" he asks as they head out to Plaza Frontenac.

"You just itching to spend. No, we are not going car shopping."

"Darn. Some other time I guess."

"Zion, no car shopping."

"Lea, I spend my money the way I want to spend it."

They hit up five shoe stores. Zion enjoys watching her shop. She's determined. When the sales-people aren't sure they have what she's looking for, Lea says thank you and moves on to the next store. She finds a pair of shoes to match the dress perfectly.

Her selection of jewelry is simple. She finds a simple gold chain with gold hoop earrings to match. Not once did she look at a diamond. Again, he wants to put her in diamonds, yet she goes for simplicity.

"Bear, this was fun. Thank you. Even though, you know, it wasn't necessary." They're sitting in Cardwell's having lunch.

"It's what I wanted to do. No arguments. I'm already missing you. Let's get out of here, I've kept you away from your mom long enough."

"Are you okay? You seem antsy, distracted. Tell me."

"Maybe it's just my nerves. I keep thinking we're being watched or followed. I know logically it's impossible. We just got back. There's no way Addison could be following me, right?"

"I don't know. Let's head home. Sometimes, we need to listen to our instincts."

With Zion driving, Lea focuses on the cars around and behind them. She doesn't notice anyone following them or anything out of the ordinary.

"I don't see anything unusual either," Zion says.

"That's a good thing, right?"

"Yes, Babe." He looks at her smiling. "That's a good thing."

Lea relaxes for the remainder of the drive. This will be the last time they'll be doing anything in public like this for a while, and they have made the most of this day. They know they can see each other anytime at their places, but must limit the public dates.

That's not a bad thing, Lea attempts to convince herself. She wants to be seen with him, but she wants to keep him and herself safe.

YOU KNOW WHAT? STOP OVERTHINKING THIS AND ENJOY IT, Sex Diva yells at her.

Enjoying.

Zion parks in front of his building. They get out of her car and lean against the passenger door hugging. "Baby, come up for a little while. We can make out and I can suck on your nipples, and you can give me a hand job. A couple of hours at most."

"No, Zion. I'm not doing that. You need to go to work, and I need to see about my mom. I'll see you Wednesday after work."

"Damn. Well, I tried. I love you, Ms. Lea Adams. Wait, why can't we get together on Monday or even tomorrow after you leave your mom's house?" he asks, nibbling her earlobe.

Giggling, Lea responds, "Because I need to work and prep for the week and if you're around and my period is over, I'm going to want to have you fuck my brains out and I would rather wait until Wednesday. I love you Mr. Zion Landon. Now go." She kisses him.

He steps back and walks her to the driver's door opening it. As she steps inside, he gets one last caress of her ass. Leaning into the window he gets a kiss. "Drive safely and call or text me when you get to your mom's."

"I promise. Good night, Bear."

"Good night, Kitten."

After Lea drives off, he stays outside looking around at the cars driving by. Still not seeing anything unusual, Zion goes into his building, stopping at the security desk to chat with the guard.

"Hey Brian, how's it going? Anything I need to be made aware of?"

"No sir, we haven't had any issues with the young lady you warned us about. We also made sure to keep an eye on your vehicles and nothing has happened with them," Brian responds back.

"Thanks man. Have a good weekend," Zion says moving onto the elevators going up to his apartment.

Mrs. Vance has unpacked for him as usual, and started the laundry. He smells beef stew and homemade bread. At least he won't be starving or having to eat fast food while working.

"Hello Mrs. Vance. How are you this fine wonderful Saturday?" He hugs her coming out of the laundry room and heads toward his bedroom upstairs. He changes clothes and walks over to his in-house gym for a workout.

Mrs. Vance stands there stunned. She calls her husband. "Sam, I don't know what kinda trip you guys had this week, but Mr. Landon just hugged me and SKIPPED off to his gym. What's going on?"

Sam laughs responding back to his wife. "Darling, he's in love. You know how that is. Hurry up and get done, we have the weekend to ourselves."

Zion was right to listen to his instincts. He and Lea were being watched. When they got back to her car, someone was staring, having followed them from her house.

"Ms. Bitch got me having to get rid of another one. Ms. Bitch goes out of town and comes back with a dick. Ms. Bitch gonna fuck around get a dick killed. Ms. Bitch is mine."

The individual takes out a gun pointing it at Zion and Lea, pulling the trigger over and over loving the sounds of the clicks. Getting aroused.

"Time to drill some ass and make a video."

The individual arrives back home.

"I hate this house. Always did. Barely furnished this piece of shit. Only the basics. Never invited anyone over. Couldn't stand the judgment."

It was gonna be great. Then this druggy shows up. Ruining my new plans. Not this time. He strips from the waist down. Fucker passed out on the couch. Without warning. Without foreplay. Without pleasantries. A camera is turned on. Legs are spread wide open. Anal ease is squeeze in between ass cheeks. He hates going in dry and this witch is dry as a desert with all the drugs she takes. Dick is plunged into ass. Pleasure and pain are taken and given. No words are spoken.

Every time. No cowering. No pleading. No begging to stop.

"Fuck! That's it! Fucking take it!"

He thinks about Ms. Bitch begging him. He pretends he's drilling Ms. Bitch. He cums. They both do. Hating themselves.

-18-

Sunday morning, Zion lay in bed later than usual. He thinks about what happened in Chicago, how he was so easily able to step back into his past and confront Addison. He doesn't consider himself a weak man but this got him questioning.

When he was in therapy, one of the therapist's suggestions was for Zion to write down what he was thinking and feeling about an uncomfortable situation. It was his first step into journaling.

The shit I wrote about. The fear, hatred, anger, the desire to hurt Addison. I laid it all bare. To feel those exposed wounds was difficult.

Going to his office, Zion takes out a pen and pad of paper. He sits down to write. To freely let it all flow. To show his anger for Addison compared to his love for Lea.

Addison
The thought of this woman makes me ill. She has changed so much from what she was in college. No fucking way will I get back into that shit. Anger and pain. That's what Addison represents.
Lea
I laugh. I smile. I become aroused at the thought of her. My desire to do for her, make her a part of my life, sometimes overwhelms me.

Grabbing the pen and pad, Zion leaves his office. Stepping into his living room, he lists the changes in his home since being with Lea and adds them to the pad.

Lea

Furniture changes, much more comfortable sectional. Dining room, I have added a new console for her camera equipment where its easily accessible. Bedroom/bathroom, her stuff next to my stuff.

Zion laughs.

Kitchen, always a fresh fruit platter, protein powders and a blender for her smoothies. Her favorite wine in my wine cabinet.

All changes that Zion loves. Changes due to the love he has for Lea. While cooking himself breakfast, he thinks back to the conversations he and the BOM's had about settling down. He's on his path. He sends a text to Bryson and Larson:

Zion: *I've found my forever half.*
BM: *Well, well, well. You in love now? You sure about that?*
LD: *Rubbing shit in ain't cool.*
Zion: *Y'all, this shit feels damned fantastic.*
LD: *As the youngest I figured I would be first to fall.*
BM: *Larson you the one to suggest we stop fucking around and you keep running from yours.*
LD: *Man fuck you. I've stopped running from her and lovin' my cougar. What the fuck you got going on?*
Zion: *Yeah Bryson, what up with you?*
BM: *Leather and lace fellas, leather and lace. In and out of the office.*

Zion: *Fellas. one of us got a wedding in their future.*
        I'm out.

BM: *Fucking wedding you say. Wholly shit.*

LD: *Dude, you whipped.*

Zion: *So the fuck are y'all. Leathers and lace. Larson man,*
        your cougar. Whipped, in love, taken off the fucking
        market.

Zion chuckles at the conversation. Returning to his office, he sits down, turning on his computer. He opens his web browser to research, of all things, BDSM. When Addison brought it up in their relationship, he had never researched it. He simply went along with what she said.

Even during therapy, he didn't look further into it. With Lea, he wants to be educated.

He types in the acronym BDSM. The first few images that appear are of toys and stores. As he scrolls further, images of women tied up in different ways appear. Then he starts reading articles regarding the facets of BDSM and how it starts to cross the line into areas of abuse.

Starting a fresh sheet of paper, Zion writes.

- *No way in hell we getting into rope play. Hell the fuck no.*
- *Forget all these items going in the ass. No ass play.*
- *Body stimulators on the nipples, for the penis? I'm willing to try.*
- *Bed straps. Good idea. Wrist and ankle straps. Good idea.*
- *Only my hands will go around her neck. Never will I strap her neck.*

- *Submission. How much submission? I like these submission poses. Fuck yeah.*
- *Spanking. Open hand. NEVER CLOSED FIST.*
- *Fetishes. What the hell kinda fetish could I have? No fricking clue.*
- *Edging. Now that I can get into.*
- *Additional toy play. Male vs female.*
- *Communication, consent, communication, consent.*
- *How vulnerable am I willing to be? To let go. Fuck.*
- *Damn, I'm so fucking excited. My Lea. Me exploring safe BDSM. Shit she the one.*

Zion flips back to the pages of the comparisons between Addison and Lea.

He tears them off the pad and walks to his balcony. Turning on the grill, he starts a fire. With a drink in hand, he tosses the pages into the fire.

Goodbye to Addison Raymond, hello to Lea Adams. One helluva future, no turning back.

-19-

On Tuesday evening, Zion goes to his parents' house for dinner. They've just returned from a six-month vacation in Europe. He knew when he became wealthy enough, he would ensure his parents could travel and experience life anyway they wanted. The trip to Europe was his and Star's anniversary gift to them. While they were traveling, he met up with them twice to be sure they were okay and enjoying themselves. The first time was before Lea and the second was right after he met her, but things hadn't progressed with Lea and him yet.

He's now ready to tell his family about her, informing them about a woman he's dating, in love with, and may be marrying someday.

Hell, not may be. Definitely.

His parents' house is located in AshlenVale Downs in north St. Louis County. He arrives at six-thirty letting himself in with his key. His nieces are screaming and running through the house. At eighteen months, Denise and Cam are pushing toy carts, attempting to keep themselves upright and mobile. Garrett is running behind Cam and Zion catches up with Denise before she can fall face first onto the floor.

I coulda been a great dad. Maybe with Lea we can adopt. Or get a puppy.

He goes to the kitchen greeting everyone, carrying Denise on his shoulders. He places her in the high chair next to her sister.

"Finally, you're here. Great. Can we eat now? I'm starving." Star says, taking food out the oven.

"Geez, sorry, I had to work you know," Zion says, walking over to the sink to wash his hands.

His mom and dad come into the kitchen laughing. He gives them both hugs. By looking at how flushed his mom is, he can tell they were back somewhere making out.

Old ass sex fiends.

Everyone sits down, serving up food.

"So, Zion. Tell me about the new headquarters. Everything going as planned?" his father, Royal asks.

"Yep, ahead of schedule by eight weeks. I'm hoping to move in floor by floor as soon as it can be arranged."

"Why the hell do you want to do that? Won't that cost a fortune?"

"I told you about Addison. I don't feel secure in our current location. I can't risk having clients come to the office with a possibility of running into her and causing issues. By the way, remember that anywhere you go, you are to use the car service and security I've hired. Right? ALL of you. Please. Thank You."

"We'll see," his mother, Patty, says. "I want to hear about Miss Lea Adams," she says and pins him with that you better talk, 'cause you're not going anywhere, look.

"And who told you anything about her at all?" Zion looks over at loud-mouth Star.

"Man, you're dating. You lucky I haven't taken out a full-page ad. Tell us. We need details."

"She's the building remodel Project Lead, sexy, inviting, warm, and caring, and we've been dating since the beginning of the project. We keep business as business and outside of business we date."

Let's see if I can get away with only that information.

"Dating? You're dating? As in spending time other than having sex?" his mother asks.

"Yes mom, dating. Even knowing about my issues, she still likes me and wants to be with me," he looks directly at his parents, hoping they don't bring up the kid situation.

"She's forty-four, never been married, no kids. That's all I'm saying about her so let's change the subject," he says.

"Nope, don't wanna. I got a few more questions," his father states.

Might as well get this over with.

"Go for it," Zion says.

"Okay, when do we get to meet her? Do you see long-term with her? Are you in love with her?" His father looks at him grinning cause he knows his son will answer all his questions. "How in the hell did she manage to pin you down into wanting long-term? And do we see a wedding, marriage in your future?"

"You will get to meet her at the birthday party and not before. Yes, I see long-term with her. Yes, I'm in love with her. Before I could even talk about temporary sexual liaison, she laid the law down, saying she only wanted long-term and she wouldn't do temporary. Wedding, marriage in the future, everything is possible. I'm not going to bring that up with her until I have this Addison mess finished and neither will any of you. And after tonight, NONE of you will discuss this. Is that understood?"

His mother gets up and hugs him with tears in her eyes. "Oh, my baby boy, you're in love. FINALLLLLYYYYY. I can't wait to meet my future daughter-in-law."

"Mom, all of you, promise me you won't talk about this night and anything future with her of what I'm thinking. PROMISE ME."

"We all promise."

"I promise."

"Not a word out of me."

"I don't know nothing."

"Pea."

"Carrot."

Everyone, including the twins chime in, making a promise not to bring any of this up to Lea.

They clean up after dinner then move to the living room and allow the girls free reign while the adults are taking up strategic points encircling them, watching them play and have fun.

"Zion, come to my office I want to talk with you," his father tells him.

Zion gets up and follows him. This discussion can be about anything. Business, personal, fun. They are alike that way. Any discussions with them can go in many different directions at the drop of a hat. His dad gets to the point as soon as the door is closed.

"Tell me more about Miss Adams and yourself. I need to know you're okay. To get ahead of any stray thoughts your mother may have."

Zion pours them a glass of Glenlivet scotch and takes a seat on the other side of his father's desk, ready to share his thoughts. He's the only man on earth that can get Zion to talk like this. Sam comes close, but his father, can pull almost anything out of him. When it came to Addison, Zion had hard limits he would not discuss.

"Dad, I don't know what it is about this woman or if it is about her. Maybe it's the timing. It feels right being with her. I keep thinking it's the newness of a relationship, but you know me. I haven't been in a relationship since college. Is this supposed to feel like this?" Zion asks.

"Son, you've never had a woman say no to you. You've been so damn protective of your feelings for fear of rejection because of being sterile, that you've never allowed it to get to this stage.

There've been women you could've settled down with and had other options for kids. Adoption for one. But you never would even consider it once a woman said she wanted a baby. You punished women for your sterilization. Sounds to me you ready to stop punishing and start loving. Tell me, how did you break the news to her, did you blurt it out in anger, as usual?"

"Yes, the morning after our first night together. She had a night terror and woke up scared. We were talking and I told her. Dad, in that moment she made me feel like a gentle giant. She told me I wasn't less of a man because I couldn't give a woman biological kids. I knew I had to get to know her better. I did almost blow it though."

"Yeah, how so? Running scared?"

"Addison. I had cut off contact with Lea, wanting to figure out what was going on and what to do about Addison. I thought it would be best to not see or talk to Lea."

"And how did that work out?"

"I went back groveling, pleading, and telling her everything she wanted to know to get back into her life."

"How much did it cost you? What did you have to buy? Some shiny expensive bauble I suppose."

"No, I bought her nothing. Dad, this woman sees me and not my bank account. Would you believe we spent the day walking in Forest Park, at the zoo, riding the paddle boats? She has a job she loves. She's 'established' as you would say. I can take off my Mr. Captain-Save-A-Heaux cape and put on my savior armor. I did splurge last week, totally my choice. It felt natural to do. I couldn't risk being away from her, so I arranged her business travel with me and used the company resources. I did buy her a pair of chocolate diamond earrings."

Zion takes out his phone and shows his father a picture of Lea on Wednesday in Chicago. She's walking into the hotel; completely unaware he was snapping pictures. Then there's the one of her getting dressed for their dinner date in Atlanta. Putting on makeup and looking down putting on her shoes.

God, this woman is beautiful and sexy and doesn't even know it.

"My, my, and you say she's forty-four. Are you sure about that, she looks about late thirties? Wait. Do I see a woman with natural hair? No weave. Okay take this back. I'm not going to say another word. One more thing. No double 'D' tits. My man, you're maturing."

"I know, right? Dad, I had an 'Addison' episode with her."

Zion has never gone into details about the sex and how truly painful it was with Addison, with his father. They agreed he would refer to them as episodes that get out of hand and would leave him feeling inhuman.

"When I came out of the episode, Lea didn't judge me. She comforted me. She held me. In minutes, she destroyed every evil moment about Addison, and I fell head over heels in love with her. And I told her. I didn't hold back or hesitate. I just said it."

"I'm proud of you. You know that, don't you? I'm happy you've fallen in love. We all are."

"Dad, you said I punished women because of my sterilization. Do you really think that's what I was doing?"

"Yes. Zion, if you didn't get automatic acceptance, it was the woman's fault. You never considered suggesting anything else. I hate to admit but a lot of those women were not quality."

Zion looks at his father astounded.

"Son, don't give me that look. Your choices in women were not all that great. But you were only screwing around so there was no need for me to step in. I've been paying close attention to your relationships the last few years. I thought you were close to settling down a number of times."

"Naw. There was one I had been seeing steadily but it was never gonna go past the sex," Zion says thinking about his last temporary fuck.

"Baby issues." Royal smiles at the nod of Zion's head.

"Not only that, I just wasn't feeling a connection to her. With Lea, before I even knew her name, I wanted her."

"I can't wait to meet her." Royal leans back in his chair admiring his son. *Finally, the boy is in love. About damned time.*

They finish off their conversation talking business.

Dad saying, he's proud of me and happy that I've fallen in love verifies what I have with Lea is the best thing ever.

-20-

After her workout Tuesday, Lea gets home, taking out her computer to work on the final projected change in dates for Landon Enterprises. By eleven o'clock, she has three proposals for the meeting with Tom and Zion tomorrow. Tom insisted on a face-to-face meeting.

She lays in bed wondering how Zion's dinner with his family went. She wonders constantly about what he's doing, saying, whom he's talking to, is he thinking about her as much as she thinks about him. *'cause I can't get the man out of my mind.*

Against her better judgment, she sends him a goodnight text.

Lea: *Hi Bear. My queen-size bed used to be a perfect size. Now it's too big. All your fault. Goodnight.*

Zion: *I'm hating the thought of going up to my King. All that empty space. Goodnight, Kitten. See you tomorrow.*

The next morning, Lea is standing in her dining room staring at the set of keys to her house sitting on her dining room table. She's decided to give them to Zion, along with his own passcode to her house alarm. She's walked away from the keys without picking them up four times already. On the fourth attempt, she even makes it to her car. Now she's here again for the fifth time, staring at them.

PICK UP THE DAMN KEYS. YOU GONNA BE LATE.

Lea grabs the keys, a red velvet pouch, and the card with the code on it.

I don't have to give him the key. It's not like he's said anything about it. Besides, making closet and drawer space is the prudent thing to do. He does stay over often.

OH, STOP OVER THINKIN' IT.

It was thoughtful to have his favorite body wash in my bathroom and purchasing bottles of his favorite wine and liquor.

JUST GIVE HIM THE DAMN KEY SO WE CAN GET BACK TO SEXING, I'M HORNY.

How the hell can you be so damn horny? It's not like you haven't been through a dry spell before. Years of them, remember?

YES, BUT NOW WE HAVE SOMEONE WHO CAN KEEP UP. WE GETTIN' OLD. GET BACK IN THE GAME. WE DON'T HAVE THAT MANY YEARS LEFT FOR SEX.

Chill why don't you, stop being so fucking desperate.

The Sex Diva pouts and go sits in the corner tapping her foot.

Hell, I'm arguing with myself again. After our meeting, I'll give him the key. Or maybe when I get to his place. Or have it delivered.

ARE YOU FRICKIN' KIDDING ME?

Lea gets into the office and finishes up the documentation for the meeting. It has been changed to include Zion, management from his IT department, his security detail, and hell, even, his marketing, human resources departments, and Neil from the building site. Ten people in one meeting.

I'm sick thinking about it.

Tom comes to her office. "Hey, you ready to go? I have the packets from the copy room."

"No. Yes. Sure. Let's get this over with," Lea says, grabbing the pouch with the spare key and card with the code on it. She and

Tom are using a car service today, so they can concentrate and talk more about what's going to take place.

"Lea, are you nervous?"

"Of course, I'm nervous. Do you know me at all? I want this over with and the decision made."

"I'm proud of you managing to keep business and pleasure separate. I see how happy you are with Zion. Your demeanor has changed, and I like it. More confident."

"More confident? I guess. Even if things shouldn't work out, maybe the confident Lea will stay for the duration."

"Not work out? Why wouldn't it work out?" Tom sees marriage and a happy future for Zion and Lea. Not working out is the farthest thing from his and the Cupid's minds. Maybe they need to meet to make sure this Addison thing doesn't become a deterrent in this relationship.

"You know. Can't have too much happiness and all that. Well, here we are. Let's go make a deal," Lea exits the car and becomes Lea Adams, Project Lead, Meeting Facilitator. She strolls through the lobby with a sexy confidence, head held high, and gripping her tote by the hands instead of carrying it on her shoulder. Usually, she hangs back and walks with or behind Tom. Lea has him trailing after her, catching up to her as she steps onto the elevator.

They walk out of the elevator onto the sixth floor of an open balcony with the office doors of Landon Enterprises facing outward. They are buzzed in and escorted directly to the largest boardroom. The room is currently empty, allowing Lea to unpack everything and get settled. She places packets at each seat, making sure hers is as far away from Zion's as possible, figuring he would be at the head of the table. Right as she's finishing, Morgan arrives, followed by, Star, Saul, Neil, Landon Enterprises Human Resources Director, Landon Enterprises Infrastructure Manager,

Sam, then Zion. An older gentleman, who looks like Zion, enters the room. Introductions are made. Lea hears the gentleman introduced as Zion's father, Royal Landon.

Oh fuck, his father. Oh, fuck, shit.

Star, approaches Lea. "Lea, hi. How are you? I don't think Zion has told you but I'm Landon Enterprises Marketing and Communications Director. This is our father, Royal Landon. For some reason, now that he and our mom are back in town, he wants to do business meetings. Dad, this is Lea Adams, the Project Lead on the new headquarters and this is Tom Brasil, CEO of Golden Technology and Electronics Enterprises."

I send up a silent prayer, thanking the heavens she didn't say, "and Zion's girlfriend". Maybe she doesn't know.

They exchange greetings. Lea attempts to stay focused in business mode hoping and praying these two are not aware of her and Zion dating. Zion comes over and puts his hand on her back practically advertising they're closer than business associates.

Shit, Shit, Shit.

"Hi Lea and Tom," Zion caresses her hip above her ass in front of his father.

Oh, fucking great. Don't even look at him, Lea.

"Good morning, Zion. Shall we all take our seats and get started?" Lea attempts to put some business formality into the situation.

She walks away from his grasp. He grins at the maneuver. Zion wants to keep touching Lea. Lea wants to hug Zion. Sex Diva perks up.

HURRY UP AND GET THIS OVER WITH.

Lea walks away from the head of the table, assuming Zion will be sitting there, but his father takes that seat. Star sits on her father's left. Everyone else takes their seats, leaving two at the end, one for Lea and Zion next to her.

No, No, No. I'll stand, that's it, I'll go stand in the damn corner. Oh no, Zion has pulled out my chair, staring me down, forcing me to sit or make a scene.

He's sitting on her left and Tom at the other end of the table on her right.

Lea takes her seat, then Zion takes his. His meeting room table is solid black mahogany.

Thank heaven. I can wipe my wet palms on my clothes without attracting attention.

Her leg shakes and Zion looks down at it, putting his hand on her and she stops, getting control of her nervousness. They glance at each other, then Lea quickly looks away and into his father's eyes.

He knows. The man knows. He knows his son is sexing his Project Lead, and by the smirk on his face the man approves. Where are the black holes to swallow me up when I need one?

Zion addresses the group. "Thanks everyone for coming. As you may have heard, I'm wanting to push up the move into the new headquarters as soon as we can. I don't feel this building is secure enough and Landon Enterprises is not being allowed to incorporate the security ideas at this location that Sam and I have in mind. It has worked out so far because we've been traveling to see clients instead of clients flying into St. Louis. Well, I would like to cut back on some of my travel," Zion squeezes Lea's knee while saying this, "and I would also like my clients to feel they can come to our headquarters without having to worry about their well-being, confidentiality, and privacy. G-TEE is here to give us some information to see if this is feasible. Tom, Lea, thank you in advance for working on this. What do you have for me?"

Tom gives Lea that look saying "the floor is yours Lea". She practically knows this by heart so she stands, walking over to the whiteboard.

Zion turns his body toward Lea, attempting to concentrate on her words and not his growing arousal. His pride is on full display for everyone to see.

"Currently, the Landon Enterprises project is eight weeks ahead of schedule due to great weather and Neil running a tight ship on the building site. The contracted scheduled completion date is May thirty-first. With the schedule ten weeks ahead, the completion date could be February twenty-eighth. I have provided three different proposals for the changes requested by Mr. Landon," Lea points toward Zion and quickly looks away toward the whiteboard picking up a marker to have something to do with her hands. She then turns back around addressing the group taking a deep breath before continuing.

"October thirty-first, November thirtieth, and December thirty-first. I have discussed these dates with Neil and the other contractors and vendors. Comfortably speaking, they are willing to commit to the timeframe of November thirtieth with the understanding that finishing touches could carry through to December thirty-first. As we're now in June, this gives us a six-month timeframe of finishing and having everyone moved in and ready to go by December first.

"Training sessions on equipment for all your employees can take place in multiple sessions, depending on their workload. To help facilitate a smooth move, any equipment you can dispose of now and transition into new equipment and programs would be a major step forward for Landon Enterprises. The less physical equipment there is to move, the less there will be to think about setting up in the new building or finding temporary storage space for it. This will also cut down the overall expenses if Landon Enterprises doesn't have to legally and properly store old equipment."

Feeling her mouth about to go dry from all the talking, Lea pauses for questions. After getting none she proceeds, "The restaurant for the new building is willing to move in as early as December with a skeleton staff. It can commit to being fully operational by January thirty-first. Seventy-five percent of all office furniture is sitting in warehouses waiting to be installed when given the go ahead. This could take place starting September fifteenth at the earliest."

"Miss Adams, what kind of increase in funds are we looking at for this?" Zion's father asks, alternating among note-taking, watching Lea present, and Zion watching Lea.

Royal makes notes to discuss with Patty:

- Zion in love. Zion giddy. Lea business smart. Lea knows her shit. Lea doesn't look at Zion.
- Big or small wedding. Wedding gift, house or land. Grand babies questionable but always doable.
- Maybe we can stop worrying about our boy getting old and screwing around.
- Hell, yeah, we can.

Royal turns his mind back to business and what Lea is saying.

Lea tries not to do the movement of adjusting her neck because looking at Mr. Landon, she knows this is how Zion will look in about thirty years.

LORDY BE THIS MAN GOT FINE MEN IN HIS FAMILY.

Trying not to grin at the thought, Lea answers. "Normally, there would be an additional fifty percent increase in costs, but due to the build being ahead of schedule, we're only looking at a twenty to thirty percent increase. Those costs can also be offset by the recommended disposal of older equipment and furniture as soon as possible. In addition, G-TEE also has recommendations for the Human Resources and Compliance departments for packing and storing employee and client hard copy files and are willing to work with dates for the Marketing department to help in facilitating media announcements if necessary. As these options were not included in the original contract, there would be an additional fee for those services."

The meeting goes on like this for the next hour-and-a-half with Lea giving information and Zion and his staff questioning why, how, and when from her and Tom. G-TEE's responsibility is limited as far as moving into the building is concerned. All his other departments are figuring how they can make this work in the five- to six-month timeframe they are being given. Mr. Landon is silent, taking notes, letting Zion run his business.

Finally, Zion speaks up forcibly, "Everyone, listen. This is gonna take place. By November thirtieth, we will be in the new headquarters. Do whatever you have to do to make this happen. I would prefer by October thirty-first, but I understand that's pushing it and everyone way too hard. Do we agree?"

Everyone in the room looks at him and nods or verbally agrees. Tom, Neil, and Lea also agree, and she informs them she'll get the addendum to the contract written up and sent over for signatures.

"Be sure to add a fifteen percent bonus for getting this done early," Zion says, "Okay, everyone. Thanks for coming and let's get back to work so we can get this done."

"Will do," Tom says. Tom and Lea prepare to leave.

Zion is in a huddle, talking to his sister, his father, Sam, and Saul. Lea focuses on gathering her things. She notices there's an extra packet left, so she walks out to the reception area and hands it over to Morgan for Zion to have if he needs it.

"Morgan, is it okay if I drop something off in Zion's office?"

He can open it when I'm not around and we can discuss it further when I get to his place tonight.

"Sure Miss Adams, go right ahead."

Lea places the red pouch on the keyboard of his computer and exits quickly. Tom is exiting the boardroom ready to leave. He doesn't notice her coming out of Zion's office, but Zion sure as heck does. He winks at her.

Dammit. I wanted him to see it when I wasn't around.

She grabs her bag and turns around to say goodbye to everyone but gets blocked by Zion.

Zion had his eye on Lea the whole time he was talking with his father in the boardroom. All he wanted to do was get her in his arms, bent over the table, and buried inside of her. He can't stop thinking how everything about this woman is a turn-on.

"Lea, may I have a moment please?" Zion asks and points her in the direction of his office. "Tom, a few minutes, or I can bring Lea back to the office if you can't wait."

"That'll be fine. We were only going back to the office to drop Lea off at her car. I can have the car service take me straight home. Lea, I'll see you tomorrow," Tom says.

"See you tomorrow, Tom." Lea turns to Zion. "You needed more clarification on something I assume?"

"Nope. I want to know what you were doing in my office. Kitten."

"Nothing. Bear."

"Well let's go see. Shall we."

They walk into his office. After closing and locking the door, he turns and sees the pouch sitting on his keyboard. He walks over, snatching it up, holding onto Lea.

"A gift. For me. I feel special."

"You don't have to open it. Actually, give it back." Lea reaches for it but Zion is quicker than she is, and he opens it up taking out the key ring with a blue smooth stone charm and card.

He puts them in his pocket. "Thank you, Lea."

He takes Lea in his arms, kissing her.

"We don't have time for what I want to do to you right now," he grips her butt cheeks, pressing her into him. "But when I get you home, woman, you just don't know."

As he is about to kiss her again, they hear someone outside his door. It's his father asking if Zion is still here.

Shit, his father!

Lea grabs her purse from where she dropped it on the floor and stands near Zion's conference table, having him wipe his mouth off. He unlocks the door and in walks his father and sister.

OMG, I just want to crawl in that missing black hole and disappear.

"Hello again, Mr. Landon. Star," she wants to be sure they're aware she's in the room before anything embarrassing is said. They turn to her and stop in their tracks.

"Oh, hello Miss Adams," his father greets her again, smirking. Star is standing to the side staring at Zion and Lea, grinning, knowing she interrupted a make-out session.

"What's up, Dad?" Zion asks him. He walks over to his desk, packing away his computer and files. He wants to get out of this office and get Lea back to his apartment.

"Oh, I just wanted to let you know I'm taking this packet home to your mother. She wants to know what's going on and if she can help with anything. Miss Adams, I was impressed with everything today. It looks like my son has found a great project lead and colleague. I'm glad I got to meet you. Star, let's go."

"But Daddy, I had a question for Zion," she stammers and turns to look at Zion. "Uh, I forget."

"Good, let's go." His father ushers Star out of the office and closes the door.

Lea collapses into a chair.

Shit, Shit, Shit.

"Hey, you, okay?" Zion asks her, grinning mischievously.

"You know darn well I'm not okay. Why didn't you tell me I would be meeting your father?" she asks him exasperated.

"I don't know; it's just Dad is all," he smiles at her. "Come on, let's go."

"It's just Dad is all? Remember that when it comes to you meeting my mother," she says to him. "And why did you have to caress my ass in the boardroom? You put our relationship on display for your executives to see. Is that appropriate? I mean now they know for sure you are dating the—. Oh, crap what am I saying?"

"Lea, I would be surprised if they hadn't known. I know we're not going out in public, but I'm not going to hide any affection I feel for you either. I'm the boss. They don't like it, they can quit."

"It's just—."

"It's just what, Lea?"

"I'm still not used to men displaying affection or acknowledging a relationship status the way you did. It's something I'm still adjusting to. I think I'm still stuck in the hiding and making excuse for hiding type of relationship phase."

"Well, stop it. Get out of that phase. I'm not hiding my affection for you. Let's get out of here."

"Where are we going?"

"My place, and we won't be leaving until tomorrow morning. I'll drop you off at work."

They walk out to Landon Enterprises front office to Sam waiting for them. He takes their computer bags and walks out to the lobby standing by the elevator.

"Morgan, if you need anything, I'll be at home. Good night. On second thought, take off. Go, get out of here."

"Okay sir. Good night," Morgan responds walking toward the conference room to clean up.

Zion turns to Lea with a mischievous grin.

"What's with the look Mr. Landon?" Lea asks him grinning back.

Zion walks up to her and bends down whispering in her ear, "Oh simply relieved to be getting out of here. Miss Adams."

"You really don't care about who sees what, do you? Or what issues this could cause?"

"Nope. You don't work for me. You work for G-TEE. I'm not in any way according to my legal department doing anything against my company rules. Contracts where negotiated before we even met. The deal with G-TEE was legally complete before we became an item. So, when I'm dating you, devouring you, making you scream and whimper from pleasure, nothing and no one can say shit about it."

"Nice to know that. What do you have in mind about making me scream and whimper tonight? And should I be worried?"

"Kitten, of course not. Simply making up for lost time."

Sam, Zion, and Lea step off the elevator into his apartment. Sam walks to Zion's office, greeting his wife, Mrs. Vance on the way, to drop off their computer bags. Lea walks over to Zion's bar and makes them drinks, taking them out to the balcony. Zion and Mrs. Vance have their daily discussion. After she and Sam leave, Zion join's Lea on the balcony.

"Finally, it's just us. I can now give you my full attention." He picks up her feet and places them in his lap, taking off her shoes. He massages the balls of her feet, watching her flex her toes. He's never been a foot man but the sight of her doing this is arousing him.

"Yep, just us." Lea presses her feet into his crotch. Zion doesn't take his eyes off her and presses them harder with one hand while picking up his drink in the other, sipping it. He sits the glass down and unzips his pants giving Lea full access to him.

OH MY GOD, THE SIGHT OF HIS DICK IN THEM BOXER BRIEFS GET'S ME WEAK EVERY TIME.

Lea uses her feet to stroke him up and down. Again, he squeezes her feet pressing them into his growing arousal. She unbuttons her blouse, stripping it off. Lea caresses her breasts causing her nipples to harden even more. Zion licks his lips.

"Damn woman yes. Squeeze them."

He puts her feet down, moving between her legs. He latches onto a tit sucking and soaking the thin fabric covering it. He pulls the other one out. Opening his mouth, he latches on squeezing the one he just released.

"Oh, baby yes, suck."

Zion licks her chest between her breasts twirling his tongue around, up and down. He stands, pulls her up and strips off her skirt and underwear. Undressing himself, he uses their clothes to create a soft pallet on the table.

"Zion, here on the balcony? What if I scream?"

"Baby I want you to yell to the heavens. I got the top floor and no one can see. He puts her on the table, laying her on her back and lifting her legs straight up pressing them against his shoulders. Moving between her legs and closer to her vagina, he slides into her moist folds. Lea growls as he slips into her.

"Lea, forget all about my pain of last week," he says stroking slowly in.

"Oh, fuck yes, its forgotten. Damn."

He grips her wrists, wrapping his arms around her legs. Zion's desire tonight is to erase the memory of him hurting himself and to show Lea the primal desire he has for her and only her.

Zion slowly strokes in and out of her moving left and right. Lea tries to mimic the movements, but he has her pinned to him in such a way she can barely move her body.

He bends his legs a fraction of an inch to ensure his penis strokes her g-spot. He watches Lea's reactions, looking for those glorious signs of pleasure.

Lea whispers more, more, each time Zion strokes in. "Fucking yes, deeper Zion. Shit fucking more."

With this all-clear to go ahead from his love, he pulls her to the edge of the table gripping her thighs. He pounds into her faster, keeping her legs pinned to his chest. Zion kisses her calves attempting to stave off his orgasm.

"Lea, Baby. So good. Cum for me."

"Yes Zion. Zion. Shit. Yes." She screams. Lea explodes lifting her bottom off the table. Zion keeps pumping into her, through her contracting around his penis. She finally stops bucking. He pauses and explodes inside of her, jerking with each squirt of seed leaving his body.

"Oh shit," he yells.

After a few minutes Lea says, "Ow, ow, ow. Zion my legs." The feeling is starting to return to them in the position they're in, and its becoming uncomfortable. He lets them go, and they dangle over the edge of the table.

Zion pulls out of her. She can feel the warm ooze seeping from inside of her, flowing to the crack of her ass onto their clothes. He grabs one of the chairs and drops into it, his body tension leaving, laying his head onto her stomach. Lea wipes away the glistening sweat from his head and shoulders while he caresses her legs and feet.

The Sex Diva is stunned silent.

A deep rumble of a laugh gives her pause.

At Lea's office, a car is sitting outside the garage entrance waiting. The driver is strumming fingers on the steering wheel, waiting for a Gold Acura to emerge.

After about two hours of waiting and having to drive around Clayton, making sure of not being approached by the cops, the driver parks their car and walks into the garage checking every level looking for the Acura. It's still here.

"If she's here, maybe just maybe, I can speak with her."

Going to the office, standing a distance away from the newly installed cameras, the individual notices the lights are turned off and all is locked up tight.

"Fuck, where the hell is she? How the fuck did she get out of this fucking building without my seeing her? What the hell is going on? She always leaves at the same time going to the park for a walk. I know her schedule like the fucking back of my hand. Some bullshit ain't right. Not right at fucking all."

"Maybe I'm trailing the wrong person. Maybe someone needs to stoke some fires."

-21-

Zion and Lea are finishing dinner after their sexual escapade on the balcony. They are sitting at the dining room table, Lea in one of Zion's t-shirts and Zion in pajama bottoms. He takes their empty dishes to the kitchen, loading them into the dishwasher. Returning to the table, he refills their wine glasses. Without saying anything, Zion hands Lea the folder sitting on the dining room chair next to him.

"What's this?"

"Some research I've been doing."

Lea opens the folder. The first sheet of paper is the BDSM list of items Zion came up with. Before reading the list, Lea attempts to look at the other sheets of paper.

"Kitten. One sheet at a time," Zion admonishes her.

"Hm, ok." Lea reads the list. Finishing it she says, "I understand, but I don't understand."

"With what happened with me in Chicago, I wanted to know how I could so easily step back into my past. It's something I learned in therapy. Write down the pros and cons and analyze. I want to understand more about BDSM and what I would be willing to partake in with you," Zion pauses, watching her closely. When she doesn't interrupt, he continues.

"I know I want none of what Addison and I did."

"Neither do I," Lea says.

"Good. I like the dominance and submission aspects. The body stimulators sound fire."

Lea looks down at his list again. "Can I now look at the other sheets?"

"Sure."

Flipping them over one at a time, Lea studies them.

Sheet 1 – images of submission poses
Sheet 2 – explanation of edging
Sheet 3 – list of different fetishes with whips, wax,
      bondage, foot and sensation play,
      highlighted
Sheet 4 – list of fantasies
Sheet 5 – list of sex toys; Shibari wand, nipple
      clamps, restraints, blindfolds, sensation
      wheels

FUCKIN SHIT. THAT IS SOME LIST.

Every time Lea flips a page to read, Zion grins broadly at her reactions. She flexes her fingers, rubs her hands up and down her thighs. Picks up the wine glass with both hands and sips, then sits it back down. She blows out air, fans herself, and bites her lips.

Sex Diva is sitting on Lea's shoulders swinging her legs back and forth.

"Lea?" Zion softly whispers her name. She doesn't react.

"Kitten?" He scoots closer to her. "Baby? You okay?" He touches her leg.

Lea jumps, knocking over her wine glass, spilling the wine on the table.

"Oh shit. Damn Zion. I'm so sorry. Fuck shit." To keep the folder and papers from getting wet, she swipes them onto the floor.

She tries to wipe up the wine with her hands.

Zion grins, hopping up and grabbing a towel.

"Lea, stop. You making a mess. OCEAN," he says sternly.

Lea stops and wipes her hands down his t-shirt, staining it.

"Oh fuck, dammit," she mumbles, looking down at the red streaks on his what used to be stark white t-shirt.

"Lea, sit down," Zion tells her, moving her to the chair. He finishes cleaning up the wine, moves the glasses and bottle to the kitchen and returns, picking up the folder and papers from the floor.

"Baby. Are you okay?"

Lea looks up at him, pops out of her chair into his arms, kissing him, hugging him, telling him how much she cares about him. He holds onto her, enjoying the onslaught of love.

"Well, I guess I did right, huh?" he says laughing.

"Zion? Did right? You are absolutely fucking amazing." She kisses him over and over. He tastes her tears.

"Kitten." He stops the kisses, forcing her to look at him. "Why are you crying?"

"Zion, you heard me. You listened. You did research. You. You. YOU. You want to do it," Lea says, grabbing the folder and tossing the papers above them in the air.

She hugs him again, burying her face into his chest. "I love you so much. When can we start?"

Zion flexes his pectoral muscles and Lea kisses them. "Oh baby, I'm glad I pleased you. Let's start tonight. With some submission poses to see which ones we like."

"Okay. Okay. Okay. Submission poses. Gotcha. Watcha want me to do." Lea, leans back looking up at him.

"I want you to calm down. Breathe. In. Out. In. Out."

Lea does as she is told, taking deep breaths.

"Good. Now let's start from the beginning with this."

"Okay. Okay. Sure. Sure. Beginning."

"Woman, you got me losing my train of thought with your excitement." He pushes her back into her chair.

Lea sits on the edge of it. Sex Diva is cheering, jumping up and down, waving pom poms.

Zion brings his chair over to sit in front of her. They are not touching. Lea doesn't realize it, but he has started.

"Calm down. We are gonna test dominance and submission. Me dom and you sub. Do you consent to this?" One of the biggest things Zion learned with BDSM is both parties must fully and verbally grant consent and both parties must understand this consent can be withdrawn at any time without judgment.

Lea shakes her head up and down, "Yes, I consent."

"Would you like a written BDSM contract? At this point, we are in a learn-as-we go situation."

"No. No contract. But can we get a book and keep it handy, writing down what we like, don't like, willing to do, not do and use our initials as confirmation?" Lea rushes over her words.

"Yes. I'm willing to do that. Now, is there anything that you have been wanting in BDSM I can provide?"

"Yes. Sometimes I would like to be in the dom position and you the sub."

"Okay. We will work out what that means for us. Is that understood?"

"Yes. Understood."

The Sex Diva is now doing the Michael Jackson thriller dance. CAUSE I AM SO FUCKING THRILLED. THIS IS OUR MAN AND HE WANTS TO DO BDSM.

Zion picks up the sheet of paper that has the submission poses. He grabs a pen from the chair. Adjusting his posture in the chair to one of a commanding in charge position, he asks Lea, "Which of these poses are you agreeable to trying?"

Lea takes the pen and paper from him. She circles; attention, inspection, waitress, trophy, wall, cross, Egyptian, and nadu. She puts a question mark on humble, table, and kneel. Sex Doll, ready to please, floor, and stool are x'd out.

"Dang it. I think I was supposed to ask you for the paper and pen first," she says handing both back to him.

"Baby, it's all good. We'll do what works for us." He stares at the page. "I believe we have done the attention and a modified inspection pose. Tonight, we are going to do the wait and at your service pose."

Lea impatiently waits for his instruction.

"I want you to go upstairs and take a shower. Alone. When you are done, you will put on a matching bra and panty set that is laid out on the bathroom sink. This is a special set for this particular reason. You will only wear this set and others like them when I tell you. Is that understood?"

"Yes. Zion. Understood."

"When we are in our dom/sub personas and they will be personas, you will refer to me as 'Z' and I will refer to you as 'My Kitten'. If you do not refer to me as 'Z', that is breaking persona and everything stops. And a punishment is administered. Agreed?"

"What kind of punishment?"

"You may be instructed to stand in a pose. You may be asked to apologize. Or we stop completely and everything ends. No sex. Nothing and I mean no punishment other than these will be administered. Never will I abuse you, disrespect you or humiliate you. Nor will you do that to me. Agreed?"

"Yes. Agreed."

"When I instruct you to do something in our dom/sub persona, you will always look me directly in my eye. I don't like the idea of your eyes down. I know you sometimes can't hold my gaze, so we are adjusting that aspect to accommodate us. Agreed?"

"Yes. Agreed." Lea doesn't look away. "Z, may I go shower and change?"

"Yes. My Kitten. You may go shower and change. Do not run."

Lea gives Zion a big grin 'cause she was about to speed up his steps to his bedroom. Instead, she slowly stands and calmy walks up the steps. Once she is sure she is out of eyesight, she rushes to the bathroom, stripping off his t-shirt. Lea examines the bra and panty set.

I see why he said these are to be used while in our dom/sub personas. Sex Diva look at these. There's a slit across my nipples. The crotch is cut out of the panties. My pussy is out there for, oooooweeee. I love this man.

NO, WE LOVE THIS MAN. HURRY THE FUCK UP. SHOWER AND GET DRESS. I CAN'T WAIT TO SEE WHAT HE GOT PLANNED.

She showers and changes into the fuchsia-colored bra and panty set. Zion didn't say where to stand, so Lea goes and stands in the bedroom in the wait pose.

Five minutes later he comes into the bedroom, dressed in a different pair of pajama bottoms. These will be his dom/sub persona clothing. He is freshly showered and smelling good.

When Lea walked upstairs to shower and change, Zion stood up and ran to the downstairs bathroom to shower. He was finished in record time. Reviewing the second folder that Lea didn't see, he goes over the commands used in dom/sub. He takes a shot of vodka and rushes upstairs. Not hearing the shower, he assumes Lea is in the bedroom in one of the requested positions. He takes a deep breath and enters.

She is in the wait pose, standing at her side of the bed, with her hands folded in front of her. As he walks into the room, she looks him directly in the eye. Lea doesn't move a muscle focusing on controlling her breathing.

The Sex Diva is jumping up and down with excitement.

"Hello. My Kitten."

"Good evening. Z." Lea whispers.

"Say our safe words," he instructs.

"Ocean to stop. Halo to ease up."

"Good. You are free to revoke your consent at any time. Understood."

"Yes. Z."

"Do you consent?"

"Yes. Z."

Zion approaches Lea and kisses her lips, cheeks, neck. He moves her hands to her side and licks and sucks the skin between her tits.

Unsure of what to do with her hands, Lea leaves them at her sides and enjoys Zion licking and sucking. He caresses the area above the 'v' of her clit through the panties. He goes back and forth from one side to the other.

Lea is smiling at him, not looking away from his beautiful gaze. He slides his fingers between the slit of the panties and glide them between her pussy lips. Feeling the slickness, he rubs her lips together. Zion bends down to her womanhood and kneels at eye level. Licking his lips, he presses his face into her pussy, eating her through the opening of the lace underwear. He loves that he can leave them on and not have to rip them. Each time Lea moves her hands to touch him, Zion says, "Don't."

He stands and turns Lea around.

"My Kitten, I'm going to bend you over. I want you to touch your ankles. Don't let go. Is that understood?"

"Yes."

Lea bends over, spreading her legs and gripping her ankles.

WE GOTTA INCORPORATE SOME YOGA INTO OUR WORKOUTS.

Zion puts his hands between her legs, stroking her inner thighs up and down. He slides his hands up to her pussy, using them to stimulate her. Taking one hand and placing it on her thigh, he uses the other to squeeze and rub her pussy lips and clit together.

Lea can barely keep her balance, but Zion helps steadies her. "Oh, Zion."

He stops.

"My Kitten, what name are you to use?"

"Z."

Zion presses Lea's pussy lips again, squeezing her clit, hard. She's still bent over, grabbing her ankles.

Zion pulls his penis through the opening fly of his pajama pants. He purposely purchased these silk ones for this reason with the idea of fucking Lea from behind in this submissive pose while dressed. He slides her panties open wider, slightly baring her pussy to him. Stroking her wet pussy lips, he spreads them open and slides inside of her.

Lea inhales, "Z."

"That's my girl," Zion says, praising her.

Lea releases the grip on her ankles and attempts to lift up, but Zion pushes her back down and pulls out.

Frustrated as hell, he knew he had to stop. Lea broke formation. Therefore, she has to be punished.

"Do you know why I stopped?" he demands of her.

She turns to look back at him but he turns her around facing the bed. "My Kitten. I am awaiting an answer. If I don't get one, we can call it a night and go to bed." He growls, straightening and stepping back.

Damn, I wanna fuck, he thinks to himself, *but I have to get her in line understanding when we are in dom/sub persona, she is to do as she is told, unless safe wording or asking.*

Whispering she asks, "I removed my hands?"

"And what else?"

"I, I changed position?"

"Correct. Now what are we going to do?"

Lea bends over, back into position. Gripping her ankles, legs spread, ass up. She scoots a fraction of an inch closer to the bed to use it to brace herself in case she needs to.

"My Kitten. I'm proud of you."

Moving back into place, Zion caresses her pussy to get her wet again. She is soaking.

Well, damn.

He slides in. Concentrating on Lea, he goes slowly up and down. Bending his knees a few inches, he is able to go a little deeper. Lea is trembling in his hands.

She mumbles, "Shit, shit, shit." Her back bumps softly against the bed, but she doesn't care.

YOU BET NOT SAY ONE FUCKING WORD. OH SHIT YES FUCK US Z.

Lea digs her nails into her ankles, lifts up on the tip of her toes and cums. She screams, "Yes 'ZZZZZZZZ'."

Zion, fucking her from behind, harder and harder, releases her hips and braces himself on the bed. He presses into her with one more deep push and explodes.

"Oh. Got. Be. Fucking. Damn." He grips the bed and rides out his orgasm, loving the sensations of the lace panties, the silk of the pajama bottoms, and Lea's pussy.

He pulls out and adjust their clothes. Helping Lea to stand upright, he pulls her into their bed with him.

"Z. May I do one thing?"

"Of course. My Kitten." Zion is worried, thinking he did something wrong.

Lea sits up, grabs a pillow, stands up, brings it to her face and screams into it. A full-throated, leaving her hoarse, and coughing scream yelling, "Oh fucking hell yeah. That was the utmost in heaven fun I have ever had." She puts the pillow on the bed, and screams into it some more, even punching it.

Zion is laying in bed and laughing so hard, his stomach hurts.

God, I love this woman.

-22-

The next day, Lea is on the phone to Gordon.

"Hey, where are you?"

"Sitting in the airport. I got about three hours before I board my flight to California. What's up? Everything okay? You sound winded. Don't be calling me after you just got through doing it." Gordon walks to a corner for some privacy.

"No, I haven't just got… Oh stop it. I'm walking back to my car from my jog." Lea gets in her car and puts Gordon on speaker.

"I can't and won't go into deep details but uhhhhh…"

"Uh what? Zion proposed?"

"Oh heck no. Nothing like that."

"Then get to the point. Geez sometimes you like to draw shit out, it gets…"

Interrupting Gordon before he can finish Lea says, "Zion and I did dominance and submission last night. Gordon, I got my in-between."

"…on my nerves. Wholly shit, Lea. Well promise me you will keep it safe. As much as you have read up on the topic, don't get stupid and go overboard."

"I promise I won't. Gotta go now, getting on the highway but I fucking had to tell you. I'm so excited. I gotta find a book so we can write down what we like and don't like. Bye Gordon. Have a safe trip."

Before Gordon can say bye, Lea has hung up. Staring at his phone he mumbles, "Bye Lea. Thanks. Oh and one more thing, if he hurts you, I'll bury the guy under my garden."

Lea is sitting in her office staring at the book she purchased to help she and Zion track what they like in their foray of the dom/sub world. Unable to find what she was looking for in a bookstore, actually she was kinda embarrassed to even ask if they carried something like a BDSM journal, Lea went online searching.

Putting in the key words BDSM journal into Amazon search, she found a book called the Naughty Sassy Journal with the word Caution on it. The description was of a journal with blank lined notebook pages of BDSM categories such as kinks and fetishes, bondage and toys. The image of the holographic couple in a sexual position had her sold.

She and Zion's love life is explosive now. Neither of them has ever been this open and honest with their lovers as they are with each other.

Even though Zion considers himself to be superb in the sex department, being with Lea and her appetite for more and different sex is extraordinary. Especially with their foray into the dom/sub world. And it is nothing like the degrading sex he had with Addison.

Thinking of her, Zion hasn't heard from her in a couple of weeks now. No emails, no pop-ups at his building.

Maybe I overreacted to this. One person shows up from my past, and I flip out and hire extra security and cars. He makes a note on his calendar to consider easing up on this after the birthday celebration. *Then Lea and I can get out and socialize. Yep, ease up on security after my birthday if I haven't heard from Addison.*

Zion will be traveling the next couple of weeks, and he hates it. First time he can remember he has wanted to stay home. Being away from Lea that long annoys him. He'll be back in town in time for the combined birthday celebration Star is throwing.

Lea and Zion are sitting in Zion's living room watching TV. Lea is cleaning her camera equipment in preparation for the July fourth get together he's having at his apartment. Another change in his life that would have never taken place before he met her. Holidays were either spent at his sister's or parent's house or were elaborate catered events at his place.

"Did you ever think about becoming a professional photographer?" he asks her.

"Sure. Being an introvert and behind the camera is the best place to be. I never pursued it beyond taking pictures of friend's, wanting to hone my skills."

"What's your style of photography?"

"Journalistic. I like being in a room full of people and taking pictures of them enjoying themselves. You get the best shots. The posed pictures caused people to be stiff and forced." She aims her camera and snaps a picture of him listening to her talk while caressing her legs. She shows him the image on the camera screen. He's in a relaxed pose, looking calm and serene.

"Anyway, I had put my camera away for about fifteen years."

Zion gives her a stunned look. He can't think of anything he owns that's fifteen years old. Not even a piece of jewelry.

"Yes, it's that old. Don't look at me that way. As long as you take care of your equipment, it can last forever. I was focusing on school and other stuff."

"Why haven't you upgraded?"

"Haven't had the time to research for one. I can't decide if I want to turn my basement into a studio. I can't decide if the cost is worth it and I'm going to leave it in the closet gathering dust."

"Sounds like a lot of excuses to me."

"Must you point that out?"

"Yes. I don't deal in excuses. Anymore. Kitten." He stares at Lea giving her a pointed look. Moments like these with her excite him. The change from being on the go and traveling to sitting, watching TV, and talking with his girlfriend, has become invaluable.

"Subject change." Lea knows where that look can lead to and before it does, she has a touchy subject to discuss with him.

"So, the birthday party. You're scheduled to arrive back in town the same day. What time shall I meet you there?" This is her subtle way of bringing up the topic of her arriving alone.

"What do you mean meet me there? You're my date!"

Star has invited close family, friends, and business associates for their celebration. She was born on July twelfth three years after him. There will be about seventy-five to a hundred guests in total. For Zion, it will be his first birthday with a date. Past celebrations were dinner with family if his parents insisted on it or traveling and partying. He's looking forward to this one. Not only turning fifty; but turning fifty, being in love, and having a date. Being seen, introducing her around. Arriving together.

"Zion, remember. We're not displaying our relationship in public like that because of Addison. We arriving together would probably give her ammo." Lea looks at him waiting for his disagreement.

"We're arriving together," he says flatly.

"Are you sure that's a good idea?" she prods.

"I want you by my side. This damn situation is getting on my last fucking nerve." He gets up to go fix himself a drink. "I'm tired of this."

Lea watches him from across the room splashing cranberry juice in the glass with ice, skipping on the alcohol. She recognizes this look well.

"Zion, I want to be by your side, I want to arrive with you, but have you heard from her?"

"No. Nothing. Shit, Lea we can't keep putting our lives on hold because of what someone may or may not do. I'm considering easing up on security after the party." He walks back over and sits down beside her.

"Really? Easing up on security? Have you heard from her?"

"No. A part of me thinks I may have overreacted."

"Now that's a shocker. I never thought you would be one to over react." Lea grins at him softening her words.

"Beautiful, stop being a smart-ass. I do question some of my decisions."

Lea leans her had on his shoulder. He brings his hand up to caress her cheek. After kissing his palm, she asks him, "Are we arriving together or not?"

"No. I don't know. Let me think about it," he says.

Zion is quiet, probably thinking about how he can make it work for him and Lea to arrive as the couple they are. Lea recognizes this look from when he's concentrating on something for business. After he works it out in his head, he then returns to the present and moves to the next task. This time she assists him.

"Hey, whatever you decide I'll go with it. Me, arriving alone is no big deal. It gives me extra time to get dressed and be extra extra fly for the evening."

He looks at her. "I want you by my side, Lea."

"And I'll be there. Mentally and physically. Always."

-23-

July fourth weekend arrives and Lea, Star, Garrett, and the girls are preparing to watch the fireworks from his balcony. Because Denise and Cam are still so young, they figured this would be the safest way for them to enjoy the excitement of a fireworks display without the crowds.

His parents are having dinner with some friends they met while traveling, who have a layover in St. Louis. His mother tried every way possible to figure out how to come to Zion's, for the opportunity to meet Lea as she's the only member of his family that hasn't met her yet, but she made these arrangements long before he met Lea and his mother always sticks to any plans she makes. Zion has yet to meet any of Lea's family. Now that he thinks about it, the only one she talks about is her mom and a few cousins. Maybe it's time they have the family interview.

Mrs. Vance and Sam have the holiday weekend off so they can get away and enjoy their family. This will leave Zion and Garrett manning the grill with, Lea and Star preparing side dishes.

While waiting for the sun to set and the fireworks to start, Lea and Star spend time with the girls playing board games and Zion and Garrett playing a few rounds of checkers. Not letting this opportunity pass, Lea takes a lot of pictures of everyone, especially of Zion interacting with the girls.

He will love the images. It's sad that he can't father his own kids.

Lea sometimes wonders if he ever thought of adopting. She often thinks that if they were to marry, would she be willing to do what it takes to give him a child? Even at her age, the risks involved, would she be willing to go through them? When she looks at him playing with his nieces, she decides yes. She would. Or even adopting, she would do that with him. He's only mentioned marriage once, so at this point she's dreaming.

Star and Lea are in Zion's kitchen prepping the food for dinner. Lea is making potato salad and Star is making fettuccine with a homemade lobster sauce. The girls are sneaking fruit from the fruit tray.

Now that they're alone, Lea decides to approach Star about Zion and kids to get a feel about his desires to be a father.

The man can afford to do anything. Why not a single father?

"Star, do you mind if I ask you a personal question about Zion? I would ask him, but I don't want him to focus on his anger when talking about it."

"Let me guess. Kids?" She smiles at Lea.

It's nice having a woman other than her mother to talk with. Lea being with Zion is fun to watch.

"Yes. Has he ever mentioned anything about adopting?"

"No, never. As soon as a woman talked about carrying his child, they were dismissed from his life. He wouldn't waste his time. Why do you ask?"

"With his money, he could adopt and be the father he always wanted to be. I was curious why he hasn't?"

"Zion is not the single father type. So, doing it alone is something he would never pursue. He wants what our parents had. All of it. He could accept and live with not having kids, but I know he really wants them."

"Please don't tell him I asked you about this. I was just wondering."

"No problem, Lea. I'm glad to help." Star hopes she's pointing Lea in the direction of considering adoption with Zion when they get married.

"Maybe someday he'll get what you all have. Even if it's not with me."

"Lea, why would you say that?"

"Oh, I don't know. Human interference, world intervention. Anything and everything could happen. Just thinking out loud."

My brother needs to hurry and propose. Star keeps to the promise she made about not bringing up marriage but that doesn't mean she'll let Lea believe she isn't important to him.

"Since my brother has met you, his thoughts and way of living have changed from his days of screwing around and not wanting to get close to women."

"Lea, we know about Zion's hard-living bachelor days. He's a grown man. He took steps to ensure his playing around didn't interfere with family and business. How, I sure as hell don't know. But since meeting you he's softened. He's relaxed, he smiles more, he's playful. He's even let his guard down some. That's all your doing."

OH HE PLAYFULL ALL RIGHT. WE PLAY A LOT.

Sex Diva hush.

HEEHEEHEEHEE. I'll go be in the nadu pose.

Yes, you do that.

"Please don't give me that much credit. It could be because he's aging and looking for some peace."

"Oh, there's that. He knew he couldn't screw around forever. There were times I would introduce him to women thinking they would be the one. Been doing that for years on the sly. Each and every one got the 'hell no' attitude from him. He's been ready to settle down for about five years. He doesn't know I know that. I watch him and I listen. I'm glad he's fallen in love with you."

"Star, I think we better change the subject. You'll have me planning a future I'm not so sure I should be thinking about."

"Go ahead and plan. You have two flower girls waiting to show off." Star laughs at the girls tugging on Lea's skirt begging for attention from her.

"Thanks for the talk. I appreciate it," Lea says bending down to eye level with the girls. They give her sticky fruit kisses.

"My pleasure," Star says grinning and grabs Lea's camera to snap some pictures.

Zion comes into the kitchen checking on the ladies, "So, how we doing here?"

"Great. Side dishes are ready to go. Are you worried we may over-cook them?" Star asks Zion.

"Nope, I came to get my kiss that Lea owes me." He looks at her mischievously, remembering what she said to him the first night she arrived.

"Cam and Denise, let's go so we can give your uncle some privacy." Star snatches Lea's camera on her way out and sits on the balcony taking pictures of her and Zion.

"So, Bear. You hadn't forgot?" she asks him, walking into his embrace.

"Kitten, I never forget."

Lea lifts her head to give him multiple kisses for allowing her to take pictures of the fireworks from his balcony.

Grabbing the girls and holding them in his lap, Garrett asks his wife, "Do you really think Lea is the one?" They had started discussing the status of Zion's relationship during the drive to his place. Patty told them to find out as much as they could about Lea and whether she was a good fit for him, even giving them questions to ask Lea. They ignored her suggestions.

"Yes. Yes, I do. Have you seen all the personal touches of her around here. Not to mention how he re-arranges stuff to include her. And the PDA." Star snaps away getting pictures of them hugging and kissing. "When have you ever seen him even hold a woman's hand other than in a gentleman's way?"

"Never, now that you mention it. So, what are you going to tell Patty?"

"That Lea and I talked about shopping and shoes and purses, played games with the girls and watched you and Zion play boring checkers."

"Good luck darling, cause you gonna be in trouble for not doing as you were told."

"We both know that if I did everything my mother wanted me to do, you and I wouldn't be together with twin daughters." Star snaps pictures of them kissing and hugging Garrett.

"So so true." He responds hugging his girls.

-24-

Zion leaves town on business, traveling up until the day before the birthday party. Lea keeps busy with work and catching up with friends. She and Zion talk every day and night, even texting although that's something he hates to do. He says texting can never say what he's thinking and feeling, and he loves the sound of her voice.

He finally made the decision they won't be arriving together to the party. Lea will drive herself and will meet him there, which he's totally against. Not only will she be arriving without him, but she'll also be alone with no one to talk to. She's representing G-TEE alone as Crystal and Tom won't be able to attend.

I know I'll be hiding out as much as possible or sitting and staring into space, attempting to make small talk with the other guests. Wish I could have at least brought Gordon and Lily with me. Fuck, I hate this.

Saturday arrives and Lea is getting dressed at her mom's house. Her mom wants to see what she'll be wearing. Tonight's selection is the third dress Zion purchased for her when they were in Chicago. A wine-red, long-sleeve dress made of soft flowing chiffon. Slits are in the arm, from shoulder to wrist, with a V-neckline. The dress hits at mid-thigh. She elects to wear the wine-red heels they found when shopping together, along with the dangling gold necklace and instead of the gold hoop earrings, Lea is wearing a pair of spiral gold earrings. Tonight, she blow-dries and flat irons her hair, wearing it straight. It hangs down just past her shoulders with bangs brushing her eyebrows. She spritzes on Flirt, another pheromone-infused scent. Mom approves of the results. Well, kinda. She keeps reminding Lea not to bend over certain ways as the dress could rise up and show more thigh than expected.

Yes, mom. That's my plan. Gotta make sure Zion sees and likes my smooth legs.

Lea is supposed to arrive at seven, but her nerves are shot, so she arrives thirty minutes late, wondering how far she'll have to park.

Maybe they have a valet service. Who the hell am I kidding? Of course, they have a valet service.

As she pulls up in front of the Trinity Jazz and Dining Venue, Ryan steps to her door and opens it. "Hello Ryan," she addresses him. They haven't seen one another since Chicago.

"Good evening, Miss Adams. Mr. Landon has requested that I personally park your car for you. He's been awaiting your arrival."

"Oh, fricking joy." She hands him her car key off her key ring. "You didn't hear me say that, and I'll deny it if you report back to him."

"Ma'am, I heard nothing, but thank you and have a good night."

"Thanks, Ryan." Lea points toward the entrance. "I guess I'm supposed go that way, right?"

"Yes, Mr. Landon is aware you've arrived."

"Snitch."

Ryan laughs, getting in Lea's car and driving off.

She walks toward the entrance concentrating on not falling, tripping, or bumping into anyone.

So many people, so much money, so much eliteness in this place.

When you walk into The Trinity, you walk onto a balcony overlooking the lower level.

Why do so many places design themselves with balconies and lower levels?

With this one, no seating is on the top level, just spiral staircases, four of them leading to the lower level. A throng of women are standing near the main two staircases posing for effect, making sure all eyes are on them, so when they walk down, they have all the attention.

When Lea steps onto the balcony to go right, a gentleman halts her.

"Damn baby, you looking sexy as hell. You 'bout the realest thing up in here. Can I get you a drink and maybe we talk about you ending up in my bed tonight?" he asks, leaning into Lea's personal space.

WHOA NELLIE, BOY BACK UP WITH YO STANK-SMELLING BREATH.

Sex Diva we gotta chill. And, yes, ole boys breath do stank.

"You know, I'm gonna pass. But you keep trying with the other beautiful women. I'm sure there are more here for you to choose from," Lea says stepping back, attempting to move on and away from his breath.

"Another uppity low-class female trying to land a rich man. I hear the richest man in the room is already taken, so you really should give in to me." He's now fully blocking her path.

HOLD UP WAIT A MINUTE. DID YOU HEAR WHAT SMELLY BREATH JUST SAID? PEOPLE KNOW ZION IS TAKEN.

"You're right, the richest man in this room is taken. By me. How do you think he'll react when I explain to him about this further delay?" Lea stares him down.

"Yeah, right. Like Zion Landon is bedding you. I doubt that. You don't seem to be his type."

That comment strikes at Lea's insecurities. Hearing that people are aware Zion is taken bolsters her confidence.

FUCK HIM. GET TO OUR MAN. CHECK STANK BREATH FIRST.

She listens to the Sex Diva, plays it off by smiling and shaking her head. "Tell you what, move away and watch me walk to my man. If he rejects me, I'll suck the soul outta you tonight. When he doesn't, you be sure to not trip over your feet running outta here. Okay?"

Lea walks over to the farthest staircase and descends knowing 'ole boy is staring her down. She gets to the fifth step before the bottom, and Zion is standing there with his hands on the railings waiting.

God, this man is gorgeous.

He has on a black suit, a black shirt, and black shoes, and a wine-red handkerchief is in the pocket of his suit jacket peeking out.

"You, my beauty, are late. I think I'll need to spank you later to get you to understand seven p.m. instead of seven-thirty p.m." He looks her up and down from her shoes to the top of her head staring at her hair.

Lea places a leg on the step in front of Zion, and he reaches out to caress her ankle up to her calf squeezing it. Lea feels the goosebumps rise to her inner thighs. "What was Howard saying to you?" Zion looks up the staircase at the man who was talking to her. They make eye contact, and Howard walks away in the opposite direction.

"He wanted to talk about me ending up in his bed tonight. Especially because the richest man in the room was taken. He figured he would be the next best thing, considering I'm low-class."

"Low-class. What the fuck?" Zion moves to go after him, but Howard has exited the venue.

Lea puts her hand on his chest stopping him. "Don't worry. You'll be the only one having the soul sucked outta him tonight."

"Soul sucked outta him. What?" he asks, smiling unsure he should have even asked.

"I told him if you rejected me, I would suck the soul outta him," she says smiling.

"Lea, I'm speechless. I'll talk to Howard later. After I get my soul back."

"Hello, Bear. Happy Birthday."

"Hello, Kitten. Thank you." He holds out his hand for her. She accepts it and descends the remaining stairs.

-25-

Zion almost thought Lea was not going to show. He got here right at six forty-five as per Star's instructions as they are the guests of honor. Along with their parents, they have been greeting and talking with their guests. At seven o'clock, he kept his eye on the door looking for Lea with her spiral curls and red dress. Every few minutes, he would scan the room searching for her knowing she would be in a sea of strangers, probably in a panic, so he wanted to latch onto her quickly. He finally sent Ryan outside to watch for her car and to make sure he drove it to his apartment garage. At seven twenty-five, the text from Ryan informed him she had arrived and was entering the building. He grinned like the love-struck man he is.

When he looked up at the balcony entrance and saw that dress, he could finally relax. Then he looked up at her face and saw a halo of straight golden-brown hair. He could have fainted.

My Lea is sexy as fucking hell.

Her bare legs glistened. She commanded everyone to look at her without trying. She didn't walk toward the main spiral staircases everyone else was using. She walked to the right taking stairs that were in the dark. To see an old high school pal talking to her made him angry.

Not my Lea.

Zion doesn't remember whom he was talking to, but he excused himself and made a beeline straight for Lea. Her ascending the stairs made his groin ache. His fingers gripped the railing, wanting to run them through her hair, caress her legs, wrapping them around his waist. Her lips glisten for a kiss he knows if he gives her, it will not stop at a kiss. And leaving early is not an option. The V of the dress lightly caresses her cleavage with every move and breath she takes.

Damn, I chose well with that dress.

He takes deep breaths and adjusts his cock in his pants, telling himself to get a grip.

Party first. Play later.

As Lea steps off the last step, he puts her arm in the crook of his and clasps their fingers together.

Fuck this Addison hiding shit. I'm done hiding Lea and our relationship.

He walks her straight over to his parents to introduce them to the woman he's in love with. Being one of the guests of honor, Zion of course has a lot of attention on him tonight. Walking the room with a woman attached to his arm generates even more. People are in small groups murmuring about who this woman could be. Lea can feel the curious glances and squeezes Zion's hand tighter.

Sending up a silent prayer, *please don't let me trip and fall, embarrassing myself tonight*, she takes a deep breath and readies herself for introductions.

Interrupting whom his parents are talking to as politely as he could, Zion directs their attention to Lea. "Excuse me, Mom, this is Lea Adams. The woman I told you about. Lea, this is my mother, Patty Landon, and you've met my father, Royal Landon."

Lea attempts to dislodge her hand from his so she can greet them, but Zion won't let it go. His parents catch this.

"Lea, how are you? Son, let go I want to give this young lady a hug," his mother says.

He releases Lea but re-takes her hand almost instantly after the hugs from his parents.

"It's nice to meet you, Mrs. Landon. And it's nice to see you again, Mr. Landon."

"It's nice to see you again also, Lea. You don't mind me calling you Lea, do you? With the way my son has staked his claim in and outside the office, Miss Adams seems rather formal."

"No sir. Not at all." Lea looks at Zion with an I-told-you-so look.

"And I still don't care," he responds back.

Star comes over and greets her with an enthusiastic hug. "Lea, hi, you look great," she whispers in her ear. "Love the entrance, he could not take his eyes off you."

She pulls away and smiles. "Happy belated birthday, Star." Lea takes an envelope out of her clutch and hands it to her. It contains a gift card to one of the stores Zion mentioned his sister liking when he and Lea where shopping for accessories for the dress she's wearing. Star takes it giving Lea another enthusiastic hug.

Lea looks up at Zion, "I'm sorry I was so late. Nerves. You know me."

Zion bends down, kissing her on the cheek. He couldn't hold off any longer for a taste of his Lea.

"It's okay. You're here now. Let's get you a drink."

"Excuse us, Mom and Dad."

Before Lea can say anything, he ushers them off to the bar.

His family stares at them walking away.

"She's nothing like the other women he was screwing around with," Patty says.

Star asks her wondering how she would know. "Mom what do you know about the women Zion was screwing? He never brought them around you."

"No, but I had plenty of catty women friends who wanted me to 'introduce' their daughters to my son thinking they were the one to settle him down. Each bit of information came with a picture or description. Your mother isn't clueless."

"Never thought you were. I'm just surprised you never mentioned this. That's not like you."

"What the hell is that supposed to mean?"

"Mom? Seriously? Patty the well-meaning meddler held back? Again, that's not like you."

"You know smart-ass, I can still throw a shoe and hit a target. Even in a room full of people."

Royal steps in before the ladies get out of hand even though he knows they're joking. "Star, go mingle. Patty, let's dance."

Garrett walks Star toward the outdoor balcony of the venue. She gives her mom a mischievous grin saying, "Yes, Daddy."

"Glenlivet Code on the rocks and a glass of Château Suduiraut," Zion orders from the bartender.

"Zion, you tracked down my favorite wine? I only mentioned it once."

"I brought it back with me on this last trip. Two cases. And a case of Quinta do Noval. You liked that one when you had it in Chicago. I'll admit, I'm not a sweet wine drinker, but I could get used to the Suduiraut."

Lea leans in close to Zion, with him putting his hand on her waist. Uncaring of the stares, they put their love on display for all to see.

"Thanks, Bear. Now I really feel bad about not having a birthday gift for you. It's a good thing I'm driving."

"No, you're not. Your car is already at my place."

Just then, Ryan walks up to them handing her car key to her.

"Thanks, Ryan," Zion says to him and turns, staring at her.

"You just took away my excuse for not drinking. My plans have been foiled."

"Lea, is that why you insisted on driving tonight?"

"Well, it was one. The other being I didn't know how this would play out tonight."

"What do you mean?"

"It's your party. You are the guest of honor. If you started ignoring me, hiding me, I wanted to have control over whether I stayed or left. Especially if something with Addison was to pop off."

"This is what I mean when I say I am done with this hiding bullshit. It was a bad idea. Lea, I would never let any harm come to you. Understand?"

"Yes."

"And no more driving yourself. Well outside of work. Anything we do together from this moment forward, I drive, Sam drives us or I'm in your car with you. Is that clear? My Kitten."

"Very clear. Z." Lea doesn't break his gaze.

He smiles. "Now we enjoy ourselves. The Suduiraut is your drink for the evening. We'll make sure you pace yourself."

"Yes. Sir," she accepts the drink taking two sips. "Zion, you're ignoring your guests."

He moves in closer, barely leaving any room between them. "Sweetheart, I don't give a fuck about these people. I want to get you home and open my birthday gift." He's about to bend down and kiss her, but two women interrupt him and wish him a happy birthday.

This continues throughout the night. Even during dinner. People come over for birthday greetings, sliding him envelopes, hoping to get an introduction to the young lady sitting next to him.

All don't get an introduction though. Mostly women do not. Especially one woman in particular.

Lea finally asked Zion about her as she kept interrupting them numerous times for the most asinine reasons to talk to him. Having Zion recommend a drink, reminisce about when they were young, ask if he remembers so and so from high school. She looks down at Lea with a look of, 'you're nothing to him and she is'.

"Zion, who is the lady that keeps interrupting us and have you sexed her?" she asks him bluntly.

"One of my sister's high school friends, Shauna. Yes, I sexed her. I know she's making a spectacle of herself; I haven't seen her in years. Straight to the point, no chaser. I adore that about you," he laughs caressing her leg under the table. Lea closes his hand in between them as he edges closer to the hem of the dress, not taking her eyes away from him.

"Just wonderful. Well, I must go to the bathroom. I know she's going to corner me, I want you to be prepared. Brace yourself for what you may hear after I get back."

Zion stands, holding his hand out for hers and assisting her with her chair. As she stands, he brings her hand up to his lips, kissing it. "I look forward to it." Lea squeezes his fingers then releases his hand and walks toward the ladies' room. He watches her, beaming.

I haven't been able to let her leave my side all night. Every interruption has got on my nerves. We need to get out of here.

Zion walks over to his parents and sister approaching them from behind. His mom turns and gives him a hug. She takes the envelopes out of his hand, playfully hitting him with them.

"My baby's in love. I cannot contain myself." She has been watching the interactions between Zion and Lea all night. He has kept Lea to his side. They have danced and displayed so much

PDA that Patty is questioning is this her son? *Not my lil bear. He hates PDA outside of family.*

Zion hugs her back. "Mom, people are watching us. You must contain yourself," he says, laughing.

My son is laughing. I can't believe this. It's not one of his fake low laughs. "No. Now where is that beautiful young lady of yours?" she whispers.

"She went to the bathroom and when she comes back, we're leaving. And remember, you promised me you would take it easy and not say anything to her."

His mom and sister speaking at the same time, "Bathroom, alone. With these female vultures?" And they take off toward the ladies' room.

212

-26-

Lea comes out of the bathroom stall and is confronted by Ms. Wanna-Be-In-Front-Of-Zion's-Face.

Okay, let's get this over with.

Lea looks her up and down and says, "What?"

"Where in the hell did he find you?"

Lea attempts to respond but is cut off.

"Oh, never mind. Let's get something straight. You don't belong with him, and it's not going to last. You don't have what it takes to make him happy. The sooner you get out of his life, I can step in and claim my rightful place next to him. He's getting old and needs me to get him in line, settle down and start a family." Shauna is waving her hand and rolling her neck so hard, Lea is trying not to laugh. Instead of interrupting her, she lets Shauna finish her little speech.

"This world Zion lives in; you don't fit in it. Look at you. Where in the hell did you get such a cheap-ass dress? I mean seriously, couldn't you have done better than that?"

Lea glimpses herself in the mirror. *Bitch I look hot.*

Shauna continues, "It's his birthday for heaven's sake; these are his friends and clients. He needs a woman on his arm who will understand how to impress these people. You have completely embarrassed him tonight. Get out of his life and stay out. Do you understand me?" She runs out of steam, thinking she has scared Lea into leaving Zion. Or embarrassed her.

Lea walks over to the sink to wash her hands and put on lipstick. She wants to punch this faked up no-class bitch in her fucking face and pull out her spleen, feeding it to her up her ass.

PUSHING HER HEAD THROUGH THAT WALL OF MIRRORS WOULD BE SO WONDERFUL. JUST SO

FRICKIN' WONDERFUL. The Sex Diva, is bouncing around fist punching the air ready to fight.

Calm down Diva. One thing we not gonna do is embarrass ourselves.

"Hey I'm talking to you. Do you understand? You need to get the hell out of Zion's life. Tonight. Make this the last time he ever sees you." Seeing Zion tonight, Shauna wants him. She busted her ass ensuring she got invited to this party. Reading about his new office, moving his company back to St. Louis, and hearing from his mother how she was wanting him to settle down. This was her opportunity to get in front of him. Then to see this woman glued to his arm all night. Following her to the bathroom to scare her away was her chance and she wasn't passing this up.

It must be the liquor, the heat, the moon and the planets aligning, because before Lea knew what was happening, she walks straight up to Shauna, and gets in her face. The woman flinches like Lea was about to hit her.

GET IN A GOOD PUNCH FOR ME, TOO.

"Bitch, please. If he wanted you, he would be here with you. So you fucked each other years ago. Obviously, you didn't have what it took to keep his interest, and you sure as hell not about to get another chance." Lea is on a roll and is almost running over her words, attempting to get out what she wants to say. She's so close to Shauna, Lea can smell the vodka on her breath.

Homegirl needs a breath mint or some gum.

"As you stated, Zion needs a woman on his arm who can impress. Not the embarrassment you bring. Stay away from MY man. I have no problem kicking your ass. Seriously, you telling me I look cheap? The glue and lace are showing on your lace front."

Shauna reaches up touching her forehead, feeling the sticky glue on her fingertips.

"See, look in the mirror. Sweat is not your friend. Up your game and stop paying for the cheap weave. Your hair should move with your head, not against it. Oh, by the way, MY man purchased this dress for me. It matches the handkerchief in the pocket of his jacket. I'll be sure to let him know you think he has cheap tastes." Lea turns and walks out.

Sometimes, you have to stake your claim. Zion is mine. All mine.

Shauna stands there speechless. She turns toward the mirror grabbing a paper towel wiping her forehead. In the process, she removes foundation along with specks of glue. As Lea leaves, Shauna turns to make a move to attack from behind but is stopped by Zion's sister and mother coming in the bathroom.

Lea bumped into Star and Mrs. Landon on the way out. "Hi ladies," she said and kept moving straight to the bar.

When Lea gets there, she orders two Hot Damn shots. Telling Shauna off was good, but having her and Howard point out areas Lea feels she's lacking, thoughts she has considered many times before, makes her wonder why Zion is with her.

She glimpses him out the corner of her eye making his way toward the bar. Before he reaches her, she downs the shots. Upon reaching the bar, Zion picks up the glass sniffing.

"Glass of water for the lady, please."

"No, not a glass of water. Another shot please."

The bartender slides a third shot to Lea and a tall glass of water to Zion. Lea grabs the shot and downs it. After the third one she feels dizzy and silently belches.

Oh shit.

Zion, grabs the glass of water and walks her outside for some air. "Lea, what happened?"

"I'll tell you what happened," Star says approaching them. "That bitch Shauna confronted Lea telling her to get out of your life. Twenty years later and one week of you dating, and she has the gall to tell Lea she isn't good enough for you," Star tells him. "Don't worry I set her ass straight. I've been wanting to tell her off for years. Lea, don't let what she said rattle you. Zion, would never be with her. Why don't you two get out of here, I got this."

Lea giggles. "Her weave moves left when she turns her head right. Why do women wear such cheap hair? And what is with the caterpillars for eyelashes? I mean seriously. Zion is that a turn-on for you?" By now, Lea is feeling her body break out in a cold sweat from the top of her head moving down her body. Beads of moisture appear on her upper lip. She fans the 'V' of her dress against her chest, generating a breeze.

YOU KNOW WE CAN TAKE HER. SNATCH HER ASS INTO NEXT WEEK. I'M READY.

Zion looks inside the room and sees Shauna staring at them. He puts his hand on Lea's back and kisses her temple. Shauna sees the wine-red handkerchief in his pocket, confirming what Lea said. She turns away in a huff and stalks out.

"Sweetheart, she was years ago. You're now, today, and my future. Let's go home. And no, nothing about her is a turn-on for me."

Lea looks up at him and sees the desire in his eyes. Taking the water out of his hand, she drinks it. She fans herself, feeling the shots warm her. "Sure. Let's go home. Maybe, let's go find Shauna, so I can push her into traffic or hook her up with Howard. She's pretty uppity low-class for his tastes." Lea turns, looking for blood.

Zion takes two steps and snatches her at her waist pulling her against him. "Lea, baby. Calm down."

She turns around looking at him, wanting to kiss him. "Why calm down?"

He watches her intently then whispers, "Ocean". She deflates instantly.

Lea blows air up to move the bangs from her forehead and runs her hands up and down her arms in the open slits of the dress. "Ugggghh." She feels chastised like when her mom calls her to attention for doing something she has no business doing.

Great, Lea. It's the man's birthday, and you let a jealous woman throw you off your game back into that world of uncertainty you thought you were done with.

They cross the room to the steps, him saying goodbye to everyone, especially his mom and dad. Lea says goodnight, thanking them for inviting her. Howard, Shauna, and now Zion made her feel less than. She's hating this night more and more. She's ready to cry tears of frustration.

Lea massages her neck causing the dress to rise up. This movement catches a few admiring looks from gentlemen in the room.

Zion takes her hand, lowering it blocking others view. Drawing Lea into his embrace, he whispers in her ear, "Kitten. I love the view. But you gonna make me get into some fights, showing off to other men what I get to enjoy."

Lea giggles again.

"Zion, you would fight for me?"

Looking down at her with all seriousness, "Lea, some days I think I could kill for you."

She brushes her lips against his exposed skin between the opening of his shirt.

Zion moans softly. He directs her toward the steps with him close on her heels.

Shit, it's hot. I wish he would back up off me.

Upon arriving at the top, he places his hand right at the nape of Lea's neck on her collar bone. Caressing it. The feeling tickles and courses down her back to her tits and clit.

Shit, the 'spot'.

She concentrates on staying focused and walking, looking around for Shauna. They get outside away from everyone, and she rolls her head to the left and right in an attempt to move out of his grasp. Zion doesn't let go.

"Lea, stop trying to get away from me. You aren't going anywhere."

"Zion. Let go."

"No. You need to calm down before I put you over my shoulder and carry you to the car."

Lea turns, looking up at him, wondering how far she can take her attitude.

"You know I will. Do you want that?"

"No. Sir." She looks away into the dark parking lot.

"Sir, my ass." He growls, running a finger across her cleavage, lifting her face to look at him.

They get into another staring contest with Lea losing. A tear slips out of her eye.

"Where's the car?"

"Baby, why are you crying? What's wrong? Not this Shauna shit."

"Howard, Shauna. Zion why are you with me? All these women, beautiful women—."

"Have nothing on you. Understand me. They have nothing compared to you. Nothing."

"Can I go find Shauna and at least bump into her making her trip and fall? Please?"

He kisses her quickly, then turns her toward the Porsche, walking behind her.

"No, my feisty little drunk."

-27-

When Zion saw Lea make a beeline to the bar, and take not one shot, but two, he knew something was wrong. Hearing about what Shauna did made him want to rip her to shreds. Whiskey, rum, vodka, and orange juice, all in one drink. Lea hates vodka. She's pissed. He can see the flush in her neck, and the rise and fall of her chest arouses him. He gets her to the car and presses her up against the passenger door. "Lea, look at me." She looks up at him staring at his lips. He smiles, knowing she loves seeing it.

How a smile from him makes this woman melts has him walking around all day with a grin on his face.

"Tipsy baby?" he asks her, pressing his lips to the skin below her right earlobe.

"Yes," she nods her head, whispering, leaning her head on his chest, giving him access to her neck.

He presses his dick into her pelvis. "Horny baby?"

"Yes." Lea slides her leg between his, raising it to caress him.

He kisses her deeply. She grasps the back of his head refusing to break the embrace, gripping him under his jacket, rubbing her pelvis against his.

He breaks the kiss.

"Zion, don't you want me?"

"Lea, I want you every chance I get. Kitten, we're in a parking lot where anyone can see us. As much as I wanna be buried inside of you, right now is not the time." He gently bucks into her, then opens the car door and places her inside.

I shoulda made Sam drive us. Fuck, now I gotta concentrate on getting us home with this fricking third leg. Lord Jesus help me.

He gets in, turning to look at her. She's staring out the window. "Kitten, would you like to talk about it?"

"Nope, not really. It's done, it's over with. She had her say and I had mine. All I wanna do right now is go home," Lea says and realizes Zion purchased the Porsche in black.

He watches her, wanting to reassure her in some way. "Lea, look at me," he coaxes.

She turns to look at him and smiles. "Really, it's all good. I expect this will happen some more. I'm not getting into any more catty arguments with your former sex tramps," she assures him. "Let's go for a ride. I have something to show you."

He pulls her face toward him kissing her. "What Kitten?"

Lea leans back in the car seat and takes off her underwear. Before she can slide them in her purse, he snatches them and puts them in place of his handkerchief. The black and gold lace stands out.

Lea laughs at the sight, still feeling the liquor in her system. Sex Diva and the liquid courage have taken over.

IT'S TIME TO GIVE OUR MAN A SHOW.

Zion touches the panel between them and her car seat leans back. Lea raises her dress and takes his wine-red handkerchief from his lap, laying it closer to her. She is shaved smooth. She slides her fingers between the lips of her pussy. He enjoys hearing the sound of the wetness.

"Baby, give me a performance."

Lea plays with her pussy, caressing it.

"You wanna taste?" She holds out her fingers to him. He smells, then licks.

"I taste a hint of pineapples. Nice."

Again, Lea giggles. All thoughts of Shauna, Howard, and Zion's birthday party have evaporated. This her man.

LET'S DO THIS.

Lea hikes the dress up above her ass, placing the handkerchief below her to catch some of the juices. Taking off her shoes, she places her feet on the dashboard.

"Oops. Sorry. I guess feet shouldn't go up here, huh?" While she's saying this, she opens her legs wider and uses her right hand to take her left breast from her bra. Pinching her nipple, she moans licking her lips.

"Open them legs as wide as you want. Damn woman." He leans over and sucks on the exposed nipple, opening his mouth wide and swallowing as much of her tit as he can.

"Oh. Zion."

Zion pulls away sitting back in the driver's seat. "Lea, look at me." He caresses his dick through his slacks. "Do it, but don't make yourself cum. Keep bringing yourself closer but stop."

He starts the car, driving to his apartment and keeping a close eye on Lea.

Lea and Zion only had eyes for each other when leaving the birthday party. Neither noticed the man and woman watching them sitting in their separate cars.

"She's involved with him? When the fuck did this happen?" The man vents, pounding on the steering wheel of his car. "No, this can't be. They can't be dating. I can't fucking believe this.

I've done everything to keep men away from her, and she hooks up with him. I fucking thought that was a business lunch. Not a god-damned date. How the hell did I misjudge that. No, this has to stop. This has to end. They won't end up together. That is not the plan. Mine dammit, all mine. Bitch is fucking shit up. Not this time. This time things will end my way. Fucking tired of waiting."

The woman, in her car, stares at Zion. Never has she wanted him as much as she wants him now. He will be theirs. Forever. Nothing and no one will take that away from them. Not even the bitch he's making out with.

She gets home and looks at herself in the mirror, lovingly stroking herself.

He'll want this. No worries. I'll be giving him what he desires most in this world. Me. Not her. And I'll get what I want. To be Mrs. Zion Landon.

"That's okay Zion. Another temporary fuck. You can have this for your birthday. We'll be together. Just like we should be. All of us. No more screwing around. Get that woman out of your system."

Love's Awakening

225

-28-

By the time they get home, Lea has brought herself to the brink of climaxing at least three times. Her gyrating and moans have Zion sweating bullets, but he has something better planned for them tonight.

Lea notices her car is sitting in the garage across from his other vehicles. He parks the Porsche next to hers.

Opening her door, he tells her, "I have a surprise for you." He takes the hand she had been playing with herself, licks her fingers and palm, saying, "Hhhmmmm. I like."

Lea walks into his arms for a hug. During the ride up in the elevator, she tries not to think about the other parts of tonight.

This is her man. He's taken her home with him. He's making love to her tonight, not some past sex tramp.

She presses her body against his, unbuttoning his shirt to kiss his chest and breathe in his scent. He grabs her ass and presses her into him, nibbling her neck. She looks up at him and he kisses her. He pulls away grinning, shaking his head, just when it's getting good.

"Zion!!!"

They arrive upstairs and exit the elevator. Lea notices a change in his foyer. Where glass vases, art pieces and statues stood, pictures of his family have replaced them. Many from the July fourth weekend and a few of when he and Star were kids. His parents. He even has pictures of Lea and him. She had left her camera equipment here and he downloaded the images.

There is the one she took of him caressing her legs, one of them standing on his balcony, and another of them playing with his nieces. His sister was snapping away. And he's displaying them. He's displaying pictures of his girlfriend. He even has the one of him she has saved as her phone screensaver blown up and displayed as a piece of art on pressed glass. She stands there gawking.

"I can't stop looking at them either. It never occurred to me to display pictures of family, old or current. My apartment was a show place, a work of art. Since meeting you, dating you, it's turned into more of a home. But this isn't the surprise. Come with me."

He takes her hand, and they continue into the apartment, upstairs into his bedroom.

NOW WE TALKIN', the Sex Diva chirps in.

A pair of silk PJs lay on his bed next to a wrapped box.

"Zion, what's in the box? It's your birthday. Shouldn't I be giving you gifts?"

"My Kitten. You're my gift.

Zion has stepped into his dom persona by addressing Lea as My Kitten.

Lea asks, "May I open the box? Z."

"Yes. You may open the box while I change."

While Lea is opening the box, Zion strips and puts on his dom PJ bottoms.

In the box is a Baby doll green teddy. It has spaghetti straps of red and gold. The bra cups of the teddy have thin bands of lace material that stretches across the breasts, held together with a golden circle. The gold circle lays directly over the nipple, ensuring they stick out. The underwire bra of the teddy pulls the breasts up and together. The bodice of the teddy flows down and away from the torso.

DAMN GIRL. HURRY UP AND PUT THAT ON. SHIT YES, I LIKEY THIS.

"What do you think of it?" he asks her, "I hope you like it."

Holding it up higher and looking at him through the lace of the teddy Lea breathes out, "I fucking love it." She lays it back on the bed and starts taking off her clothes.

Zion says, "Attention."

Lea stops what she is doing and stands in the sub attention pose.

"Good girl."

Zion slowly undresses her. This has become a part of their before care. When he and Lea first practiced the attention pose and undressing, it took them an hour to get through it. Each time one of them would break persona and they would have to start over. It didn't help there was a lot of laughter and shots involved.

After she is fully dressed, Lea asks, "Where are the panties?"

"Panties. We don't need no stinkin' panties." Zion takes the panties out of the pajama pants pocket. They are ripped down both sides and stretched out of shape.

"Now was that the same as ripping them off me?"

"Nope, but thinking about you and having them wrapped around my cock while I was out of town helped me to jack off. Sorry. I couldn't help myself. When I kept picturing you in them, I had to."

"We'll discuss this masturbating without me at a later time. It's your birthday. Proceed."

"I like your hair tonight. Very sexy, but I like the spiral curls better. Something to play with. This hairstyle would be good for pulling when I'm fucking you from behind." He's standing without touching her. A repeat of their first night together. Testing her patience.

The seduction game has begun.

"My Kitten. Have you been enjoying our foray into dom/sub?"

"Very much. Z. Have you?"

"Hell yea. Are you ready to include more?"

She stares at him astonished. Lea hasn't wanted to push him into more than they could handle.

"Don't look surprised. I want to try restraints. Specifically, restraining you."

"Restraints? So, you've been fantasizing about me tied up and at your mercy. I'm all yours."

"Come with me," Zion leads her to one of his other bedrooms.

Zion holds out his hand, and she places hers in it. They walk into the smallest of his three bedrooms. It's decorated in earth tones, browns and greens, and has a small bathroom. Next to the queen-size bed, is a dresser and a small writing desk.

The comforter has been removed from the bed and ankle and wrist restraints lay on top. A bed bondage restraint system. Laying on the nightstand is a leather riding crop, a larger tickler and whip teaser, and a leather pleasure whip and blindfold. Candles are lit all over the room and glow in alternating different colors. They are non-burning candles operated by a remote control running on batteries. Lea looks at him but says nothing.

The Sex Diva is jumping up and down screaming, YES, YES, OH FUCKING YES.

"My Kitten. Do you consent to me restraining you?"

"Yes. Z."

"What are our safe words?" he asks her.

"Ocean for stop and halo to ease up," she whispers.

He walks her over to the end of the bed. "What are we going to do about your hair, I wonder? I hadn't planned on you wearing it like this."

"I need my purse; I have a hair band in it I can put on."

"Good, don't move."

Lea stands, looking around and not moving from the spot he placed her in.

Zion grabs her purse from his bedroom and looks for the hair band. He checks her phone to be sure her mother hasn't messaged.

Perfect. Nothing pressing. This night is ours.

He goes back to the bedroom, handing her the hair band. She puts her hair in a ponytail.

Watching her arch her neck, the lifting of her breasts with the movement of her raising her arms high, has Zion running his hand across his face, grinning sexily.

"Is this okay?" she asks.

"Yes, perfect."

He walks over to the nightstand and grabs the tickler, whip teaser, and blindfold. Lea is bathed in the soft glow of the candles. He comes back and stand in front of her and caresses his cock. Lea stares at the movement, her nipples hardening. He puts the blindfold on her.

"Are you okay? My Kitten. Does this freak you out?"

"No. Just weird."

Zion bends down kissing her neck, trailing kisses down to her cleavage and latching onto a nipple.

Lea moans from the licking, nibbling and biting. He alternates between each breast. She lifts her arm to touch his head but he pulls back, stepping away from the movement of her pressing his face into her cleavage.

OH SHIT I FORGOT.

Chill Diva.

OK. OK. SORRY.

"Turn around. My Kitten."

Lea turns around facing the foot of the bed.

"Walk up to the bed and press your legs against it."

She does as instructed, stopping until she can't move any farther and almost flopping over onto the bed. Zion catches her by the waist positioning her in place. Gliding his hand between her legs, he says, "Baby, spread these sexy legs for me."

Lea does as she's told, opening her legs, her pussy reacting to the flutter feel of his fingers on her inner thighs. He bends down and puts her ankles in straps. Straps that she hadn't noticed before.

He stands up behind her and runs the whip teaser up and down her arms and legs. Goosebumps are rising on her skin and she shudders from the feel of it. She allows herself to focus on the sensations instead of wanting to know what's going to happen.

Zion is smiling, unable to control his excitement. He's been planning this night for weeks, researching different BDSM items from his growing list and watching videos. He couldn't wait for the party to be over and get Lea back to his place. His dick is rock hard with anticipation. He stands next to her and glides the feather end over her nipples, staring at them. His tongue is tingling to have them in his mouth again. He returns to standing behind her at arms length and runs the feather over the mounds of her ass watching her clench them from the sensation.

"My Kitten. You okay?" Even though this is his birthday, his present from her is to please her tonight, giving her as much pleasure and enjoyment as he can, showing her he can give her as much of the sexual pleasure she has desired without anything from his past hindering them.

"Uhm hmmmmm," she mumbles.

He moves in close behind her, lifting her ponytail and kisses the spot on the back of her neck that drives her wild. She leans back toward him, pushing out her breasts to the heavens, shivering, rolling her shoulders, and moaning.

Lea is ready to be fucked, and she's using every ounce she has to allow Zion to lead her where he wants. She wants him and needs his touch so much right now she can scream. He bends her over, having her lay on her stomach reaching for the second set of restraints for her wrists, stretching her arms out on each side. Now she understands why they're in this bedroom. Her arms would not have been able to stretch across his California King like this. He puts her wrists in the straps.

"Lift your arms for me, I don't want these to be too tight."

He wants her to be able to move, but not too far.

"I'm fine." She lifts her arms and flexes her wrists moving them around doing a modified Superman move. She's positioned where she can either lay flat against the bed or prop herself up on her arms. She's getting wet thinking about what could possibly happen.

He walks behind her and bends down spreading her ass cheeks. He stares at her splayed out like she is, with her ass up and legs open profiling her pussy.

Shit, yes, she looks good like this, he thinks while stroking his face, licking his lips and smiling.

Zion moves standing to the side of Lea while rubbing her ass. *Nice beautiful sexy ass.*

He presses one leg against the bed, and the other outside of Lea's left leg. This position has his dick pressed against her thigh. Flattening his palm onto her right ass cheek, he squeezes it. Lea moves her lower body to get a better feel of his penis pressed against her.

Zion halts her movements, lifts his hand, and slaps her ass. She jumps. He presses his dick to her thigh and slaps her ass again. She moans. He slaps it again and rubs his hand print. She grunts and moves toward the bed this time, pressing herself against it. He pulls her back. He slaps her again. She whimpers and sucks in her breath. He slaps it one last time.

Oh yes, baby. Happy birthday to me.

He jiggles and squeezes her behind making the mounds shake like a bowl of Jello.

Lea's ready to explode with her orgasm. She hates being unable to see what he's doing next, so she controls her breathing and listens. He moves to the right of her and it sounds as if he's removing his bottoms. He's touching himself by the sound of the moan he's making.

Fuck, I want to see. The bed just dipped. He has climbed up on it. What now?

"Stop moving around so much. I'm sitting right in front of you. My cock is right at your mouth," he lifts her head up and places her face close to his dick.

I can smell him. I lick my lips wanting to taste him.

"May I taste you? Z."

"I thought you'd never ask. Open your mouth and stick your tongue out."

Just as she sticks her tongue out, he puts his dick in the path of it so she can barely touch the tip, then he pulls back. She opens her mouth again and licks her tongue out and he puts his dick in the path of it. She licks it, sucking it into her mouth.

Even restrained she can suck my dick so, damned, good.

"Oh fuck. Suck it. Yes."

Zion leans over her, placing his dick closer to her mouth so she can continue to suck in more of him as he puts his finger in her pussy, fingering her. She moans and presses her pelvis against the bed attempting to orgasm. Right as she gets into her rhythm to bring him off, he pulls out and sits back getting himself under control, breathing heavily. She whimpers from losing the taste and feel of him. He hops off the bed and turns her face toward him and kisses her.

"You ready to cum for me?" he asks her.

"Yes. Z."

He moves back around to her ass rubbing on it again spreading her legs open, bending down opening her pussy lips.

"Shit, you so damn wet."

He swirls his fingers in her juices, sticking three of them in her. She jumps then closes herself around them moaning. He rubs her.

"Oh Zion. Yes, shit yes!"

He pulls out his fingers. He has never eaten a woman from behind like this and he's been thinking about doing this to Lea since he ordered the restraints. He bends down, pressing his head into her pussy licking it. Licking up all her juices, sucking on her clit.

Fuck, she tastes so damn good.

He moans on her clit and she fucks his face wanting to get off.

OH GOODY, GOOD LORD SUCK IT.

He stops, making sure she doesn't cum yet.

WHY THE FUCK HE STOP? BRING THAT TONGUE BACK TO THE CLIT. SHIT.

Lea digs her nails into the bed, pulling the sheet to the point it pulls away from the mattress. She's been brought to the point of cumming so many times tonight it is straining her nerves.

Zion wants to be inside Lea to feel her contract around his cock. He stands up pressing his dick in between her ass cheeks sliding it up and down. The tip of his cock leaves pre-cum on the crack of her ass. He pulls back and pushes his dick into her pussy.

They say "Oh fuck," at the same time at the feel of him sliding into her. He spreads her legs open and presses her into the bed, bending over grabbing her breasts. With her hair in the ponytail, he can kiss the back of her neck, licking the spot, driving her wild. She grinds against him, and he keeps fucking her hard, holding on. Lifting up, he grabs her hair wrapping it around his fist, placing his other hand on her back. Long and slow strokes with each thrust into her pussy is driving him over the edge.

"Lea. So. Good."

He grabs her waist, making sure he doesn't slip out.

Fuck. We're so damn wet. Pussy juices, pre-cum, sweat.

He keeps stroking in and out of her drawing out the pleasure. Sometimes moving slowly and other times pumping fast and hard, taking them to the brink. To the mountain top but not over it.

TH*is man* IS D*rivin*G M*e* NUTS. I *WANNA CUM.*

At this point the Sex Diva and Lea have merged into one.

He moves his hand to her clit, squeezing it between his thumb and forefinger. She whimpers. He then flattens his hand on her pussy, forcing her to rub against it with each pump into her. She's pressing her pussy into his hand forcing him to rub her clit even harder.

"Shit, you wanna cum? Ready to squirt on my hand. Fuck. Your pussy so good. Maybe I should stop and not let you cum," he teases her, knowing damned well that if he stopped now, he would hate them both.

"Z. Don't. Stop. Please. Need. This. Cum. Please. Harder," Lea says with each thrust.

They move faster and their moans and groans of sexual pleasure are all they hear in the room. He uses one hand to hold her in place pounding harder into her with one final push and presses his other hand into her pussy. They cum, bucking like wild horses. He bends over kissing and trying not to bite into her neck. She buries her face into the bed muffling her screams of pleasure.

The sheet pulled away from the mattress, balled into crumpled heaps in her hands.

Oh, damn I can't stop. Shit. Another orgasm. Fuck. Dammit Lea, yes. Shit.

Zion jerks out after his second orgasm knowing if he stayed in, she could probably bring him off again.

Shit, her pussy, feels so good.

After releasing her around the waist and pulling his soaked hand from her pussy, he reaches over and un-snaps the restraints from her wrists and ankles, pulling her into his arms. He holds her, pressed up against him, praying she doesn't reject him, that she enjoyed this as much as he did.

She turns around kissing him, grinding against his dick.

"Z. Put it in. Fuck me some more," she commands.

He lifts her onto the bed laying on top of her, not sure he'll be able to get hard again. But after a few strokes, he gets hard enough to slide back inside her. He allows her to fuck his dick as hard and fast as she likes. She wraps her legs around him, pressing him into her, grinding into his pelvis.

"Oooooo shit," he groans.

Zion can tell she's about to cum. He grinds into her pressing her into the bed. She holds onto him shaking from the force of her orgasm, and he cums again. Growling like a lion, roaring like a bear.

"Oh fuck. Yes. Dammit. Fuck. Yesssssssssssss."

Lea moans her orgasm into his mouth kissing him nibbling on his bottom lip.

DAMMIT, I THINK WE BIT HIM. HOPE WE DIDN'T GO TOO FAR.

She raises his hand, and they lick her pussy juices off his palm and fingers.

"Oh Zion, baby. Happy Birthday, Bear," she kisses him, holding onto him, hugging him.

He kisses her, holding on, caressing and stroking her.

"Lea, I'm never letting you get away. Never," he says.

They climb up into the bed with Lea crawling into his arms cuddling up to him.

Happy fiftieth birthday to me.

Zion drifts off to sleep, feeling loved by his Kitten.

The Sex Diva is splayed out in the corner of Lea's mind, unable to move or talk.

A deep voice mumbles, *DAMN, WE GOOD TOGETHER.*

-29-

Waking up Sunday afternoon, Zion and Lea are still in the small bedroom in the queen bed. Throughout the night they cuddled, talked and managed to get in one more round of sex. The bed sheets are across the room in a pile. Lea has sweated so much, one side of her hair is no longer as straight as the other. She even has a couple of hickeys on her chest.

Zion's legs are sore. He can bench press hundreds of pounds, but walking and carrying and fucking at the same time was something he never thought he would need to stretch for. A soak in the tub will loosen them up. After their soak, Zion grabs some gray sweatpants to put on and Lea grabs a tank top and underwear. She leaves his bedroom walking toward the small bedroom to clean up.

"Woman where you going?" Zion asks her, stopping her in her tracks.

"Zion, I can't leave that room for Mrs. Vance like that."

"Lea, we gonna go eat. Maybe make out. Have some more sex. Mrs. Vance is off until Tuesday. We got time to straighten up later. Leave it."

"But Zion—."

He picks her up and carries her down stairs. "Kitten, I said leave it. Now let's eat. And even if Mrs. Vance has to clean it up, big deal. Who do you think help me set this up? I trust her not to discuss my business. Even with Sam."

"I never even thought of Sam knowing or not knowing. Now I'm absolutely gonna clean up. Later."

Later turns into the next day.

Monday they are working in Zion's home office. He has to work on some investing options for a client, and Lea needs to troubleshoot an issue with a VIP client's computer. She's sitting at his conference table in a tank top and jean shorts. He can see the curve of her butt in those shorts. He has attempted to focus on a spreadsheet for the last thirty minutes, but her legs, all soft and smooth, distracts him.

Shit fuck this. I can't concentrate on anything but her.

He goes over, taking the seat next to her.

"What's up Bear?" she asks him.

Man, I love it when she calls me that name.

"Nothing Kitten. You about done?"

My Kitten. She crawls into my arms every chance she gets. I was never one for affection. She has me craving her touch daily.

"Sure, I was about to call and let her know the results. Why?" she asks looking at him cautiously.

She knows I'm up to something. I've never been this playful or devilish in any relationship in my past. With her she brings it out in me unknowingly. The last couple months of their dom/sub world has been so much discovery between us.

"No reason. You keep working away. Could you stand up for a second?"

"Of course."

She stands and he walks up behind her moving the chair to give her a hug from behind. She relaxes into his embrace, then connects the call with her client.

"Hi Mrs. May. I wanted to let you know I was done with your computer. You're all set."

While Lea is talking, Zion plays with her tits. She swats his hand away and continues with the conversation.

"No ma'am. I had to update your virus software and run some scans on it." Lea presses her ass into him and puts her hands over his pressing them into her waist.

Zion unbuttons her shorts and slides them down her legs, bending down kissing her ass and thighs.

Yep, I kissed my girl's ass.

"Could you hold on a second please? Thanks," Lea puts Mrs. May on hold and takes a deep breath moaning. "Zion Landon. Can you wait until I'm done?"

"Nope," he tells her, splaying his hands across her butt and squeezing her sexy mounds. She goes back to her call.

"Sorry Mrs. May, was there anything else I can do for you today?" Lea asks her client wanting to end the call.

Zion stands up and reaches down and rips off Lea's underwear tossing them toward his desk. His sweatpants follow. He spreads her legs open fingering her pussy, getting it wet.

"Uh no ma'am, I'll have—. I'll have Crystal send you the bill like we always do," Lea puts her hand over her Bluetooth mouth piece. Zion bends down and moves in front of her French kissing her pussy. Lea takes in a deep breath and her client hears her.

"Huh. No, I smashed my finger in the draw. If everything—. Is okay—. I'll let you go and disconnect from your computer now. If you need anything else drop me an email or give me a call—. Yes, ma'am it was good talking to you too. Take care," Lea slams her laptop shut, disconnects the call making sure she has hung up and whispers. "Oh, fuck Zion yes, lick my clit. Shit baby, lick."

She's bent over the table attempting to keep herself up right while he licks, sucks, flicks and kisses away.

Shit this woman tastes so good. I can replace her with a meal or snack daily.

"Please let me sit down, baby. Please."

Instead, he stands up and puts her on the table, lying her on her back bringing the chair over and sitting down. He pulls her toward him and attacks her pussy. He sucks on her clit harder, really getting into it, sticking three fingers inside of her. She fucks his face, spreading her legs, holding them open. Zion takes his fingers out making sure her pussy lips aren't hiding her delectable button.

"Oh, shit baby. That's it, eat it, suck my clit," she begs him.

He gives her a few more sucks and she cums. Hard. Bucking up and down. Screaming. Before she can come down from her peak, he stands and presses his dick inside of her and fucks her feverishly. She kisses him, licking her pussy juices off his face. Within minutes he's cumming in her, unloading semen and moaning in ecstasy. She's cumming again begging him not to stop. He doesn't and they cum again.

"Fuck. Lea. Dammit. Oh, fucking shit your pussy good." He slows down pumping inside of her, coming down from their orgasmic high.

"Baby, you see why we could never work in the same office now don't you. We always end up fucking. Hard," she says to him.

He lifts up looking down at her. "No, I don't. Your pussy is too damn good to be at work all day."

She laughs and kisses him. "I love you."

"Not as much as I love you baby," he doesn't take his eyes off her. She puts her hands on the sides of his face looking at him deeply.

"For the first time in my life I believe I won't die feeling I was never loved. Or alone."

"Baby, I hate it when you talk like that. Stop it okay. Just know we love each other. And are meant to be together," he says to her. "And thank you for my wonderful birthday weekend."

"Birthday sex. You don't feel cheated, do you?" Lea asks him.

"Hell no. You allowed me to have the celebration I wanted."

Love's Awakening

-30-

It has been ten days, fourteen hours and thirty-five minutes since Zion and Lea last had sex. The Tuesday after his glorious birthday weekend with Lea, Zion had to leave town going to Canada, Spain and London. He laughs at the idea counting down until he sees her again. There have been no stalker issues which worries him. But as Detective Greg told him, there isn't much Zion can do unless Addison makes herself known. So, Zion has decided to keep on living.

He's decided to take Lea to Charleston, South Carolina, upon his return. He's forcing himself to take a break from work, family, and other interruptions. And the only way to do so is to get out of town. Normally, it would be a meetup with the other BOMs hitting celebrity parties. But now its about traveling with his girlfriend and he knows Lea will keep him away from working.

He calls her from London to give her the details about their trip. "Hello my beauty, miss me?" he asks after she answers the phone.

"Every minute of the day. When are you getting home? I need a hug."

"Glad you miss them. I'll be home Tuesday, and then we fly out Thursday."

"Zion what do you mean we fly out? Aren't you tired of traveling?"

"Kitten, I'm wore out from business travel. Our trip will be pure leisure. You and I. We're going to Charleston. Leaving work, family, and stalker behind. Or do you want to stay at home."

"Heck no, I don't want to stay home." Lea hops up and starts pulling out clothes to pack.

Zion hears all the background noise. "What are you doing?"

"Pulling out clothes. You said Thursday, right? I gotta get packed." She tosses more clothes on the pile to choose from to pack.

"Well, don't pack too much. It's not like you'll be wearing much of it. I've been away ten days."

"Oh yeah right. Who needs clothes? Ha. Okay. Gotcha."

"Zion, I have a question."

"Go ahead."

"This weekend, can we switch up?"

"Explain."

"Can I be dom and you sub?"

Zion stares at the pen he is twirling on the desk. He and Lea have only participated in their dom/sub personas with her following his lead. It has become rather intoxicating for him with the power she has granted him in their sex life. Outside the bedroom in their daily lives, she easily steps back into the powerful business woman he admires. But him becoming the sub.

Shit I don't know.

"Bear, please. Trust me. And if you don't like it, remember consent can be withdrawn at any time. No judgement."

He lets out a breath. "Okay, Lea. I agree to a switch up. You dom/me sub. I trust you."

"Thank you baby."

Zion laughs and then yawns. "Me a sub."

"Bear, get some rest. Sleep. I'll see you when you get home. Love you."

"I love you too Kitten. Goodnight or is it morning? Hell, never mind. Bye Kitten."

"Bye Zion.

Ryan picks Lea up from her house on Thursday taking her to the airport for departure. Zion will meet them there as he's finishing up, closing out any issues to free up this weekend, telling Morgan to take off as well.

Sitting on the plane, waiting, Lea gives her mom a call.

"What up my child?" she answers.

"Oh nothing, waiting for Zion. What up with you?" Lea asks her.

"Not a gosh darn thing. You get to see your man finally. You been cranky. Have fun and enjoy. Bring me back a souvenir. By the way, you still in love with him? Do you want to marry him? Do you see a future with him? Will I be referring to him as my son-in-law? Please, not too soon."

"Yes to the first three questions, and I don't have a clue to the last question. But I would like for you to. Very much so," Lea admits. Zion is walking onto the plane while she's talking, looking at her and smiling. "Mom he's arrived, I think we're taking off soon, I'll call you when we land."

"Okay. Have fun and don't worry about me, I'll be going to the movies and dinner and that's all. Bye my child."

Lea hangs up staring at Zion.

"Hi Bear. Everything okay?"

He sits down next to her and buckles in. Ryan and Sam take their seats for take-off.

"It is now. I got a call from my realtor in Charleston. Some property has become available for sale on the beach. A fire destroyed two beach homes, the owners want to sell instead of re-build. I like the location, and I can get them both for a good price. If things work out, I'll tear down the remains of both and build a new beach house with enough privacy on either side. I've wanted to have a house on the beach," he tells her.

"Are we staying in a hotel in Charleston?"

I'm getting excited about this trip.

"Nope. I currently have a house. We'll be staying there. If everything works out, I'll be putting it up for sale and getting these properties. How's your mom? Everything okay?"

"Yep, checking in."

"Lea, why are you looking at me with such a look of innocence? Should I be worried?" he whispers kissing her.

She caresses his leg. He takes a blanket and throws it over his lap hiding his erection. "Of course not. I was simply wondering if you want to take me to the sleeping quarters and make out?"

"Yes, you know damn well I do."

"But."

"But we switching. Remember. Or does this start on the plane?" He leans into her.

Lea turns looking at Sam and Ryan. They are sitting in seats closer to the front and have left Zion and Lea toward the back. Both have gotten comfortable, reclining their chairs watching movies.

"No, it doesn't start now. I still have some planning to do."

"Nice to hear. I want you anxious. I want you soaking wet, so by the time we get to Charleston you can't stand it. I want to have you ride me, baby. And I know you will, when you've been deprived of the opportunity," he says.

"See you wrong for that, just wrong,"

I can't help but laugh 'cause he has pegged me right.

For the entire plane ride, Zion blocks her attempts at convincing him to go to the sleeping quarters. They joke, kid. Lea cajoles, pleads, and begs.

UGH, THIS MAN, THIS MAN. HE KEEPS SAYING NO.

"You're not nice. Remember this. I'll get you back."

"Oh, baby I look forward to it," he says unfazed.

They arrive in South Carolina, taking a limo to Zion's beach house. Hell, freaking beach mansion. Sam and Ryan leave, bidding them a good night and telling Zion they will see him Monday morning.

Driving into the circular driveway, Lea and Zion are dropped off at the front door. A forest green Lexus LC is parked on the side of the house sitting in front of the three-car garage.

"Monday morning. Aren't they here to protect you? Securely? From me?" she asks him.

"No sweetheart. Sam is here to see his son and Ryan is here to see his girlfriend. They're available if I need them but they're off duty. Except for Ms. Helen and her husband who came to open the house and stock everything I requested, we're on our own."

Zion walks to an elderly woman standing at the entrance of the house. She steps aside as her husband takes the luggage upstairs to the main bedroom. Ms. Helen, greets everyone jovially with a heavy southern drawl.

"Good evening gents and Lady. Mr. Landon, here are the keys to the car. I will get everything unpacked for you. As requested, I'll return as needed to take care of any cleaning and restocking of food. Otherwise, please do have a wonderful weekend and buzz me if you need me?"

"Thanks Ms. Helen. I appreciate you." Zion turns to Lea, "How about a late dinner and a walk?"

"Wonderful." Lea smiles. Turning away and walking into the house she stares in awe. It's not that Lea is unaccustomed to seeing big beautiful mansions and homes. It's just that every time she walks into one, the feeling of excitement overwhelms her. She wants to walk around and peak into every nook and cranny, see what's behind doors, ask the owners what they were thinking when they chose the colors, furniture, layouts, and everything. Walking into million-dollar homes gives her goosebumps.

Entering the front door, they step into the foyer. Steps lead to the upstairs. To the left is the living room and to the right is the office. Walking directly past the stairs, there is an open kitchen, dining area and family room. Off the family room, doors open to a screened in porch. The house has four bedrooms, four bathrooms, and two half baths. It backs up to a forest.

Lea peaks into the rooms on the first floor from the hallway. Glancing toward the back, she see's an in-ground pool and an outdoor kitchen reminiscent of the one he has at his apartment. This time the colors are muted grays, black, white, and blues. From the front of the house, you would never think it had all this to offer.

"You selling this? I assume you're going bigger?" she asks him.

"Yes. I want to build a vacation house on Atlantic Beach in North Carolina. My parents used to bring Star and me there during the summers. When considering having both families, security, you and your clothes and shoes, well that's a lotta space needing bedrooms and bathrooms. I figure six to eight bedrooms, at least six bathrooms and a chef's kitchen will take up a lot of acreage. That doesn't even include outdoor entertaining space. This house has been great but it's too far from the beach. It's more of a bachelor's pad. If I can go bigger and design what I want, I will. I have a great architect. He designed my new office space."

"Some bachelor's pad. You should keep it and rent it out. It's still a money maker if you ask me."

"Kitten, maybe I will and let you handle that. Let's get change and go to dinner."

Zion drives them to Oak Steakhouse. He called ahead placing a request for the meal and seating. They will be dining on shrimp cocktails, oak house salad, lobster tail, filet mignon's, and whipped potatoes.

After being seated and confirming the menu with the waiter, Zion decides to approach the subject of kids with Lea.

I wanna marry her, and I wanna give her everything. But can she really be happy without kids? I need to know for sure.

"Lea, may I ask you a question?" Zion asks, looking serious.

"Sure. Go ahead." Lea places her silverware down next to her plate and pours herself a drink.

"Why haven't you had any kids?"

Fuck, that question again. Oh well here goes.

"I always thought there would be time. In my twenties and thirties, I was around plenty of friends having kids and all they did was complain, never having any time to themselves, wishing they could start over. Many of them got pregnant because it was the thing to do. I tried finding the 'him' I could tolerate being a part of my life the rest of my life. In my thirties I decided it was time. I had a plan." Lea takes a sip then continues on. She hates talking about why she doesn't have kids. She feels inferior even though she knows nothing is wrong with being forty-four with no kids.

"Find a man, settle down, have a baby or two and be done with it. I failed. By then the men my age, were done having babies, the younger ones were dropping seed all over the city, and the older ones would only date women who were fixed. I thought about adoption for a hot minute and discovered I didn't want to do it alone. Eventually, I gave up the plan and accepted it was never gonna happen. The strange thing is, all those friends that bitched and complained back in their twenties and thirties are so happy and proud of their kids now. Guess it wasn't meant to happen for me."

"Do you honestly think you can't conceive now, or do you think it's too late?" he asks.

"Hhhhhmm, not too late but a fear. I still don't want to do it alone. Who knows what kind of medical procedure I would have to go through to do it at my age? Will I have a healthy baby? I think that scares me the most. Why do you ask?"

"You're great with the girls and kids are drawn to you. I'm wondering if that's something you would miss with a future with me?"

"I accepted long ago it wasn't going to happen. And no, I would not miss it with a future with you. Not at all. In a way there's a selfish part to my not having kids. I want to be the center of a man's world. I want to be his focus. At my age, I'm looking to be with a man whose kids were grown, with grand-babies who was done with popping out babies. Zion, if we end up married—."

He stares at her with a look of 'oh we gettin' married'.

Scoffing at him, Lea says, "Oh don't give me that look. If we end up married, us not having kids won't bother me, break me, or keep us from being happy. I hope you would feel the same way."

"Kitten, I want to give you everything. I don't want you regretting anything about us. Ever," he says not taking his eyes off her.

"Zion, I have no regrets. The only regret I could have is not being with you anymore."

The server approaches their table with the check. Lea mouths to Zion she loves him. He winks at her, and mouths the same back. They leave the restaurant and go for a walk.

As they arrive back at the beach house, Zion receives a call from a client he has to take.

"Lea, I know this is supposed to be our weekend but this is important. I promise it won't take long."

"No worries Bear. I'll roam around and check out the house."

"Baby, roam away." Zion says walking off to the office.

Lea walks into the kitchen opening doors, pantry, a door leading to the garage and a door leading to the basement. She goes to the double doors leading to the back of the house. Turning on a light switch, it lights up showing the pool/hot tub combination, an eating area, and two separate lounge areas.

Back inside the house, she goes upstairs. In the master bedroom, she notices their bags have been unpacked, with the empty suitcases standing in a corner. She looks in the closet and drawers seeing their things. Being really nosy, she goes and looks at the other bedrooms and bathrooms. Back in the master, she undresses and takes her shower. After about fifteen minutes of laying in the big California king bed, she drifts off to sleep.

WELL, I GUESS NO SEX TONIGHT.

Zion walks into the darkened bedroom. He switches on the bed side light and looks down at his Lea sound asleep. Thinking about the time she mentioned how he wanted to be happy to see her lying in bed waiting for him, gives him the most contented feeling he's had in years. He goes and takes a shower, then join her drifting off to sleep, unbothered about any kind of punishment she can give him.

The next day, they meet with his realtor at the burned-out beach houses. Lea keeps quiet, listening to him do business and walking around being nosy again. He loves the location and he's excited. Based on the asking price, Zion makes a full offer for both, which he will have torn down and build a new one, ensuring privacy.

From there, they go sightseeing and shopping. Lea doesn't see much she wants but Zion sees plenty he wants to buy for her. Clothes, shoes, jewelry, purses. It's tough reigning him in. Because they didn't have sex last night and they are switching personas, she takes him into a store that sells accessories, spotting the scarf rack upon entering. Selecting colors she like's, she settles for six silk oversized scarfs.

"Baby, that's it? Don't you want more?"

"Nope, I'm good." He looks crestfallen. "Okay I wasn't going to say anything but I need a few sundresses." He drags her off to a store and once there he has her model numerous dresses, selecting the ones he likes with little disagreement from her. When he pays for them, she stands in silence.

Shit, he spent that kinda money on me on fricking sundresses.

"No objection?" he asks, daring her to do just that.

"Nope, I'm not crazy."

"That's my Lea. Let's head back to the house. We're having dinner in tonight."

"Wonderful," she says in a southern drawl.

"Why do you say it like that?"

"Why do you think? Z."

"So it has begun. My Kitten."

"Only if you still agree."

"Oh I agree. Most definitely do I agree. But I wanna know what I am agreeing to." Zion is enjoying this immensely.

Lea turns and struts out the store, walking to the car. She has taken off her underwear and her ass is jiggling under her dress, brushing against the soft material.

Zion laughs, catching up to her. "Loving the view."

"Good."

When they get back to the beach house, Lea prepares dinner with Zion's help. He keeps asking her what she has planned for him but she doesn't respond.

"Why so many questions. Don't you trust me?"

All kidding aside, he turns her face toward his, ensuring they are looking at each other. "My Kitten. Of course I trust you.

Always and fully. But the gleam in your eyes say I'm in for a world of I don't even know the hell what and it makes me slightly antsy."

Lea leans into him. "I promise you, this will be a night you won't forget and a memory that will forever be seared in your deep conscience. I will keep you safe but I also promise to drive you mad with pleasure. Now, why don't you go take a shower, and I'll bring you a drink. What would you like? Z."

"A brandy would be wonderful. You have me intrigued. Shall I meet you in the bedroom? My Kitten."

"Yes. Z."

Love's Awakening

255

-31-

Lea pours Zion a glass of Courvoisier and takes it to the bedroom putting it on the nightstand. She places a glass of ice and a can of whip cream on the second nightstand, hiding it under one of the scarves Zion purchased earlier. She then goes to the other bedroom and takes a quick shower. Standing in the bathroom she spritzes her body with Victoria's Secret Pear Glaze.

Looking at the other scarves, she's undecided how to use them. Carry them in while walking naked? Have them wrapped in a box? Leave them in the bag?

WRAP THEM AROUND OUR BODY.

Nice idea.

Picking up a scarf, Lea pulls it around her chest to cover her breasts. She ties it in a bow in the middle and repeats with a second scarf. Wrapping two around her waist she ties one in a bow on her left hip and the other on her right hip. She ties one around her head, leaving the ends brushing her shoulder. She walks barefoot to Zion, careful not to walk too fast.

YES, SLOW DOWN. DRAW THIS OUT. OUR MAN AT OUR MERCY. I LIKE THE WAY WE THINK.

She walks into the bedroom, and he is standing at the end of the bed, glass in hand and the towel still wrapped around his waist.

Zion almost chokes on his drink, watching Lea walk toward him wrapped in the scarves he purchased. He couldn't understand why she selected such long scarves. Now he gets it. The scarves don't hide much. Her rock-hard nipples are waving hello to be licked. He licks his lips. "Miss Adams. What in the name of all sexy heaven do you have planned for me?"

"A lot of fun, Mr. Landon." She lifts her face for a kiss, which, of course, he obliges. "Remember our safe words."

"Yes. My Kitten."

Lea stretches out her hand, palm out. "Glass."

Zion hands her the glass. Lea takes it and places it on the side table.

"At attention. Z."

Zion lowers his arms to his side with legs slightly spread a part."

"Z. You can withdraw consent at any time. Is that understood?"

"Understood. My Kitten."

She takes the towel off him. Folding it in half, she lays it on the bed in about the spot where Zion's waist will end up.

YEP, GOTTA COVER UP THAT WET SPOT, CAUSE OH BABY, IT'S GONNA BE SOAKIN.

"Lie down in the middle of the bed."

He does as he's told, directly on top of the towel as planned.

"Have you ever been tied down, restrained?" she asks him. He looks uncertain.

"No, never," he deadpans, sitting up on his elbows.

At this stage in their relationship and the comfort they have with one another, Lea can ask almost anything of me. This being tied down shit, I ain't too sure about that. What the fuck she thinking?

"May I tie you down, restrain you?" Now that Lea thinks of it, it would be a better idea to ask Zion than to do it. She doesn't want to scare him and he pulls the bed apart.

"Is this a payback?" he asks.

"Our sex life is never about payback. I enjoyed immensely what happened that night. Right now, its about me wanting to give you this, that's all. I have no ulterior motives and never will. But if you don't want to proceed, say so," Lea is patiently waiting for him to decide, refusing to pressure him in any way. He has a lot of trusting to get beyond what happened with him and Addison years ago, so in no way will she ever push him to do something he doesn't fully agree to.

"Go ahead. My Kitten," he says looking at her.

"My job tonight is to please you and keep you safe."

"Proceed." He props himself up on the pillows for a better view, relaxing the tension in his body. Releasing memories from his past.

Ensuring he's watching her every move; she removes a scarf from her chest. She takes his left leg and straps it to the bed post. Walking to the other side of the bed, she removes the second scarf, not looking away from his gaze. He watches her, clenching the bed sheets.

"Are you okay?"

She's standing at the foot of the bed, still wearing the scarfs around her waist, breasts bared to his view.

"I want you to proceed."

She walks to the top of the bed. "May I have your arm?"

He reaches out to her and she presses his hand onto her cheek, kissing and licking his palm. She unties a scarf from her waist and straps him to the bed post. She walks to the other side of the bed. He doesn't take his eyes off her. Removing the fourth scarf, she straps his other hand to the other bed post.

Lea climbs onto the bed. He lays his head back on the pillow thinking she's going to use the last scarf to blindfold him. Instead, she pulls a mask from under the pillow, distracting him with a kiss.

"We are going to partake in some sensation play. If at any time this brings back any memories you're uncomfortable with, make me stop," she says.

"Don't worry. I will."

She puts the mask on him. Lea sits in between his legs running the last silk scarf up and down his body. She starts at the balls of his feet, twirling it around, then glides it up his legs over his waist and down his other leg. She goes back up and gently glides the scarf over his manhood, which grows stiffer with each caress.

She leans over him not touching and glides the scarf over his nipples back and forth numerous times. He inhales and moans. She moves to his side and positions herself to use the scarf to caress his arms, under his arm pits, the bend in his elbow and his palms and fingers. He makes a fist attempting to hold onto the scarf but she moves it quickly and sits on his stomach.

"Z. Am I too heavy?"

Hoarsely he answers, "No."

"May I continue?"

"Yes," he groans.

Lea glides the scarf across his face, his lips, his chin, his neck. He laughs each time turning his head in the direction of the scarf. It smells like her of course. Searing the scent in his nostrils. Lea bends over, kissing and licking his neck. When he moves his head to attempt to kiss her, Lea moves off him reaching for the can of whip cream she had hidden under the last scarf on the nightstand. She sprays a line of it from his neck down to his navel. He lifts up from the unexpected cold.

"Ooooooohhhhhhh," he says.

Lea puts a little of the cream on her finger and feeds it to him. He licks her fingers hungrily.

"I like that. The same way you lick my clit," she says.

"You know it. My Kitten. You know it."

Lea licks the whip cream off him. She spreads it around to lick on his nipples slurping it up. Zion laughs at the sound.

"What's so funny?" she asks with a smile in her voice.

"You and that sound. And the sensation of course. Please don't stop."

"I'm just getting started." She travels down to his sides, licking, nipping and biting. She moves down to his stomach and licks. His penis is now standing straight up.

Lea lifts up and takes an ice cube out of her glass of melting ice. She puts it in her mouth and straddles him again. She kisses him, allowing him to suck on the ice cube. He groans, enjoying it. She sits up grabbing two more ice cubes and moves down to his penis.

Lea takes one of the ice cubes and inserts it into her vagina. "Wheewww baby," she says reacting to the cold inside of her that's now coursing through her body. She shivers.

"What the fuck just happened?" Zion asks her.

Clenching her inner walls, she concentrates on keeping the ice cube inside of her. She murmurs hoarsely, "Nothing. Z. All's good."

Lea trails the other ice cube down his chest to his belly button and into his pubic hairs.

"Z. You know what's about to happen, don't you?"

"Yes."

"I can stop now if you like." She shudders again, feeling the water from the melting cube in her vagina drip down between her legs, leaving her thighs slick.

"Please."

"Please what? Tell me. Please what?" She growls, concentrating on clenching. He's straining against the scarves but not hard enough to pull free. In anticipation.

"Please. Continue."

Lea puts the partially melted ice cube in her mouth and crawls in between Zion's legs sitting on her knees. She caresses his penis up and down and then goes down on him with the ice in her mouth.

"Oh fucccckkkkk," he yells lifting his head off the pillow turning from side to side.

Between the cold of the ice and the heat of her tongue, Lea gave Zion a sensation he will never be able to describe. She continues to suck him off. He's moving all over the bed, from left to right, up and down, moaning and groaning, cussing like crazy. The coldness from the ice keeps him from cumming, but Lea gets a lot of pre-cum out of him. She stops after the ice has melted. His pubic hairs are soaking wet from the combination of his pre-cum, her spit, and the ice.

"You want me? You want inside me?"

"Shit, yes, fuck me, shit fuck me."

Lea sits on top of him. Zion feels the moisture on him from the ice in her vagina. He assumes incorrectly that Lea is extremely wet and ready. She slides his penis into her. The ice cube, which is practically a pebble now, slips out and lands in his pubic hairs. When he makes contact with her cold inside pussy walls he bellows, "Oh what the fuck!"

Lea leans over his chest and kisses him. As she glides up and down, he warms up quickly. Instead of untying him, she rides his dick, the way he likes it.

"Got damn, fuck!" He yells. "Shit! Damn!" Zion is attempting to fuck her but with his legs tied to the bed posts he can't lift up enough to push into her. It's all on her to bring him his release. She scoots back farther onto his waist over his pelvis so she can grind into him harder with her clit rubbing against his pubic hairs.

Shit this action feels so good.

"Oh. Z. Yes, shit your dick is so good." She leans over and licks and sucks on his nipples.

"Fuck, dammit. Yes, oh fucking yes. OOOOOOOOO shit," Zion cums, jerking and shooting inside of Lea. She continues riding him, making sure she cums after him so he can feel her having an orgasm and not see it.

"Oh shit, yes, yes," she screams and jerks, cumming on his dick.

With her riding him like this he's getting to that point of aching. The cold, the heat, her grinding. His eyes are tearing up behind the blindfold. He tries to keep himself from hyperventilating through the orgasm that doesn't seem to want to stop for both of them. Lea finally flops down on his chest out of energy.

"Kitten, untie me now or I'll break this damned bed into pieces." He's pulling on the scarves.

Lea reaches up and unties the scarf from his left hand and he reaches over and unties it from his right then removes the blindfold. He sits up holding her, squeezing the breath out of her.

"Oh, my Lea," he whispers, holding her in his arms. Burying his hands in her hair, he turns her face toward his forcing an opened mouth passionate kiss on her. Lea responds back feverishly.

His penis may be limp, but every other sexual nerve ending on his body is screaming for this woman's physical touch. Zion kisses her lips, cheeks, closed eyes, neck, pressing her into him. Lea holds on, hugging him around his neck in almost a death grip. The goosebumps on his body flare up, each time she caresses him.

Lea feels him attempting to move his legs. Breaking the kiss and holding his face in her hands, she says, "Zion, let me untie your legs."

He releases his hold on her shoulders and places his hands on her waist allowing her to bend back, reaching the scarfs to untie his legs. He grasps her again, laying them down, staring into her face.

Unsure of herself, Lea asks Zion, "Was that okay? Did I do good?"

OMG, my baby sounds like a child in trouble, Zion thinks. "Lea, Babe. My Kitten. You did fucking fantastic. Like you said, you have given me a memory that will be forever seared in my brain. No matter what. Shit woman, you can tie me down and punish me anytime you like. If you got those kinda ideas for switching, hell yeah me sub, you dom.

Lea giggles. "I'm glad you liked it."

"I loved it."

The Sex Diva watches Zion and Lea drift off to sleep. WHERE IN THE HECK SHE COME UP WITH THE IDEA OF THE ICE IN THE VAGINA? WE'RE AN AMAZING FREAK.

AND I AM LOVING BEING ON THE RECEIVING END OF IT.

OK, WHO THE HECK THE DEEP VOICE BELONGS TOO?

CALL ME ADONIS.

-32-

Lea and Zion laze around the house on Sunday. She would suggest a walk on the beach but Zion would veto it with a cuddle, hug, and kiss.

"Lea, don't you get it? I don't want to share you with them ugly outsiders yet. God, woman, I can't get enough of you. After last night, all I think about is wanting to be submissive. Again. Shit that was real nice, real nice."

"You're crazy you know that? Come on we're going for a walk and oh, I don't know, find me a funnel cake. Put some clothes on. Now." Lea pulls him up and he reluctantly gets dressed.

Zion indulges her craving. Hell, by now, he will give this woman anything she wants. Diamonds, money, furs, cars, houses. Anything after last night and all she wants is a funnel cake.

At first, I was nervous when she was tying me to the bed and making sure if I was okay with what she was doing. I was about to say no. Shit. Tying me down. Who does she think I am? Some kind of wimp? Oh, hell no! Then it hit me. This was about trusting her. It took every bit of concentration to not say our safe words. After she blindfolded me, I decided to completely give in. And oh, my fucking lord, did this woman do her thang.

Ice, whip cream, lick, suck, fuck, and ride. Ooo wee, I get hard just thinking about it. I had to kiss, suck, lick, and caress her all night and day. I don't have to leave the damned house for the rest of our lives. But here we are, getting her funnel cake with strawberries and whip cream. I'll never look at an ice cube without a shudder and getting a hard-on.

"Woman, you killing me right now. You know that, right?" he tells her, helping her to eat her sugary treat.

"What are you talking about?" she asks grinning and kissing him. "I loved your reactions. I'm glad you relaxed and let me take charge."

"I had second and third thoughts about what was going to happen, but in the end, I loved it. Back to normal tomorrow. This crap with Addison. I hope it's over soon, and they find her and lock her up. Thank you for being so understanding," he says staring at her lips wanting to suck the whip cream off the side crease. He adjusts his dick in his pants under the table. *We need to get back home. Shit. Now.*

"I've only been experiencing a little bit of cabin fever, but it's all been good," she says. "I've taken the time to get some things done around my house. I look at it as some forced spring-cleaning time and tackling small home repairs. I like being with you on vacation, having you all to myself." She lays her head on his chest listening to his heart.

"Let's head back. Sex, then sleep," he says grinning.

"Aren't you worn out yet?" she asks him.

"Nope," he says pulling her into the crook of his arm. They walk back to the house enjoying every minute of being together without the troubling thoughts of home.

-33-

After they get back to town Monday evening, Lea sends him home. "Zion, I'll talk to you tomorrow. I'm meeting Gordon for dinner. Go home. Tomorrow, okay?"

"Hhhmmm, okay tomorrow. Good night, Kitten."

"Good night, Bear." He gives her a bear hug then leaves.

When Zion arrives back into the office the next day, he's smiling, thinking about this past weekend. When he opens his computer case, he sees one of Lea's scarfs in it.

How in the hell did she manage this?

After smelling it, he slips it in his desk drawer, and gets to work.

About an hour into his afternoon his phone vibrates. Thinking it's Lea finally getting a break in her day from client meetings, he prepares for a tantalizing conversation. Looking down at it, he doesn't recognize the number. "Zion speaking," he answers.

"Zion. This is Wendy. I'm glad I caught you. Please don't hang up. I need to talk to you. Can you come by my place, anytime that works for you? Please," Wendy gets it all out in a rush.

"Wendy, hello. That was a mouthful. Is everything okay?" Things are good between him and Lea and he doesn't want anything else screwing it up. Especially something with Wendy.

Wendy Noelin was Zion's last temporary fuck before he met and started dating Lea. Before he fell head over heels in love with Lea, Wendy was as close to consistency with another female he ever had. Their sex was never the intense over the top sex he and Lea are having. A relationship should be about more than the sex, but with the temporary ass he was given, he wasn't pressed into anything more. He doesn't consider Wendy a bad person or someone he wouldn't help out down the road. There wasn't a connection between them beyond sex. He had no desire to give her more or ask more from her. So, this phone call from her, he doesn't mind taking.

I'm curious to see how she's doing at least and to say goodbye and give her some closure if she wants it. I'm not a total ass. Well not anymore. Amazing how love can change a man.

"Yes and no. Things could be a lot better. I need to speak with you. Please. I'm running out of time. Please Zion," she begs.

"Okay, how about now?" Zion doesn't want to do this but something is telling him to get it over with as soon as he can.

"Perfect, that's fine. I'm at home now."

"I'll be there in thirty minutes." He hangs up and grabs his phone and keys. "Morgan, I have to make a run; I don't know when I'll be back. If anything, urgent comes up, give me a call."

Zion gets to Wendy's apartment in twenty minutes. She opens the door for him before he can even knock. He's about to step over the threshold when he looks down and sees she's pregnant.

Well, it sure as hell ain't mine.

-34-

"Wendy? What's up?" Zion asks staring at her stomach.

What the fuck kinda shit is she bringing me into?

"Come in. Please." She opens the door wide. As he steps in, she directs him to the living room. "Have a seat."

On his hesitation, she points out the obvious. "Yes, I'm pregnant and no it's not your baby. We both know that. Just listen to me and keep an open mind before you go all crazy on me. Okay?" she snaps.

"Excuse you!" Zion snaps back at her, backing up toward the closed door.

Zion and Wendy may have a sexual history but snapping at him, he ain't having it. "You need to fix your attitude, Wendy. As you said, we both know that baby ain't mine. I can easily turn around and leave." He checks her, ready to leave on an objection.

"Zion, please don't leave. I'm sorry. You're right. Please, accept my apology."

He can't walk away now that I have him here. Chill out Wendy. He isn't yours. Yet.

"Fine. Apology accepted." Zion walks into the living room and takes a seat on the edge of her couch.

Wendy has been planning this for weeks, about how she would approach Zion about her pregnancy. She feels if he can just keep an open mind, just maybe he'll go for her idea and everything will work out and be okay. *Time is running out and she doesn't know what else to do.* She thinks silently without displaying her inner turmoil. And a nasty attitude with Zion won't help. Especially with him.

"I'll get straight to the point and skip the pleasantries. Please interrupt at any time, but I would appreciate it if you would just let me get this all out," she says.

"Go on." Zion sits in silence, waiting to hear what she has to say.

It looks like it's way too late for an abortion so she calling me and involving me has to be an extremely good-ass damn story.

"In a nut shell, I gave up on finding a husband and got artificially inseminated," she explains. "I have always wanted kids. I never told you this but I'm an orphan. After giving birth to me, my mother walked out of the hospital never to be seen again. I don't know who my parents are. Lil black babies were not being adopted. I grew up in the system until I aged out. Hell, I don't even know if my name is my name from my mother or the government."

She takes a sip of water then proceeds. "Back to the pregnancy. Everything was going great up until I got past the three-month threshold. While running some tests, the doctors found something out of the ordinary and, well, I won't survive the birth of my babies. Yes, babies. Two. Fraternal twin boys. There's nothing that can be done for me. As it stands, I may not even survive to see them born. I could be put on machines to keep them alive if that's what it takes. Zion, I don't want my kids to wind up in the system or split up. None of my so-called friends want them. I know you want to be a father to your own biological kids and that's not an option for you. But what about adoption? A private adoption of two healthy babies. You won't have a baby mama or daddy to contend with. You won't even have any long-lost relatives to deal with. I've spent years searching for anyone. According to what little information I could find from the government, medical records and retired nurses from the hospital, my mother was pretty much on her own when she had and then abandoned me." Wendy tears up but, controls herself.

"I'll meet with your lawyers, give you any information you want and need, you can run any kind of background checks to find out if I'm lying. I'll give you access to all my medical records, everything you need to know. I can't allow my babies to end up in the system. So, I'm begging you, please, take my babies after they're born. Love them and become the father you want. I'm giving my life to make sure they survive. I want them to have a loving home."

Zion sits there stunned. *Okay, this was something I never thought I woulda heard. Pregnant with no father. Dying. Wanting me to be the father of her kids. Wholly fricking fuck!*

Then he thinks, *God, I can be a father. This is my chance to be a father. Do I want this? Hell yeah, I want this. God help me, I want this, just like that, instantly. No second thought, I want these kids. I can give Lea a future with kids. With a family. In a pretty fucking unorthodox way, but here's our chance. My chance to be a father.*

"Zion, please say something," Wendy pleads.

Zion wipes his hands across his face and head, stalling for words. Then he asks, "Why me? Why have you come to me with this?"

This can't be happening. This can't be for real. No, hell no. This cannot be for real. My life can't be falling into place like this. Falling in love, thinking marriage, now kids? Shit, has everything I've done in life led me to this glorious future?

Zion wants to stand and pace the room. The businessman in him has taken control, and he sits, not displaying any of his agitation. *I can't let Wendy see my reaction. I need to keep the upper hand in this conversation. This could go so many different ways. Shit. Me being a father at fifty.* He refocuses on the words she's saying.

"In the time I have left, I know no one with the money, means and I hope the desire to do this. I would say go home and think about it, but in all honesty, I want you to say yes. Now. I have all the paperwork right here in this folder that proves everything I've told you. You say yes, and I sign the documents that gives you power of attorney over me and the kids to make whatever decisions you want as long as they include you adopting them and keeping them out of the system and together. I beg of you please do this Zion. Please. Don't you want to be a father?" Wendy asks him again.

I wish he would react. Fuck Zion. Here I am giving you the opportunity to become a father and your ass just sits there all calm and cool and shit. This is not the reaction I envisioned. Where is my fucking display of love? Where is my fucking proposal of marriage? Where is my fucking happiness? I'm dying here. Don't I deserve some loving words and thank you's?

"Yes, I want to be a father. Hell. I've even considered adoption. I'm speechless and stunned. Shit. Wendy." Zion sits staring at her. He can't let this opportunity pass. He can't. His business mind has clicked into overdrive.

Hell, is this a business deal or a fucking, I don't know, relationship deal? How do I keep this as business? I want these kids, and I want Lea. Wholly, shit, shit, shit. Zion man, focus on business. Keep it business.

"Okay. I'll do it. I'll adopt your kids. I hate to ask this, but what are you dying of?"

Wendy picks up the glass again taking another sip. This is the first time Zion has shown any level of emotion in front of her. The man she experienced was always stoic, standoffish. He barely smiled. His limited display of affection was during sex and the standard gentleman duties of opening doors, standing, and holding out chairs. But this man here, the narrowing of eyes, looking heavenward, clenching and unclenching of hands, Wendy has never seen this Zion.

Before she can respond to his question, he says in such a heartfelt way it makes her wanna cry, "Wendy, I'm so sorry. So damn sorry. Your babies. Oh my God, you won't see them grow up."

Wendy feels how Zion is heartbroken for her. Hating having to say the words, she clenches her teeth and purses her lips letting the words hiss out, "I have a brain tumor that can erupt at any time. At twenty-five, I was diagnosed with a lower-grade glioblastoma. I was single, living and loving life, never imagining I would be ill at all, let alone have a brain tumor.

"After one rowdy night of partying, I had a seizure. My friends thought it was from all the alcohol I consumed. Who wouldn't be seizing after indulging in bottles of Cisco, Boone's Hill, and Mad Dog Twenty/Twenty? I was rushed to the emergency room. After throwing up and seizing three more times, the doctors ran tests and discovered the cancerous tumor.

"I went through surgery and had it removed. After months of chemo and radiation, I was given a clean bill of health and was declared cancer free. The doctors informed me, contracting this at such a young age, I had a better than average chance of living a decade or more."

She decides not to tell him the rest. After recovering, she set out to find her a husband and start her family. Kids and all. Meeting Zion Landon, she knew she would be set. Having discovered he was sterile was a "what the hell now" revelation she was not expecting. Instead of walking way, she agreed in theory to be his temporary while she looked elsewhere for the hubby. Nearing that ten-year mark, and without any actual symptoms, she had to get plans set.

And this is why she is here now, artificially inseminated from a sperm bank via IVF, begging Zion to take her babies and raise them. She hopes he will fall in love with her and make her Mrs. Wendy Landon.

"I'm currently six months pregnant. I need to make it through my seventh month of pregnancy to ensure the babies lungs are viable and can survive. If I can survive the entire nine months that's ideal but, well, I'm pushing for seven months. I'm doing this without meds that will affect the fetuses, but sometimes the days get hard. Headaches and fatigue. A nurse is staying with me."

"You have a nurse staying with you? How can you afford something like that?"

"I found a service that offers in-home hospice services to wealthy elderly dying patients. They have nurses for families that don't want to be bothered with their dying relatives. I never knew something like this existed. My neurologist referred me. With the money I've saved, I'm able to afford her. But the expense leaves for little else. With me dying, my expenses become the adoptive parent's expenses." Wendy says nothing more giving Zion the opportunity to understand what this is going to cost him.

When he says nothing, she continues, "It's all here in the paperwork. Take it, read it and have your lawyers look it over. A private adoption can be costly, but since I'm agreeing to it and there's no father or next of kin that can contest it, I know things will go smoothly. Thank you, Zion. Thank you very much. I can now rest easily and plan other things."

"What other things?" he asks.

"My burial," she says flatly.

And getting you to react favorably to me and all of my plans.
I'm getting all of what I want before I die. That's for damned sure.
274

Love's Awakening

-35-

After Zion leaves Wendy's place, the nurse comes into the living room. Although Becky is accustomed to her invisible position when caring for elderly hospice patients, it doesn't mean she ignores what's happening.

Nurse Becky, as she insists on being referred to, got into the business of caring for elderly hospice patients when her parents were dying. Her parents were living in a senior-assisted facility, insisting they would not burden their kids as they got older.

Going to visit them daily, Becky was heartbroken to see the number of abandoned elderly people. Sitting in halls, wanting a visit, accepting a simple hello from strangers. When Becky would ask the nurses why no one would come visit them, the nurses would merely shrug. This is when she learned how these patients were "abandoned" by family whom they ignored or abused early in life.

One nurse stated, "I used to think it was sad, seeing them wither away with no one caring. Then I got to hear the stories of abuse and neglect they heaped on their family. Some of these families only want the death call to collect the paperwork. I stopped stressing."

"Is it okay for anyone to visit them?" Becky asked. "I'd like to."

"Look, if you elect to stop by to say a hi when you're visiting your parents, you do you. After your parents pass away, you won't be allowed. Unless you work here. Or become a private hospice nurse. Hey, there's a business in there somewhere. Hospice nurse for the elderly for those who don't have anyone who cares," the nurse said.

And this is when Becky started working with the elderly as they were dying in hospice. It became a lucrative business. For weeks to months, she becomes the invisible Nurse Becky doing things the family members don't want to be bothered with. For a hefty price, of course. Once the patient dies, she collects her fat check, maybe a little mention in the will, then goes on a detox vacation to release all that sadness.

And here she is again, invisible Nurse Becky to Wendy Noelin. But this time it's different. Wendy is young, pregnant, trying to get a man to marry her and adopt her babies. As unorthodox as this is, Becky couldn't pass up the money or opportunity to see how this plays out.

Another reason Becky gets paid as she does, is she knows how to keep her mouth shut. She has never discussed any of her clients or family business. Even when approached with more money, Becky looks at things as, "It ain't my business. If you don't know, I'm not gonna tell."

"See Becky, I told you all I had to do was to get him here and he would want my kids." Wendy proudly informs Becky.

"Want your kids. Yes. Want you. No." Becky shot back.

"Why the fuck you gotta be so harsh about this? Zion came. He listened and he said yes. It's only a matter of time before I become Mrs. Zion Landon."

"Wendy, we've been keeping it one-hundred with each other since the day we met. No holding back or beating around the bush. So, I'm going to lay it straight on you. That man will not make you his wife. Look at him. A black billionaire, sterile and having two babies dropped in his lap. And the best part being, he won't have baby mama drama to deal with. Again, being straight, you're not going to live. And you won't ever be his wife. He doesn't have to make you his wife. Talk about getting the cow and milk for free without effort. Girl, please."

"I now see how you can work so well with dying patients. You have no fucking heart. All I need is time—."

"Time which you don't have an abundance of. When you got home that night, you said you saw him kissing another woman. Why didn't you ask him about her tonight?"

"Because I don't care about her. I'm giving him what he most desires."

"And Wendy after you're gone, she could be the one giving him the life you'll never be able to. Focus on the health of your sons. You fixed the running out of money issue. I'm not going anywhere now. You can take out all your anger on me you want, but in the end, accept that Zion Landon ain't gonna marry you. That's just yo baby daddy."

Before Wendy can retort, she grabs the trash can next to the couch and throws up. Becky rushes to her, becoming Nurse Becky, comforting her dying patient.

After Wendy's bout of nausea passes and Becky helps her into bed, she says, "Becky, he's gonna love me."

"Wendy, yes, he will. He will love and adore you for giving him two healthy boys. Remember that always."

Wendy drifts off to sleep.

Love's Awakening

279

-36-

Zion leaves Wendy's place in a daze. He gets on the phone to his parents, calling his father's cell. "Dad, are you and mom home?"

"Yeah, Son. What's up? Everything okay?" Royal asks, alert at the shaky tone of his son's voice.

"I don't know. Can you call Star and make sure she and Garret get to your house? I need to talk to you guys. Right away. It's important." He looks over at the thick folder of documentation.

"Sure. I'll get them here. See you in a few." Royal puts down his phone looking at Patty.

"What was that about?" she asks.

"I don't know. Zion wants to talk to us all about something. I didn't like the sound of his voice."

"Maybe it's about proposing to Lea. That could make any man shaky. As I recall you couldn't almost get the question out when you asked me."

"Whatever. No. This is different," he responds.

"I'll call Star." Patty reaches for the home phone.

"Where's your cell?" Royal asks her. She's always laying it down and walking away from it. He picks up his cell and calls hers. He hears the ring coming from the fridge.

He opens the door and grabs it from the top shelf. "Really, Patty?"

"At least the ringer was on." She turns to her conversation with Star when the call connects and tells her that she and Garret need to get to their house as soon as they can.

Zion decides to take the streets instead of the highway to his parents' house. It takes him longer, but having the chance to stop at the stop lights, gives him the chance to look at the paperwork. Or so he thought. Whenever he reaches for the folder, the light turns to green. Finally, he pushes folder onto the floor and give into his racing thoughts.

Shit. I'm going to be a father. In three months, more or less I will be a father. God, Lea, don't leave me please; we're going to be a family. Please Lea, understand this. Please God, help me make her understand this and that it's for both of us.

He gets to his parents' house and they're waiting on him. Sitting down at the dining room table, with the folder in the middle mocking him, he tells them about the meeting with Wendy. They're just as stunned as he is. The looks on their faces would be comical if it weren't so real.

His father asks, "So, you are going to do this? To adopt her kids?"

"Yes dad, I am. I don't want them to end up in the system or be split up. I want to do this. I want this chance at being a father. I need to do this. I've been thinking about adoption with Lea after we're married."

His mother perks up at the word "married". She gives Royal an 'I was kinda right' look.

"No, mom. I haven't asked Lea to marry me. Yet. I'd planned to ask on her birthday in a few months. I love her and I want to marry her. I want us to have kids and I had planned on discussing adoption or trying artificial insemination. But this. A surrogate. I hadn't considered that. I can't pass up this chance. Something in me is screaming not to let these babies go."

"We're here for you whatever you want to do, however you want to handle this," Star offers. "Oh, big brother, I'm so happy for you, and feel so sick to my stomach about Wendy. Where's Lea? How is she handling all this?"

Zion takes a deep breath, again running his hands over his face and head. That conversation he's not looking forward to having. "I haven't told her yet. I came straight here from Wendy's place to talk to you guys. I don't want to lose her, but I'm praying this does not tear us apart. Me, adopting the babies of a woman I used to have random sex with. Dammit, how do I break this to her? How do I do this without losing her?"

His mom speaks up. "Zion, I don't believe you'll lose her. It'll be difficult for her to adjust to. Sweetheart, you need to tell her right away."

"The lawyer. I need to get in contact with our lawyers and have all this paperwork reviewed," Zion says, staring at the folder.

His father stands, placing his hands on Zion's shoulders, "Son. Go talk to Lea. I'll call our lawyers, set up a meeting, and we'll go from there. Go talk to Lea. Now," he gives him a reassuring squeeze.

Royal walks him to the front door, watching him stand at his car. "Zion, go talk to Lea." Royal closes the door on him ending any objection. After hearing the car door close, he walks back to the dining room. To stunned silence.

"Okay everyone, we have a lot of work to do. Let's help Zion all we can," he says. They all nod "okay". Royal empties the contents of the folder on the table, and they all reach for a stack of papers and read.

After Zion starts his car, he pulls out his phone and checks Lea's location. She's somewhere in O'Fallon. He looks at the time, its eight-thirty already. *Damn it.* He calls her.

"Hey Bear, how are you?"

That name coming from her comforts me. Lea, I love you. Please accept what I'm about to say to you tonight.

"I'm good, where are you?" he asks, trying to sound calm. "I want to see you."

"Finishing up dinner with Gordon. Are you okay? You sound tired, worn out. I wasn't with you last night," she laughs, teasing him.

He smiles. "No, but I want you with me tonight. Come by my place, I'm on my way home. I need to talk to you."

"Okay, we'll finish up here and I can be there in about thirty minutes."

"Perfect. See you then. I love you, Kitten," he whispers.

"I love you too Zion," Lea looks at the phone after Zion disconnects, then looks at Gordon.

"Everything okay?"

"I guess. He wants me to come by tonight. I thought he was having a business meeting at the smoking club."

"Well, I'm done here anyway, let's wrap this up. You got some sexing to do," Gordon leers at her.

"Yeah right, okay," but Lea is sensing something ain't right about this visit.

-37-

Okay Lea, let's not over think this like you normally would. He's at home, and he wants you there. I mean sure, he could have gone to your house instead, but he went home and he wants you there. Go. Just go.

As Lea enters his apartment, Zion is coming out of his home office into the living room with a drink in his hand, his shirt open, pulled out of his pants, and barefoot.

Okay what the heck is going on?

"Have you eaten? I brought dessert. And it's not me." She says walking over to the kitchen and placing the bag on the counter.

"Hi," she says as he reaches her.

"Hello Kitten."

He pins her against the countertop kissing her. She tastes the whiskey on his tongue.

"Oh, Lea, I need you so much right now," he says unbuckling her jeans, pulling them down and off. And there goes another pair of underwear as she hears the rip. He bends down, spreads her legs and presses his open mouth to her vagina. Normally Zion starts eating Lea out by kissing her stomach, moving to her thass, the crease between her thigh and vagina, because it tickles her so much. Instead, he spreads open her pussy lips and French kisses her vagina. Swirling his tongue around her folds, he sticks two fingers inside of her, trying to get to her g-spot.

"Fuck!" Lea exclaims. She attempts to move from his fast and furious licking.

He looks up at her. Wrapping his left arm around her left leg and using his right arm to press her against the counter he says, "Lea you need to stop, you not going anywhere."

Lea takes in deep breaths. She relaxes her body and gives in to him. After a few more licks Lea explodes, screaming.

WHAT THE FUCKING HELL, SSSSSHHHHIIIIITTTTT.

Zion stands and unzips his pants, drops them to the floor and takes out his hardened penis. He maneuvers her over to the dining room table. They bump into a chair. As if he doesn't recognize it, Zion kicks it out of the way. He approaches Lea, placing one hand on her waist and the other on her neck in a light choke hold. Lea places her hand over his, drawing his head down with her other hand for a kiss.

He backs her against the table. Lea makes a peep noise as her ass touches it. Zion grips her by the thighs and lifts her on the table. Bringing her to the edge, he takes his fingers and strokes her pussy lips. Lea starts gyrating, loving the feel of it. She grips his penis and strokes him up and down, flicking under the hood.

He presses fully into her pussy, stopping when she displays the arch in her back warning him, he's touching her cervix.

Pulling back, he pumps inside of her, slow and controlled thrusts, pausing with each one and flexing his dick.

"Zion," she exclaims excitedly, wrapping her legs around his waist.

Zion grips her ass, digging his fingers into her butt cheeks for deeper penetration making sure the tip of his dick strokes her g-spot.

"Lea. Fuck. Yes."

Lea gives herself over to him, allowing him to control the speed and penetration. She wraps her arms around his neck and turns his face to her to kiss him. He moans with pleasures of ecstasy.

He's fucking her so hard and fast, that they break the kiss. He buries his face into her neck. "Oh Lea. I love you so much. Damn baby. You feel so good." He keeps pumping inside her harder and harder. "Baby, cum for me, hurry. I want us to cum together. I can't hold it any longer." He says, wanting them to be in sync, orgasming, screaming and moaning their release.

"Zion! Shit! Now!"

Lea trembles feeling her orgasm explode through her legs, arms and clit. Zion grips her ass tighter, holds her in place, and cums, lifting her off the table, jerking inside of her.

He pulls out, picks her up, and carries her upstairs to the bedroom. He finishes undressing them. Lying in bed, Zion wraps her arms and legs around him, kissing her. Not letting her talk or think. He's feverish in his lovemaking, like he can't get enough of her.

Lea wants to tell him to ease up, stop, slow down but she's never experienced a man wanting and needing her the way Zion is needing her right now.

He finally runs out of steam. Lea is in his arms, unable to move.

GIRL, I'M WORE OUT. I'M GOING OVER HERE, THERE, SOMEPLACE TO CHILL.

YEP, I CAN USE SOME SLEEP AFTER THAT PERFORMANCE. The deep voice whispers.

OK WHERE DID YOU COME FROM?

Sex Diva only gets a soft laugh in return. She walks to the corner of Lea's mind and sits staring into the fog, glaring at the silhouette of the voice.

"Zion what was that all about? Don't get me wrong. I really enjoyed it."

He inhales, hoping he's saying the right words and tells her about his meeting with Wendy. "Lea, I want to adopt these babies.

But Kitten, I don't want to lose you over this. Tell me I'm doing the right thing."

Lea suddenly cools. She emotionally detaches while listening to him tell her about Wendy, the pregnancy and about her dying. He has rambled on and she hasn't tried to interrupt him.

What the fucking hell. No. No. No.

"Zion, of course you're doing the right thing. I'm here for you. Do what you need to do to get these babies. Bear, you're going to be a father. A wonderful, loving and caring father. You're doing a wonderful thing in keeping them out of the system. I love you Zion, and I'm so proud of you. Most men would run screaming, especially at the age of fifty."

I hug him hard and hold on for dear life pushing all my emotions and feelings aside. He doesn't need to hear what I can't verbalize yet. Reassure him. He wants this. He's going to be a great father. Oh God, he could leave me and be with her. He could decide to be a single dad and go back to temporary fucks.

Sex Diva perks up from the fog.

HE'S ADOPTING KIDS FROM THE TEMP FUCK?

I thought you were sleeping? What the fuck am I gonna do? How? Shit. I wanted to give him a baby. Me dammit. Me. Not some skank tramp from his past. Oh, I feel sick.

LEA, GET A GRIP.

How the fuck do I get a grip? He could end this. Fuck I could be out and she could—. Shit, shit, shit. Ugh, I need to get out of here.

BUT YOU CAN'T.

Lea's emotions are in retrograde turmoil even though she hasn't moved an inch from Zion's embrace.

He falls asleep.

HOW THE HELL CAN HE SLEEP? WE ARE WIDE AWAKE.

After about four hours Lea slides out of Zion's embrace. She climbs out of bed and goes to the bathroom. She feels sore, anxious and pissed. Looking at her body, she sees she has a hickey on her thighs and stomach.

Fuck, I don't even remember him sucking that hard.

She grabs one of his t-shirts and hastily puts it on. Walking out of the bedroom, she goes downstairs and puts a hand over her mouth tempering her scream.

Lea, you can't do this right now. You can't. You gotta think. It's gonna be a long night.

Love's Awakening

-38-

Zion wakes up the next morning with Lea in his arms.

She wants me to continue with the adoption. She supports me. I hug her, thanking her silently. She caresses me reassuringly.

"You have a lot of legal stuff to take care of mister. You need to get to the office and me to work?"

I truly adore this woman.

"I can just as easily do anything I need to do here, with you by my side," he says, ignoring that he will be meeting with his lawyers today to review Wendy's paperwork.

"Nope, I need to get to work. And we know what happens when working in your office together," Lea stretches, moving to get out of bed to take a shower.

Zion pulls on his t-shirt, pulling her back into his embrace forcing her to look at him. "What's with the clothes? We sleep in the nude. You okay?"

DON'T BLINK. WE MAY CRY.

"Zion, I'm fine. I felt a chill when I went downstairs to get our clothes. No biggy." What she leaves out is her need for the security of clothes to consider her future.

THIS MAN HAS GIVEN US A FRICKIN HEADACHE.

They shower together, making out. Lea puts on jeans and a shirt, and Zion goes full business attire. She sits on one of the dressing settees in his closet watching him, twisting the ring on her finger in agitation.

He's going to be a father. He's adopting the kids of a former sex liaison. He had made the decision about adopting them before even telling me. I hope at some point I get included in the decision. Or get dumped before he announces he's going to marry the tramp.

"Lea, baby you keep looking at me like that, we'll never get our day started," he says walking over to kiss her. He lifts her hand and kisses her fingers, stopping her from twisting the ring on her left hand. It's now red with welts and she has fingernail print impressions in her palm.

He sits down, linking their fingers together, stroking the stone on her ring. "I know. I'm nervous about all this, too. Becoming a father."

He incorrectly assumes my thoughts. Me! Nervous about him becoming a father! Hell, fuck no! I'm nervous about me losing you. Man, Zion, you don't know the half of my nervousness because I frickin' don't!

"Yeah nervous." Lea murmurs. Zion doesn't catch her sarcasm.

Thank heaven.

WHY ARE YOU SO DAMNED CALM? YELL, JUMP, SCREAM. WE JUST FOUND HIM, AND NOW HE'S ABOUT TO BE A FATHER TO SOMEONE ELSE'S KIDS.

I can't do this now, Sex Diva. This isn't about sex anymore, so grow the fuck up and go sit in the fucking corner.

OH, GIVE ME A GOD-DAMN BREAK. EVERYTHING IS ABOUT SEX. IMA MAKE IT ABOUT SEX.

Goodbye, Sex Diva.

"I can't help it. I love watching you get dressed. I'm proud of you Zion. You're doing a wonderful thing. No matter what happens, always know I'm proud of you."

"Thank you, Lea. That means the world to me."

Going downstairs, they greet Mrs. Vance in the kitchen.

"Good morning you two. Breakfast?"

"Nothing for me Mrs. Vance. I need to take off. I'm running late as it is. Thanks."

I just need to get the hell out of here, so I can scream and cry.

"Lea, no breakfast? You sure?" Zion asks, looking at her intently.

First, the t-shirt and now no breakfast? We always sit for breakfast.

"Sweetheart, I'm sure. I can have a protein shake at the office. I'll be okay. Call me later if you need me. Remember what I said. Do whatever you need to do to make this happen. Okay? Stay here, have breakfast."

Lea reaches up to give him a kiss. He picks her up in a hug.

"I love you," he kisses her and walks her to the elevator.

"I love you, too, Zion. Very much," Lea whispers.

She gets on the elevator remembering he can see her on the camera. She stands through the descent, not moving, thinking, *I just need to get out of this garage. A few more minutes and I can break down, just a few more.* She gets to the garage and almost bumps into Sam getting on as she's getting off the elevator.

"Oh, sorry. Hi Sam. How are you?" Lea asks shakily.

"I'm good. You okay Miss Adams?" he asks stepping aside.

"Pretty good. Running late. Take care." She practically jogs to her car, getting in and putting on her sun glasses to hide the tears she feels are coming.

When Sam gets upstairs, Zion has him and Mrs. Vance take a seat with him at the dining room table to announce his baby news.

"Okay, you two. What I'm going to say is going to be a total shock. I'm sorry to make you two wonderful people the last to know, but everything has happened so fast."

"Well, go ahead," Sam says sipping on the coffee his wife has set in front of him.

He's announcing his marriage to Miss Adams. I just know it. Sam thinks silently.

"Uh. Shit. Well. Uh. I'm going to be a father," Zion says, grinning at their stunned expressions.

"Wait, what?" Sam asks. He knows all about Zion being sterile.

Mrs. Vance is silent, not knowing what to say. Zion has never shared with her he's sterile and from the look of her expression neither has Sam.

"Sam, no. Lea is not pregnant, and yes, I'm still sterile. Sorry Mrs. Vance to drop this on you. I have been sterile since I was a child. Not many people know that outside of my family. You're family, and I love you dearly. I just never. Well, we've never had a conversation where I would make that announcement to you."

"Mr. Landon, don't apologize. Your business is your business. You tell me what I need to know. That's our working relationship. But if Miss Adams isn't pregnant, how? Or should I be asking this?"

"Ask anything you want. A former lover, Wendy Noelin, is pregnant and terminally ill. Again, not by me but by artificial insemination. She won't live to raise her sons. Twin boys. She has asked me to adopt them, and I've agreed. In about three months, I'll be a father. Mrs. Vance, I know you're hired to be my housekeeper—."

"Mr. Landon, there is no way on God's green earth I would quit or abandon you now. Housekeeper, nanny, additional grandma, whatever you need. I'm not going anywhere. Sam and I aren't going anywhere. Right Sam?" Mrs. Vance says to her husband.

"As my wife said, we aren't going anywhere. We wouldn't think of it. We're ecstatic for you, young man. So much has changed. You've changed in the last few months."

"You mean since Lea has come into my life. I know. Before Lea, I was considering settling or slowing down. I've been thinking about it for a couple of years now. I never imagined at my age, love and marriage and now kids. This all happened last night, but it seems right."

"Mr. Landon, how is Miss Adams taking this? If you don't mind me asking? How should we address this with her if at all?" Mrs. Vance asks him.

"She knows I'm adopting the boys, and she's supportive. It amazes me, but she is."

"You mentioned marriage. Are you and Miss Adams engaged?"

"No, I haven't asked her yet. I'm going to marry her. We're going to be a family. This Addison mess has got to be done and over with. I can't let this continue with the boys coming. We need to get with Saul and discuss this more. I may need to bring in Essensecurity for some outside help with this."

"Whatever it takes," Sam assures him.

"Well, as Miss Adams said, you have a lot of stuff to take care of. If you don't mind, I would like to start on one of the bedrooms for the boys, taking everything out."

"Mrs. Vance you're wonderful. But please, not too much okay. I want Lea to be included. I love her and need her to know she's a part of this."

"Mr. Landon, I understand. I'll make lists and, if asked, offer. I'm here for all of you and all of this. Whatever you need."

"Thank you. I don't know what that will entail," Zion tells Mrs. Vance.

"Sam, let's head to the office. I know I don't need to say this but for now let's just keep this between us. I plan on telling Morgan and, of course, Saul and Ryan but beyond that, few people outside of my circle will know. Is that clear."

"Yes sir," Mrs. Vance says.

"Understandable sir," Sam says.

"Wonderful," Zion says getting into business mode thinking about all he has to do and what could be coming.

-39-

As soon as Lea gets out and far enough away from Zion's apartment, she calls Gordon.

"So how was the sexing?" he asks joking.

"Oh, fuck, the damn sexing, you and the Sex Diva are working my last nerve about sex right now. Okay! I need to talk to you. Can you be at my house in an hour? Please. Zion is going to be a father. He's adopting two kids," she rushes out.

"Lea, what the fucking hell. Are you kidding me? Okay, get home. I'll see you in a few," he says. "The Sex Diva is still around. Nice to know."

"Dammit, Gordon!"

"Oh. Sorry. Get home. See you in a few," he says.

Lea drives to the office and picks up her computer before anyone gets in. On her way out, she leaves a note for Crystal telling her she'll be working from home for the rest of the week.

Gordon is sitting in his car waiting for her when she gets home. He takes one look at her and holds open his arms, and she rushes into them. "Honey, it's okay, let's talk this out."

They go inside, and the second he closes the door, it all comes rushing out. "She's a former lover of his. Ha. Lover my ass. The night we met in the Central West End; he had dinner with her. Actually, they were supposed to fuck that night."

Lea walks over to her bar, grabs a glass, and the bottle of Disaronno. Gordon watches her getting liquor at nine in the morning. She fills the glass with ice, lemon juice and liquor and paces among the dining room, living room and kitchen, giving him the details.

"Anyway, she gets artificially inseminated because she's given up on finding a man. Sounds familiar, right? That coulda been me fifteen years ago, but I was too damn broke. Oh, you wanna know how she can afford this?" She takes a gulp of the drink.

Gordon attempts to respond, but Lea cuts him off, wiping her face across her sleeve. He grabs a box of tissue and starts handing them to her. As she discards them, he tries to catch each one in the trash can but gives up when her pacing almost knocks him to the floor.

"Lots of rich boyfriends dishing out money. Great tips on her job. Girlfriend been squirreling away money better than I could have ever done in my entire life. So, she gets pregnant and starts having bad mood swings and headaches. At first, the doctors said it was just pregnancy symptoms but decided to run more tests and they find the tumor. They could have operated on her, but it would have meant terminating the pregnancy. By then, she knew she was having twins. Fraternal twin boys. So, she nixed the surgery idea until after they were born. But doctors tell her she won't survive the birth of these kids if she waits."

Lea is working on the bottle of water Gordon handed her after she finished her drink in three gulps. The liquor is starting to take effect. She's not pacing as quickly, but she's still pacing. He keeps moving stuff out of her way. When it looks as if she is about to sit down, he grabs her computer bag, but she stands before her butt hits the couch. Her shoes are kicked off, one nearly hitting him in the leg.

"So, she goes through her friends asking them to adopt her kids. They either don't want to or can't afford to. She calls Zion. Money bags Zion."

Lea flips her hands around, waving erratically. Gordon was thankful the glass was empty at the time. She's filled it again, though.

"God forgive me I love that man and don't mean to put him down like that but shit, shit, shit. After he proposed, I was going to suggest adoption or anything he wanted to try. But now it's all fixed and done. Oh, don't let me forget to mention he made the decision to adopt them and started the discussion with his family before he told me anything. It's not like I would have said not to do it in the first place but fuck, couldn't I have gotten a heads-up before he said yes? Oh, no, not me. Lea was the last to know after the decision was made."

She has calmed down some or is too damned drunk to pace anymore. To Gordon, it doesn't matter. She's sitting on the couch next to him. The glass is on the dining room table. She has her head in her hands.

Yep, Lea is drunk and dizzy. Ima need to get more water and hangover food in her system and fast.

"This submitting and trusting him to make decisions for us fucking blows. And I'm not even sure he's making the decision for us. All he's talking about is being a father and raising his sons and how his family is supporting him and how much he loves me and is so happy I support this. Like I would make an ass of myself and say I didn't."

Gordon hands her more tissue. Lea is on her second box. Gordon noticed the box in her hand when she came from the bedroom in a man's dress shirt. *Must be Zion's.* He has picked up the used tissues from the floor and is watching Lea. Listening.

"At this point, I feel if I say anything negative, I'm the bad guy in this. I don't want to say anything negative. This is the chance of a lifetime. Just because my path of becoming a parent didn't work out, doesn't mean I should derail or devalue this opportunity he's being given. I have all these what-ifs going through my fucking head. What if he marries her to make sure the kids get his last name? What if he falls in love with her going through all this? What if she, oh my god, moves in with him?"

This thought causes her to stand, pace, and drink.

Fuck, I gotta get some food in this woman. She gonna be puking and I ain't for cleaning up nobody's vomit. Even my best friend's.

"Geez, she could move in with him and die in his apartment. Where does that leave me? Do I speak up or do I keep my mouth shut? If I say anything I could push them together. If I don't say anything, I could lose him. Gordon, what do I do? Why the fuck are you texting on your phone? I'm pouring my guts out and you texting. Thanks a lot."

"Lea. Sit down and no more drinking. I'm having Lily pick up some hangover food. Yo drunk ass need it."

"I've only had one drink, what's the big deal? I'm hurting here!" she yells.

"You've had four. Now sit ya ass down. If you pass out, ima let you sleep it off where you land. Hopefully, it's in the bathroom."

Lea plops down on the couch, sniffling.

"Honestly, I have no clue what to tell you to do about Zion and this baby issue. I wanna say walk away, get the hell out of this. No man is worth putting up with this kinda shit. Ain't no money worth it, ain't no dick worth it. This man is adopting the kids of another woman. Are you sure he didn't get her knocked up?"

"Gordon, yes, I'm sure. Zion is sterile."

"Lea, the timing of all this. It kinda adds up if he got her pregnant."

"God, will you stop it. I've calculated the dates. I've been up all night calculating the dates. She got pregnant sometime in March. Zion hadn't had sex with her since January. He was going to sex her the night they met for dinner in the Central West End, but he cut the date short. They ain't his, based on timing and HIM BEING STERILE!" she yells at him.

"Okay gotcha. Do you really love him that much to stay in this?"

"I'm in love with him. I want him in my life, and I want to be in his."

"And everything that goes with him?" Gordon asks.

Lea stares at him with the remanent of tears staining her cheeks. "I have no choice, do I? If I want him, I have to accept this and keep my feelings to myself."

"Yeah, pretty much, you do. If you want him and think you can handle this. Lea, I'm happy you've found love. I'm not happy who you've found love with. I don't want you hurt. And I'm not gonna sit back and keep my mouth shut. We've always let the other make decisions based on common sense. All relationships have hurdles. Except abuse, we have stepped back and allowed the other to handle them. You're choosing this hurdle. But if I see you ignoring red flags about any of this, I'll verbally shove my foot up your ass. Do we understand?"

Lea looks at Gordon stunned. Yes, they are always straight up there for each other. Such deadly calm from him, she has never heard. He keeps things light and upbeat with a bit of get it together advice. This is different.

"Lea, I asked you a question? Do we have an understanding? I will not allow you to freely walk into this with blinders on. Ima be in your ass daily. Even when you think you gotta keep things from me, I will still be here."

"Yes Gordon. I understand. Fully. And thank you. For not telling me to leave him and run."

"Oh, don't think I don't want to say that. But I see how happy and in love you are. I've seen the change in you being in love. I like it a lot. Up until this moment I even thought you found your soul mate. Hell, Zion can still fuck this up. He can become a total jackass and leave you out of all of this walking away. Or he can give you a future neither one of us ever imagined for you. Hun, I don't envy you at all. When you need to vent, you be sure and give me a call. But if you do accept to stay, there will be things you cannot say."

"What if he asks me? Do I lie to him?"

"To help him get through this, you tell him what he needs to hear. And I'll be here to help you when the freak-outs happen and more importantly if you decide to walk away," Gordon says.

"What if I do this and still lose him. If he marries her, I can't stick around and wait for her to die. I won't do that," she tells him.

"Then that will be your breaking point. If he says anything about marriage to her, you leave." Gordon holds Lea while she cries out her anger, pain, despair, and frustration. "I'm here for you and will help you get through this. I promise. And stop arguing with your inner Sex Diva. People will start to think you're mental."

"I am mental, Gordon. I thought you knew."

He laughs at her, comforting her through her misery.

Now who the fuck is that she's hugging? Dammit, I drop out of the picture for a few weeks and there's another one. This bitch is a fucking whore. Something in common. He falls for whores. Time for some fucking escalation and get this shit finished. We need to start our lives and get the fuck outta St. Louis.

-40-

Zion's meeting with his lawyers Tuesday stretched into lunch, afternoon and dinner at his office. He was determined to have them scrutinize all the paperwork Wendy provided him, every detail about the pregnancy, being artificially inseminated, her background on being adopted, and her lack of family she claims doesn't exist. Doing this adoption, he doesn't want anyone coming into the boys' lives with some kinda claim he can't fight. And he wants to ensure he is protected should Wendy change her mind.

Looking over the medical records leaves him anguished. Of course, he couldn't understand all the medical terminology, but reading the bits he could comprehend and have explained, leaves him sad for her.

When Zion and Wendy met with both sets of lawyers on Wednesday to go over the legal details, he made sure she was satisfied. She signed documentation stating that he will be adopting her kids and all her parental rights will terminate on the day they are born. He will have all legal rights to make decisions for her and the boys from this day forward regarding all issues concerning her medical and living needs. He will also be paying for all medical and living expenses. Wendy has insisted on staying in her apartment with the nurse, but Zion has the right to come and go as he pleases. The private duty nurse is to report to him on how Wendy is doing. If anything changes, Wendy will check into the hospital immediately to ensure the children are safe and taken care of. According to the documentation, everything is to be done to ensure the lives of the kids. Everything.

After everything regarding Wendy and the boys is settled with the lawyers, Zion switches to the details regarding Lea. He has draft paperwork drawn up to address her adopting them, her rights as their mother, when these rights start and how she and the boys are to be provided for should anything happen to him. By the time he is done meeting with the lawyers, Zion is at peace regarding the future decisions he has made.

-41-

Every day Zion has texted and called Lea to provide updates on what's happening. He stops by her office on Friday, hoping to see her and take her to lunch. And maybe play hooky for the remainder of the day. She's been such a strong support in all this.

Maybe they should get away for the weekend. Fly or drive somewhere.

"Zion, how are you? What are you doing here?" Tom asks, as he walks into the office reception area. Crystal is in the idea room with the team having the daily meeting Lea couldn't attend.

"I came by to kidnap Lea for the rest of the day. You don't mind, do you?" he asks Tom.

"No of course not, but she isn't here. She's been working from home since Tuesday," Tom says watching Zion's facial expressions change from happy to worried. There's something going on with these two and he wants to know. Now. "Let's go downstairs and talk, shall we?"

Zion hasn't told many outside his family, Lea, Sam and Mrs. Vance about what's going on with Wendy. Tom is one of his closest friends. Maybe it's time he opened up to him. "Actually, you got a couple hours? We can get lunch."

"Sure man. Let me get my phone," Tom walks back to his office, grabs his phone and let's Crystal know he'll be out to lunch with Zion.

They hop into Zion's Porsche and head to The Savory Club for lunch where they won't be rushed, and will have some privacy. After they have placed their orders, Zion tells Tom what's happening. "Man, a father, congratulations and, well, sorry. How is Lea handling this? Wait, is Tuesday when all this happened?"

"Monday actually. We've talked every day; I just haven't had a chance to see her. She was or is very supportive about this, even suggesting things I should consider that never crossed my mind. I didn't know she hadn't been coming to work."

"Well, I know her mother had two doctors' appointments this week and she's been going out to the build site a lot lately. Her not coming into the office is nothing out of the ordinary," Tom assures him. "Are you excited about becoming a father? Hell, can we even talk about excitement or things like that considering the circumstances?"

"Every now and then I let myself get excited. It's only been, what, four days since this all began? I call Lea to keep her in the loop of what's going on, and what I'm thinking," Zion says to Tom.

"Does Wendy know about Lea? That she'll be the mother of the kids? Or is that your plan?" Tom asks.

"Man, what kinda question is that? Of course, I'm doing this with Lea in my mind as their mother," he snaps.

"Hey, I just thought I would ask. Does Lea know you're doing this with her in mind as the mother? You have it in your mind, but have you verbally said to Lea this is what you want? I know you. You plan stuff in your head, work out a solution, and implement it. That method won't work here."

"Yes, I—." Zion thinks back on the conversations he's had with Lea. He can't remember if he has said anything to her about her being the boys' mother. "Tom, I don't remember if I have. I mean, I must have the first night. Right?"

"Zion, from what you've said, it doesn't sound like you have. All you've been talking about the adoption in terms of you and the boys. If Lea is a part of this like you say, I suggest you say the words to her. And soon. Keep reassuring her 'cause, seriously from her point of view, in my opinion, the man she loves adopting the kids of a former lover, has to be a hard pill to swallow even if she's supporting you one-hundred percent."

Zion calls for the waitress to bring the check. His urgency in talking to Lea and making her understand she's a part of this family he has in his head; is his priority right now.

Love's Awakening

-42-

Lea's plan to stay out of the office and avoid inquiries from Crystal turned out to be a good idea. Since the news from Zion, she has been a weepy mess. She keeps all her appointments with her mom and makes sure no one see's how tired and exhausted she is. She hasn't worn heavy makeup in years. It didn't take much to get back into it to hide the bags under her eyes.

She was doing fine and accepting of the situation. *Hell, it's not like I have a choice. Accept and stay or leave.* Leaving was not an option. She was even proud she managed to be upbeat and positive whenever she talked to Zion.

Then Thursday it all went to fucking hell. It began with email upon email from an address she didn't recognize. At first, she thought she had gotten a computer virus so she did some cleanup before opening the emails.

Once she opened them, she couldn't stop. They were hateful. Calling her bitch, whore, a money hungry thot, how she's going to die for being in Zion's life, how he doesn't love Lea like he loves her, how Lea better leave her man alone or she'll suffer. The pictures of Lea's face are either scratched out, x'ed out, or have knives stuck in her neck, heart and stomach. There were even a couple of emails with Lea's head blowing up over and over.

How the fricking hell did Addison find me?

Lea sat down shaking and crying.

What the hell is going on? Why is this happening to me?

Then her phone starts blowing up. Just as hateful as the emails and even more threatening she receives numerous text messages.

What to do? Call Gordon. No, I can't bring him into this. Probably being watched. Call Zion. No, too much going on with adoption. Can't go to my mom's. Won't take to her doorstep. I'm alone. Shit what do I do?

Lea paces her house, setting security booby traps, planning escape routes, making sure windows and doors aren't blocked, putting weapons in areas hidden away, even making sure a cell phone is charged and hidden for a just in case emergency.

By now she's been up almost thirty-six hours.

Drinking wine during the middle of the day. Who gives a fuck?

She needed liquid sustenance. She cancelled her meetings for Friday, being too damned terrified to walk out of her house. It gave her a lot of time to do some thinking.

It's time I spoke up for myself with Zion before this baby issue moves any further.

She's made the decision to extract some promises from him if they are going to stay in this relationship. Yep, it is time she spoke up for herself. Whether it's with him are without him, her life can be in danger and she needs to take steps to protect herself and her family. He could decide to break up with her for her own safety after she tells him about the emails and texts. Who knows? Lea has her A, B, C, and even D plans. Now it's just a matter of which one will be put into place. Going with the plan where she may never see Zion again, she takes a shower and dresses in one of his shirts. This could be the last time she gets to wear one.

Arriving at the warehouse, another failed endeavor since the bitch came back. It once housed equipment, materials, employees. Now it's a fucking desk and light. He takes a seat at the desk and power up the pc. It's time.

The AK-47 always close. Ammunition even closer.

My favorite, my Glock semi-automatic pistol. Never leaves me.

He stares at the computer screen, email open, drafts ready to send. But first a little target practice. He picks up pistol and points. Fires off shots at the multiple images taped to a wall in scattered disarray.

My love, my heart, my darling Lea. Shot to the shoulder. Fuck I'm getting good at this.

Zion. Zion Landon. Shot to the back of the head. Brain matter oozing out. Always the dead shot.

Addison. Addison and him. DEAD DEAD DEAD. Riddled with holes.

All of them DEAD. Bleeding out. DEAD.

But my love. My heart. My darling. Forever mine.

But I'm alive. Always alive. This is my show.

Us. ALIVE. FUCKING ALIVE.

-Love's Awakening III And Beyond-

Lea goes back to work, making sure everyone is acting normal and not treating her with kid gloves. Crystal is happy to see her, as is Tom. He calls her into his office to discuss what happened last week. "Hey, Lady, how are you doing?"

"It's only been the weekend. I'm sticking to a plan and a schedule. Thanks for asking."

"We don't want you hurt or stressed out, so whatever you need to do just let me know. We need to keep you safe."

"I will. I have the meeting with Saul at Landon Enterprises at two, but I was going to go a couple hours early to have lunch with Zion."

"That's perfect. Is this about the computer image and transfers? Is he needing to hire any people to help him with that? I'm sure we can get temps if need be."

"Actually, they're doing it in-house. Saul is very particular about his network. He has hired someone to help him with the transition. A company called Normalcy Assistance. He won't tell me anything other than that. I'm surprised he is even letting me see and go over what he is wanting to talk about today. It's about the best locations for users to save all their work and how to get them to do it so the transfer for each computer runs smoothly."

"Good. Well as usual keep me posted. It says in the calendar appointment you will be there until four. Just go on home from there and we'll see you in the morning. Be safe, Lea, please. No disappearing jaunts."

"Geez, this chick needs to get locked up, fast. She's messing with my lifestyle," she says smiling, hoping to ease his mind a little.

"I hear ya. I hear ya. Let me know if you need anything or if there are any changes. I do have a question."

"Go ahead."

"Will we be losing you here? Twin sons, marriage, getting settled. Will I be losing my best project lead?"

"Honestly, Tom, I don't want to stop working, but like you said, twins, marriage. I don't want to miss out on bonding. Usually that happens during pregnancy, and breast feeding. I won't have that chance, so I can only do it by being around them twenty-four seven. I love my job. Would you be willing to work something out part-time or me working from home or maybe another type of arrangement? I know we can discuss this later, but just think about it. Okay? You know me and how I think ahead."

"Lea, both of those ideas are perfect and doable. I don't want to lose you either. We're a great team here. We can absolutely consider working something out. I'm glad I brought this up. I wasn't going to at first but now that we have, well, we'll make it happen."

"Thanks Tom, I appreciate it. I'll get back to work. Did you know we're getting a second proposal from Landon Enterprises? For a small satellite office run by Star."

"Hell naw. Yes, girl, go get that money."

She sits there stunned into silence. "Lea, are you okay?" Tom asks.

"Tom, I only met him five, six months ago and we're sitting here talking about marriage, babies, combining households. Am I rushing into this? Am I moving too fast? Should I slow down and back off of this?"

"How do you feel? Seriously, when you think about Zion and being with him versus being away from him, how do you feel?"

"Like I'm exactly where I should be and everything is going as planned," she says.

"That's the answer to all your previous questions."

"Uh, thanks." Lea goes back to her office and grabs her things. She calls Ryan to meet her downstairs as soon as he can, anxious to head over to Zion's office. "I'm downstairs in the car waiting now, Miss Adams."

"Great, I'll be right down." She gets on the elevator with some other co-workers and rides down fidgeting, needing to see him, having this urgent need to be around him. It only takes them twenty-five minutes to get to his office building. She checks his calendar on her phone and it doesn't say he is currently unavailable but even if he is, she can visit with Star or sit in his office or conference room until he becomes available.

"Hi, Morgan. Is Zion available? I know I'm not due here until noon."

"He's here, just finishing up a conference call, but you're more than welcome to go into his office and wait. I'm just making sure lunch is ready."

"Great, don't tell him I'm here. I can just hang getting some work done. Thanks again." Lea goes into Zion's office and sits down on his couch to wait. After about twenty-five minutes, she hears his voice outside his office, talking to Morgan.

"When Lea gets here, show her in and no interruptions unless it's an emergency. I think I have put out all the fires."

He walks into his office, striding straight for his desk then freezes. He turns around and looks at her.

About the Author

Kia Lui

Is a graduate of University Missouri-St. Louis and Webster University with degrees in the field of Information Technology.

Kia Lui enjoys photography and museum strolling. She started writing erotic fantasies in 1994 never thinking about writing a book.

What started as a small idea to generate travel money, has evolved into a book, a series, an expression of love, laughter and happiness. Her motto is, write the opposite of what is normal, typical and expected.

Kia Lui is the owner of Kia Lui Media, LLC. Currently resides in Missouri.